ALSO, BY DAVIS MACDONALD

The Hill *(set in Palos Verdes), Book 1 in the Judge Series*

The Island *(set in Avalon, Catalina Island),*
Book 2 in the Judge Series

Silicon Beach *(set in Santa Monica and L.A.'s West Side),*
Book 3 in the Judge Series

The Bay *(set in Newport Beach), Book 4 in the Judge Series*

Cabo *(set in Cabo San Lucas), Book 5 in the Judge Series*

The Strand *(set in the South Bay beach communities of Southern California), Book 6 in the Judge Series*

 The Lake *(set in the Lake Arrowhead community of Southern California), Book 7 in the Judge Series*

The Cruise *(set on the open sea), Book 8 in the Judge Series*

The Dark Web, Vegas *(set in Las Vegas), Book 9 in the Judge Series*

The City By The Bay – A Mystery Novel*, Book 10 in the Judge Series. Out in late 2022*

I hope you enjoy The Dark Web-Vegas, and if you do, please drop a brief positive review on Amazon for me. Your review will be greatly appreciated.

Watch for announcements of future books on my Website:
http://davismacdonald-author.com/

THE DARK WEB -VEGAS-

A Mystery Novel

BY

DAVIS MacDONALD

A Note from the Author

DESIGN

I found a dimpled spider, fat and white,
On a white heal-all, holding up a moth
Like a white piece of rigid satin cloth--
Assorted characters of death and blight
Mixed ready to begin the morning right,
Like the ingredients of a witches' broth--
A snow-drop spider, a flower like a froth,
And dead wings carried like a paper kite.

What had that flower to do with being white,
The wayside blue and innocent heal-all?
What brought the kindred spider to that height,
Then steered the white moth thither in the night?
What but design of darkness to appall?--
If design govern in a thing so small.

Robert Frost, 1932

PROLOGUE

The sun was drying him out, taut, like old leather. The sun, the sand, the reflective heat, the temperature, 108 degrees. No liquid for hours now. How many hours? He'd lost count.

He'd like to see his grandson Robbie again. Just once more. Run his fingers through the boy's hair; feel him close, give him a hug. The hope for the future. But it wouldn't be. A picture of Robbie flashed in his mind, blurred, he couldn't hold the image.

As he had sat blind-folded in the SUV's middle seat, he'd thought he'd be shot in the head. But he hadn't. They'd just pushed him out into the sand. Hadn't touched him. Just dumped him. Out here. In the middle of the Nevada desert. In the middle of nowhere.

He tried to laugh through his cracked lips. But it was more a croak. As he thought about it, he realized they'd been cruel. Why couldn't they have used a bullet? This was far worse. Slow, agonizing, awful!

He stumbled and fell. Couldn't get his burned hands up in time; his face pressed into the hot singeing sand. He tried to spit the sand out. But his mouth was so dry. Too difficult.

His vision was going now. Turning the desert into a dark web at his peripheral vision. Dark in the middle of the day. Almost hiding the shadow of that predator bird overhead. Circling... waiting... patient!

He got onto his knees, a last-ditch effort to stand. But there was no strength.
He lingered there, trying to balance, thinking about it. Trying to will his body to work. It wouldn't.

He knew it was the end. He was dying.

The dark crowded out more vision. The pain in his body... the swelling in his head... everything began to slip away. They belonged to somebody else... somebody at the far end of a long tunnel.

Acceptance came over him, almost a peace. He was where he was supposed to be.

He idly felt his body crashing down again, headfirst into the sand.... Letting go....

CHAPTER 1
MONDAY
10:00 A.M.

We don't like to think about our own death. We love to think about our life. All the past fun and turmoil, the losses, the failures, the successes, the battles, the loves lost and won. We like to think about our future. All the things we're going to do, places we'll go, accomplishments we'll attempt. And what if we succeed? It's the stuff of dreams.

But never about our death. The end of existence. The Nothing. Hitting that wall...all thought stops.

A personal end waits for us some day. Like a spider in its dark web, waiting, watching, counting to its turn, death waits for you... waits for me... waits for the Judge. Was this the Spider's turn to take the Judge?

It had started as a soft morning in Malaga Cove, out on the Palos Verdes Peninsula. Cooler, with the broad expanse of the Santa Monica Bay glittering September blue. The Judge was doing his taxes; receipts and documents spread across his dining room table in a disorganized mixture of piles and stacks. The end of his extension to file was hanging over his head like the Sword of Damocles.

Katy, his wife, 20 years his junior, buzzed around the room occasionally. Like a colorful bird-of-paradise she floated in over the course of the day leaving coffee, donuts, tuna sandwiches, soda, and encouragement. Each time departing quickly. The Judge was in a foul mood, and he tended to mutter a lot. Even curse… doing his taxes. The dining room was a place to avoid on such days.

She knew sooner or later he'd lift his head toward the heavens and growl, *"Our God damn Government is turning us into a nation of God damn accountants."*

The Judge's cell phone went off with a wolf whistle it'd picked up somewhere as a ring announcement, further irritating him. The damn phone rattled around his pocket and picked its own settings. To Hell with what the Judge might have selected. The Judge grabbed the phone and snapped, "Yes!" into it in a voice that was mostly gravel.

"Is this the Judge?" the person on the other end asked, tentative, uncertain whether he had a person or a caged animal.

"Yes, yes. It's me. Just working on my damn taxes. Who's this?"

"Detective Marsh, Judge, Barry Marsh, Vegas. You asked me to keep an eye out for your buddy who went missing… Robert Hanson."

"Yes. Yes, I did, Barry. Thanks for the call. Has he turned up? I've got important papers for him to sign."

"We've found him, Judge… but I'm afraid the news isn't good."

The Judge went alert, sitting straighter in his chair, pressing the cell closer to his ear.

"Tell me."

"Deceased, Judge. Found him in the middle of the desert, thirty miles from any road."

"What?"

"Yeah. No obvious marks. No bullet holes. No apparent signs of human-made trauma, at least from what we can tell from what's left. The coroner will have to decide of course. But we think he died of terminal dehydration and heat exposure. We figure someone took him for a joy ride. Thirty miles out into the desert north of Vegas. Just dropped him off. No water, no food, no shelter, no nothing. A one-way ticket."

"*Shit!*"

"Yeah. Miserable way to go."

"Who found him?"

"A couple of young guys in dune buggies. Decided to extend their range beyond the twenty-mile network of trails. Came across what was left of Mr. Hanson. He had his wallet with his driver's license, credit cards, and several large bills. Dental records will have the final say, but we're pretty sure it's him… I'm sorry."

The Judge set the cell down and stared at the litter of receipts, bank statements and canceled checks carpeting the top of the table, the half-full file box sitting on the chair next to him, and the trash can at his feet already stuffed to the gills. He took his arm and with malice ran it flat across the tabletop, sweeping the litter into the box. It took three sweeps and two heavy press-downs on the damn box before he got everything in. But it was a satisfying. Particularly when he put the box on the floor and used his foot for the final press down. He slammed the lid down on the overloaded box with a vengeance, forcing its sides to poof out like a mushroom. Then he lugged it over by the door and dropped it with a thud.

Katy came flying into the room at the sound of the dropped box, likely concerned he'd gotten apoplexy and keeled over from the sheer frustration of his taxes. She looked relieved he was okay, and curious why everything had gone back into the sad over-stuffed box. Particularly when their deadline was so near.

He gave her his news about Bob Hanson. Hanson was one of his oldest and dearest friends. Katy had never quite approved of Bob. Her female instinct spotted right off Bob was more gambler than nester... more chaser than committer... but that was what the Judge loved about him.

"So, what's that got to do with doing your taxes, Judge?"

Katy was always so sensible, so logical. Some days it drove him nuts.

"I'm not doing my taxes. I'm going to have you drop the box at Al Womble's office. One of his whiz kid accountants can figure it out. I'm going to Las Vegas. Find out who killed my buddy... and why!"

"Judge, you can't do that. We have a dinner party tonight at the Wiggins'. And tomorrow is that fund raiser for Children's Hospital. You can't just abandon our social obligations."

"The Hell I can't. The Wiggins are the most boring people we know. And all I do at these benefit functions is drink a bit too much, express opinions destined for some reason to antagonize the people to either side of me and get a scolding from you about it on the way home."

"Oh Judge. You just can't do this to me again. It's hard enough to maintain a social life between your workaholic schedule and these Don Quixote mystery escapades you embroil yourself in. You promised this time, this week, you'd be here for me. Damn it. You even let me write it in your daybook."

The Judge cherished his small pocket calendar book and carried it everywhere. None of this computer calendar crap for him. He rarely allowed anyone to touch it, much less write in it. It'd been a blunder to let his wife write commitments in it. Commitments he might later decide to ignore. That wouldn't happen again!

"My oldest friend has just been murdered. He called me just before he disappeared. He was looking for help, desperate to talk to me. Desperate to figure a way out. That was his message on my voicemail. But I was too busy to answer. If I'd only answered, things might be different. But I was too busy. Too busy walking the damn dog for… for you. Anyway, I didn't call him back."

The Judge glared at Annie the Dog, the pesky golden retriever curled up in the corner, her smoldering brown eyes watching him with interest. She was looking for any hint he might head to the kitchen where she could be sure to get a tidbit of whatever he was shoveling into his face. "You can't expect me to stand by and do nothing. I've known Bob Hanson twice as long as I've known you."

He knew this last shot was a mistake. But it was too late. The words tumbled out of his mouth almost of their own accord. Katy's sympathetic look vanished. She looked like she'd just been slapped. He tried to think of a way to back-pedal without losing his position but couldn't think fast enough.

"You said he's been dead two weeks, Judge." Katy's eyes were blazing now. "Why can't you wait a week and then go? Fulfill the commitments you made to me first. And finish your stupid taxes."

That was his button… the taxes. She should have known better.

"I'm off for Vegas in ten minutes, before the trail grows colder. And screw the taxes. If Al can't unscramble them, we'll just ask the government to figure what we owe, and I'll send them a check."

He stomped from the room.

She called after him, "Judge… Judge…" But he ignored her. He'd spotted the hole in the line and charged through at breakneck speed. What would any sensible man do if there was a choice between taxes linked to a boring dinner party and chasing down the murderer of his oldest friend. It was no choice at all. He was going to Vegas.

Twenty minutes later at the front door she was there again, this time with a tuna sandwich carefully wrapped in plastic baggie and a bottle of some health drink, showing puke green through its clouded plastic container and likely tasting like the bottom of an oil tank.

"It's a long drive, dear. Don't stop at that ugly Mad Italian place and ruin your diet. You'll give yourself gas and be in a sorry state by the time you arrive." She handed over the tuna sandwich and her noxious drink.

He looked at her then, really looked at her. And was swept away again at how beautiful she was and how much he loved her.

Katy was tall and slender still… after eight years of marriage and the birth of their son, she was still magnificent. Her small delicate face gazed up at him with love. Her skin was pale white, as though never in the sun, providing a contrast to her eyes, vivid blue like the Caribbean, large and intelligent, framed by long lashes. Eyes that had worry in them now. Perhaps some feminine instinct that sensed better than he this quest could mean the forfeit of his life.

"I want to come with you, Judge. You might need help."

She put her hand on his arm. Then they embraced, tight, while he muttered into her lavender-scented hair, "No. I have to go alone this time, Katy. Las Vegas can be a rough town. This might be a dangerous trip."

He kissed her then, once on the lips, once on the top of her head for luck, and slid out the door and away, already calculating where he would dump the tuna sandwich and green drink.

CHAPTER 2
MONDAY
12 P.M.

Ninety minutes later the Judge nosed his way up the beginning of the Cajon Pass, the jagged and lofty trail that cut through the San Berdoo Mountains like a marauding snake and now had an uppity name: Interstate Highway 15. The primary Southern California route to Vegas. He missed Katy already. But what he had to do needed to be done alone. It wasn't fun.... well maybe. But he knew there would be risks; that it wouldn't be safe. He'd have enough trouble taking care of himself. He didn't want to worry about Katy.

Bob Hanson had been more than a long-time friend; almost like a brother. And more recently a client. They'd gone to USC together, fraternity brothers, and then on to the USC Gould School of Law. They'd been study-group pals, initiated in the Hell that was first year Law School. Held up to the scalding intellect and scathing public interrogation of overbearing law professors. Publicly humiliated each time they were called upon to stand and answer questions. Found wanting again and again and again... until suddenly they weren't. Suddenly, they were thinking like lawyers, ignoring the criticism and belittlement, with skins thicker than a rhinoceros.

Bob had been best man in the Judge's first wedding to the wife who left him; bailed to run off with her boss. The Judge had stood beside Bob at his wedding, and at a christening of Bob's only child, a daughter, Jackie. In the end neither marriage had worked out; many didn't in 21st Century America. Perhaps because females had more options now. And if they chose a career, a lot more stress.

Ten years before Bob Hanson had left the practice of law and begun developing real estate, riding the upswing in property values and initially doing well for himself. You had to be a bit of a gambler to succeed… Bob was.

The Judge stopped in Barstow and stretched his legs, grabbed some coffee, and wished he'd taken the plane. He was stiff as a board and there was another two and a half hours to go. He thought back to three weeks earlier, the last time he'd seen Bob at Bob's Vegas project, The Spire. Bob was a large man, big chest, gut and hindquarters set on short spindly legs that left him a bit breathless at the top of stairs and on marches around the perimeter of his project. An unruly shock of hair, prematurely white, had crowned his forehead, while manicured sideburns tapered down the side of his face, framing his ruddy complexion. Large vivid blue eyes under white winged eyebrows had smiled at the Judge, complementing Bob's aw-shucks grin that slightly exposed crooked teeth. Bob had always been a friendly character, filled with good cheer for everyone. If anything, a tad too trusting in the Judge's view.

But behind Bob's smile three weeks ago there'd been something. Had it been uncertainty... maybe desperation... perhaps fear? His fortunes as a real estate developer had seen many ups and downs, the nature of the business. But too many downs on his last projects. He'd told the Judge that his new project, The Spire, was his last chance to crawl out of the hole and score big before settling into his senior years. One last grab at the brass ring. Success would mean security, an expensive lifestyle, and proof of ultimate self-worth. The Judge had understood.

But now Bob was no more. Erased from the face of the earth forever, prematurely, by the decision of someone else. Someone who thought he could play God and destroy a fellow human being with impunity. The Judge was coming after whoever made that decision. He wasn't going to stop until that person was brought to justice.

Since Katy wasn't along to object the Judge stopped at the Mad Italian for a hamburger, onion rings and a strawberry shake. Back on the road fifteen minutes later he fumbled for the Tums in the glove compartment, wishing he'd followed Katy's advice. Then he brought his cell phone out and asked the car to dial a number in Las Vegas. Cindy Hanson, Bob's ex-wife, answered immediately. The soft quiver in her "Hello" told the Judge she knew about her Ex.

"Hello, Cindy. I'm so sorry."

"Oh, Judge." She let all her air out in a huge sigh.

"If there is anything I can do, Cindy…"

"No… No. Well, yes. Jackie may be missing." There was an edge of hysteria now in her voice.

"Your daughter?"

"Yes. No one's seen or heard from her since Bob disappeared. We're all going crazy. Bob just disappeared, and then so did Jackie, Judge. Shit, I'm at wit's end."

"What about Robbie?" Robbie was Jackie's twelve-year-old son, Bob's grandson.

"Robbie's okay. He's here with me. Jackie said she needed some time alone. But now I'm worried… really worried."

"Have you talked to the police?"

"Yeah. They're not much help. Said they would put a flyer out or something. Can you help? Can you help us find Jackie?"

"I can try."

"And Judge…"

"Yes."

Cindy's voice changed, rising in anger.

"Did you hear how he died, Judge? What they did? God, it was so cruel. He was eaten. Eaten alive by God damn turkey vultures." Cindy's voice wracked with a sob.

"Find them Judge." Cindy's voice was low now, menacing. "Find the bastards who did this to Bob. See that they fry."

CHAPTER 3
MONDAY
3:30 P.M.

The Judge traversed the last of the great Mojave Desert, up, over and down hills of hot sand and scrub, maneuvering the Mercedes along the grey asphalt ribbon that jagged its way through the desolate space like an errant zipper. His mind drifted back to eighteen months before, when Bob had first sought his help.

Bob Hanson had come to the Judge seeking legal advice for a new project. A typical Hanson project, a real estate play he'd bet his entire net worth on.

His project was the building of a time-share hotel in Vegas, just off the Strip. Bob wanted the Judge to do the legal on the project. And of course, the Judge said yes. It was fun to work with Bob. The guy was always up, always smiling, always seeing the best in every turn of event and every person he met. He could charm anybody with his dancing blue eyes, broad smile, warm handshake, and the embrace he instinctively gave even casual acquaintances. The Judge was going to miss his friend. It shouldn't have happened. Not to Bob. Not this way. Not any way.

They'd spent a lot of time together at the beginning, sorting out the legal and financial aspects of

The Spire. The Judge had enjoyed that time. He'd watched the project turn from Bob's vision to something tangible as it grew out of the ground. The piece of sand and scrub behind the Strip had turned into the beautiful skin of a twenty-story boutique time-share hotel.

But the hotel had gone over budget, way over budget. Surprise, surprise. And it had taken longer to construct, way longer… more surprise, surprise. Bob had run through the capital of the syndication he'd put together to raise the front money, his lender's construction financing, and his own capital, and still the hotel's interior was not finished.

Bob had pounded the pavement for additional money to carry the construction forward, courting sources he'd declined to disclose to the Judge. Somehow, he'd managed to raise more money. But it was consumed by The Spire's subcontractors practically immediately in a frenzy reminiscent of a feeding school of piranha. Meantime, the economy took a nosedive, legions of tourists to Vegas dwindled to handfuls, the bottom fell out of the real estate market, and sources of financing dried up.

Even worse, since the Las Vegas Strip was not actually in the City of Las Vegas, but immediately to its south in the unincorporated towns of Paradise and Winchester, Bob found himself under the thumb of a hostile Clarkson County Building Department that found reason after reason to temporarily stop work on his project.

The Spire's interior completion had slowed to a crawl while construction loan interest, taxes and insurance ate away at what little liquid capital Bob had left.

The Judge maneuvered through the late afternoon traffic clogging Interstate 15, finally pulling off the freeway at the Flamingo Exit. He drifted down Flamingo Road, crossed the Vegas Strip, and turned right just before the Meridian Project where he owned a condo, Koval Lane. He immediately turned again, into the sweeping driveway of a spindly unoccupied residential tower set back from the road. Its neon sign proclaimed: *The Spire.*

Driving past the glistening silver structure just behind Bally's, people instinctively slowed their cars just to have a closer look. It was an awe-inspiring tower clad in a reflective silver skin. Reminiscent of a church with its sweeping single-sided spire pointed to the heavens.

The footprint of the building was set by its first floor, a rectangular structure, its length along Koval Lane and its shorter end facing Flamingo. Above the first floor, the structure soared nineteen stories on one side, part of a giant triangle, its tall side on Koval and its angular plane running from the tip of its spire there, down to the top of the first floor facing the Strip. In the center of its angular plane was a rectangular hole cut down to ground level, creating an open-air rectangle plaza in its middle. The shared green space inside the cutout was an 'urban oasis', its two pools and verdant green-scape entwined with patios, walking paths and small waterscape features.

The Spire's shape changed, depending on the viewer's vantage point. From the west, it was a hyperbolic paraboloid or a warped pyramid. From the east, the building appeared to be a slender spire.

By keeping three corners of the block low and lifting the east portion of the building, the courtyard opened with views towards the Strip and its massive light show at night. And it caught the low western sun deep into the block in the late afternoons. The courtyard was meant to be a private space and a sanctuary for residents, but with views of the night skyline that gave Vegas its intensity and glamour. At the upper levels, the condominium units were organized on a fishbone layout, orienting the units towards the view of the Strip. Large terraces carved into the warped façade maximized the views and light into the units.

The building was... well... magnificent. And it was all built, or at least its exterior was. The interior? Well, not so much.

Half the bathrooms were not installed. And some kitchens and even interior walls needed to be completed. The City Building Department refused to issue an occupancy permit for any unit until all interiors were complete. But Bob had no money. The additional twelve million, wherever Bob got it, was almost gone. And all financing had dried up with the economic downturn. After payments weren't made, the construction lender initiated a foreclosure on the construction loan to take the property over.

Bob had told the Judge he had a signed contract extending the maturity date of the loan and deferring payments for three years, but when the time came to produce an executed extension, Bob couldn't find it.

Three and a half weeks ago, faced with an effort to foreclose on the project by the construction lender, Bob put The Spire into a Debtor in Possession Bankruptcy proceeding. Half a week later, he'd disappeared.

Was there a connection? Between The Spire's bankruptcy and Bob's one-way ride into Hell? The Judge wondered…

And what about that last critical cell message, left when the Judge was too busy to answer Bob's desperate call. The words still burned in the Judge's mind. Words from a man who sounded as though he was gasping for air.

"Christ, Judge. Pick up your damn phone. I've dug a real hole for myself on my Spire Project. This guy I went to doesn't play around. I think his people are after me now. I can't think of any way out. I need your advice. One of your Hail Mary solutions that always saves the day. God, I need to talk to you, buddy. Call me as soon as you get this."

CHAPTER 4
MONDAY
4:00 P.M.

The Judge pulled away from The Spire and headed over to the Clarkson County Coroner's Office and Morgue. The Coroner's Office looked like a library from the outside: one story, all brick, cast concrete walls in a boxy style popular thirty years ago. Detective Barry Marsh met the Judge outside.

It had been perhaps five years since the Judge had seen Barry. The Detective looked pretty much the same, except that the flaming red hair had mellowed into a blond grey. The Judge felt a tad of satisfaction to see someone else aging. Marsh didn't have a damn bald patch in the top of his head though. Wasn't becoming a Friar Tuck like the Judge.

Marsh was in a rumpled suit, his tie long since removed, and was nursing a Starbucks with two hands. In the old days he would have had a donut, but the donut shops seemed few and far between these days. He was 6 foot, 230 pounds, and had blue eyes that watched the Judge approach from a ruddy face. He'd seemed to be a good cop, had expressed views of concern about his community and the people in it, when they'd worked a case together five years before. This had created a bond of sorts that still held.

Marsh led the Judge into the office building, holding thumbs up as he passed the deputy at the front desk.

The Judge was introduced to Arthur Morales, the death investigator assigned to the Bob Hanson case. "Just 'Art'," Morales said, pumping the Judge's hand.

Art was a thin little man, emphasized by his too big shirt and jacket and his long narrow tie fashionable fifty years ago. He had the professionally sad countenance of an undertaker and walked in slow deliberate steps with his shoulders slumped. He led them into the bowels of the building, stainless steel walls and ceramic tile floors. There was a central corridor with small rooms to either side, each containing stainless steel tables and assorted knives, power cutting tools, and other instruments neatly hanging on the walls.

"How do you like this job, Art?" asked the Judge.

"It's a living, Judge. Nothing more. It pays well, and there can be lots of overtime if we get busy. I will say there is one thing that is brought home to me every day I work here."

"What's that?"

"Life is to be lived to the fullest, Judge. It's taught me to spend as much time with my wife and grandchildren as possible. To seize every chance I have to tell them how much I love them. Life is so short. And it can be a lot shorter than you expect. You turn a corner, make a wrong turn, sleep with the wrong woman, fail to pay an important debt, or piss off the wrong guy... and suddenly you're gone. No curtain call. We see it happen here over and over."

They trudged farther along the corridor, avoiding a series of gurneys stacked end to end lining the wall, each one with a pale toe sticking out from under a blue plastic cover, sprouting a blue tag.

"When multiple bodies arrive, they get laid out like this after we have done our autopsy. The organs are stored on a gurney shelf beneath the body. In due course, after all the pictures are taken, they'll be moved to our cold storage."

"You mean, unless there's a little hanky-panky, don't you, Art?" chuckled Barry.

Art blushed. "You're referring to our resident necrophile I suppose, Barry?"

"I didn't hear that story," said the Judge.

"Yeah, well, to our embarrassment, one of our Assistant Coroners on the night shift had been pimping out some of our younger bodies for sexual gratification."

"No way," said the Judge.

"I'm afraid it's true," said Art. "It's an ongoing scandal. The guy operated a cadaver brothel service for more than five years at night here. Met his customers through a private internet site he set up on the Dark Web. He advertised corpses readily available for play and for sex, charged from fifteen hundred to five thousand per sexual encounter. Price depended on the quality of the merchandise I understand. Guess he had customers from almost every state, as well as from Mexico, Europe, and Asia. There were even some Middle Eastern princes among his regulars."

Barry snickered. "Only in Sin City, Judge."

"What will happen to him?" asked the Judge.

"He's facing a total of seventeen hundred and thirty-four criminal charges of necrophilia, corpse desecration, and felony mutilation of human remains," said Barry. "Maximum sentence, maybe seven hundred years."

"How'd they catch him?"

"Investigators spent months chatting with him on necrophile forums, trying to gain his trust. Finally, he offered his services. A sting operation was organized, and he was arrested here in this corridor after he accepted three thousand dollars in cash."

"Makes you wonder," said Barry.

Art steered them into a room toward the end of the long corridor that opened into a larger room with lockers set against the walls stacked on top of each other. The lockers emitted a low hum. Refrigerated. Art consulted his clipboard, then went over to the center of the boxes and rolled out the drawer marked 10287. He whipped the white plastic sheet off the frozen lump underneath with a flourish. The Judge felt like he might be sick.

It was Bobby all right, or what was left of him. One side of his stomach was gone, his entrails consumed by the desert animals and birds. One half of Bob's chest had bleached-white ribs protruding. Half his face was gone, teeth and gums showing where his cheek should have been, and his eyes were empty sockets. But the shock of white hair was still there. The smile lines around the jaw reminded the Judge of the good times they'd shared.

"He wasn't robbed, Judge," said Barry. "He had his wallet with over eighteen hundred in cash. And we could find no indication of a wound, either bullet or knife made, nor any indication of being hit with a blunt instrument."

"They just gave him a one-way ride?"

"Yes, Judge. Pushed him out of a vehicle about sunup thirty miles from any road. Must have been a four-wheel vehicle, but we couldn't find any tread tracks. Been too long. He had his cash, driver's license, Social Security card, Triple-A card, cell phone, small change in his pocket, just as he must have been when he was picked up somewhere in Vegas. The things he didn't have of course were water, a hat, a compass, and a tent or something for shade. They knew he wouldn't be able to walk out of the desert. And he didn't."

"No car keys?"

"Nope. That was a little odd. There were no car keys."

The Judge nodded. Someone was going to pay big time. Since no next of kin had officially done so, the Judge identified for Art that it was indeed Robert Hanson and signed his form. Then he turned on his heel, and fled back down the hall toward reception, wishing he was anywhere but in the Clarkson County Morgue.

CHAPTER 5
MONDAY
5:15 P.M.

The Judge returned to his Mercedes and drove onto the Interstate 15. He transferred to Interstate 21, got off in Henderson, and headed up into the hills, to Tangiers Drive. This was a burb where some of the more affluent Las Vegas denizens pitched their tents. He parked in front of Cindy Hanson's home, a sprawling ranch style, coated in brownie-colored stucco with dark chocolate trim. The front yard was scaped in white rock with succulents here and there. A lone olive tree stood uncertainly in the middle of the yard, looking thirsty.

Cindy Hanson opened the door on the second ring and glared up at the Judge. She was an anxious little blonde who'd always reminded the Judge of a cocker spaniel, nervously shaking her torso and yapping. In the old days on Fraternity Row, she'd caused quite a stir when she walked by, a large rack on a small frame with a butt built to give an exotic jiggle. She always turned heads.

She'd set her sights on Bob soon after they'd met. The Judge had suspected it was also after researching Bob's pedigree, including his San Marino family who smelt of social prestige and money. She'd pursued Bob ruthlessly in an off-and-on romance that kept the gossip mill busy and even generated a betting pool in their frat house as to whether she'd land her big fish.

The off-and-on continued through law school, till finally Cindy had sealed the deal in Bob's last year. She'd gotten herself pregnant and presented herself to Bob's mother fait accompli, declaring she was 'having the child come Hell or high water.' Bob and his parents would have to pay for it either way, she said, threatening a social scandal the parents couldn't tolerate.

But the relationship hadn't changed much by the marriage, still up and down over a fifteen-year stretch. Cindy miscalculated her divorce, closing it out at the bottom of one of Bob's valleys in his real estate development business. The Judge heard she'd gotten only a modest property settlement, plus sliding alimony and childcare for a couple of years that floated up and down like a barometer of Bob's successes and failures.

At fifty-four, Cindy was still small, well proportioned, and still walked the wicked jiggle. But the blond hair was a little dull now from too many bleaches. Blue eyes, crinkled around the edges, still blazed out of a face tan and lined by too much stress and too much sun. The lines around her mouth suggested a grimace most of the time, likely a symptom of money issues, a constant concern. She still talked a mile a minute and acted like a dizzy blond, ignoring those who might say she was a bit old for the role.

"The bastard hasn't paid his alimony in eighteen months, Judge," Cindy huffed. "He dumped all my money into his damn Spire instead of paying me. Sure, I got investor units or something, but they're now worthless what with the project in bankruptcy. And then… and then…" Cindy's voice rose two octaves, "I've learned this morning the asshole mortgaged this house, my house, dumped the loan proceeds into The Spire. My house mortgage is now in default."

The house wasn't technically Cindy's house of course. Cindy knew it and so did the Judge. It had been the second home of Bob's parents, inherited when they died, and outside the community property laws. Bob had allowed Cindy to live here for years, an offset in part to his often-delinquent alimony obligations.

Divorce laws were strict in California. After ten years a marriage was considered long-term. The court retained jurisdiction to modify the support amount perpetually until the receiving spouse either remarried or died. Some of course married up, often initiating a new affair with a more affluent playmate of marriageable material before departing an unhappy marriage. Hop-scotching their way up the social ladder and upgrading their standard of living with all the guile of their male counterparts hop-scotching up the corporate ladder.

Others didn't age as well or, like Cindy, lacked the social base. They adopted a more pragmatic strategy. Sequential live-in boyfriends they never married, keeping their alimony rolling in. So long as the alimony continued, they'd never marry again. Why fuck up a good thing?

According to Bob, Cindy seemed to average a new man every eighteen months or so. There was a guy named Sam in her life right now, perhaps the big guy sprawled on one of the two sofas as the Judge walked through the foyer and into her living room. The guy looked territorial and not happy to see the Judge.

The living room was a step-down affair with plush desert-colored carpet and Swiss-coffee walls. Dark leather couches faced each other across a long leather carved coffee table protected by a sheet of glass. A baby grand in a high polished tan sat off to the right, near a large brass trolly with assorted booze on top and stacked cans of mixers below. Bay windows looked out across the front white gravel to the thirsty tree and beyond, down the steeply graded street toward the plain below. At the horizon, across the dry suburban sprawl, sat the jagged skyline of the Vegas Strip, looking like the painted lady she was.

On the second sofa sat a young boy of twelve. Large eyes focused on the Judge with desperation out of a small thin body. Robbie was Cindy and Bob's only grandchild, the son of Jackie, the missing daughter. Robbie looked like his grandfather when Bob was younger, blond hair and the same startling blue eyes. The child was in the in-between phase beginning teenagers hit, still a bit round in the face, but with a skinny frame that gave him a waif look.

His eyes, pockets of blue, had been filled with mirth the last time the Judge saw him. But today they looked sad and confused as he tried to make sense of events swirling around in a grownup world he didn't fully comprehend.

He jumped up and rushed the Judge, throwing his arms around the Judge's paunch, squeezing the Judge's breath away, holding on with the determination of an undersized limpet caught in the tide.

"Oh, Judge," he whispered. "Oh, Judge."

The Judge hadn't expected this. He was technically Robbie's Godfather, though he'd done piss-all to justify the title. He'd seen Robbie several times with Bob, at sporting events mostly, and on the Judge's boat once on a trip to Catalina. And he'd talked to the boy here and there, but Robbie had always been quiet and shy. The Judge couldn't say he really knew the boy. He had the sense Robbie was now clutching at straws. And he was the new straw. The Judge felt sad for the boy. And guilty he hadn't been a better friend for the boy's sake, and for Bob's.

The Judge wrapped his arms around the small bundle at his waist and squeezed back, trying to reassure the young human who seemed starved for attention and affection. Robbie muffled a small sob, squeezed harder, whispered, "So glad you're here," his voice catching a little in his throat. Robbie unwound himself and returned to his sofa, collapsing in a small lump in its corner and watching the Judge with hopeful eyes.

The Judge settled on the sofa close to the boy and leaned a bit sideway to contact Robbie's small shoulder. The boy immediately leaned into the Judge, seeking contact and warmth.

"Good to see you, Robbie. How are you? How's school going?"

"Well… you know, Judge."

"Actually, I don't Robbie. Tell me."

"Oh, well, I'm missing Mom. Grandma's worried sick about her. And what happened to Grandpa makes me so sad. And school's just… school. Pretty boring mostly."

"I'm Sam, Judge." The words rumbled out of the big guy straightening on the sofa, breaking the moment, as though jealous of Robbie's attention. "We haven't met."

Sam leaned forward in his seat but didn't get up, extending a thick paw to cradle the Judge's hand in its clutch. "I'm Cindy's special friend."

"Boyfriend?" asked the Judge.

"More than boyfriend, Judge. I'm Cindy's financial adviser and intimate confidant." A superior smile spread across Sam's face.

Sam was a well over six foot, broad of shoulder, perhaps a tackle in his youth. Somewhere in his mid-fifties, he looked a bit flabby now, sporting a padded tummy outlined under his orange floral Tommy Bahama shirt. He had a big meaty neck and arms and hands to match. The Judge wondered idly how Cindy and Sam managed lovemaking, presenting as they did the combinational equivalent of a small mouse and a Mack Truck.

Sam had close-chopped brown hair, making his ears stick out, a flexible smile that didn't tell you what he was thinking, and crafty brown eyes that made the Judge want to check his wallet.

Cindy returned with a drink, Scotch on the rocks the way the Judge liked it, but a blend, not a single malt. Any Scotch was better than no Scotch he supposed.

They sat in silence for a minute while the Judge sipped his drink. Robbie looking dully at his shoes and wiggling his feet. Cindy calming herself after her outburst of anger about her Ex. And Sam continuing to look disinterested and bored.

"Why don't you go upstairs and start on your homework, Robbie," Cindy said.

The boy got up and reluctantly headed upstairs, throwing one last longing look at the Judge.

"How are you coping, Cindy?" asked the Judge.

"How do you think, Judge? I haven't received my alimony in over a year. This house now belongs to Bob's estate and is in foreclosure. His stupid Spire Project, a monument to his enormous ego, is crumbling in bankruptcy. My daughter has disappeared. And I seem to have a permanent grandson to support. All in all, I'm swell, Judge. Just swell." She took a swig of her vodka on the rocks. "My life's rolling up into a huge shit ball, Judge. A huge fuckin' shit ball!"

Cindy slid closer to Sam on the sofa and fumbled for his hand, seeking reassurance.

"Who killed Bob, Cindy? Any idea? Or even why?"

"I don't know, Judge. I suppose lots of people were angry enough to kill him, including me. And I suspect Bob was doing some desperate things.

Particularly after those cheats at the bank denied they'd executed an extension on the maturity date for the construction loan. I think Bob borrowed a lot of money from people recently. Used the funds to make one last push to finish all The Spire improvements and force Clarkson County to issue the occupancy permit.

The pricks at the Building Department kept misplacing the file, then finding one more thing, then one other thing, then something else, deliberately delaying occupancy until Bob ran out of money. I think they were part of a conspiracy to steal The Spire out from under him. Force him into bankruptcy. I talked to Bob that morning he put the project into bankruptcy. After I got through yelling at the shit, telling him what I thought of him, he said something funny."

"What?"

"Said he may have gotten a rescue loan from the wrong guy."

"Do you know what he meant?"

"No."

"Do you know who gave him the loan?"

"No."

"How much it was for?"

"I don't know."

"Was there a deed of trust executed to secure the loan?"

"I don't know."

"Did Bob tell you anything else about it, maybe earlier, in the weeks leading up to the bankruptcy filing?"

"Bob said once he'd gotten a new loan over the Dark Web, whatever that is. Oh, and 'it was his ass' if it didn't get it repaid. I don't know what that meant either."

"Bob just got in over his head," said Sam. "It happens." He didn't sound particularly sorry.

"Did you invest in the project, Sam?" asked the Judge.

"Me? Do I look nuts? The project was undercapitalized from the start. No reserves for contingencies. I wouldn't touch it with a ten-foot pole."

"What sort of business are you in, Sam?"

"I own a marketing message center."

"You mean like a cold call center?"

"Some people call it that. But these are messages over the net to people. When someone shows interest, we pursue the contact and close a sale."

"You make a lot of money at it?"

"Not that it's any of your business, Judge, but soon, not quite yet. My partners and I are just starting it up here in Vegas. But it's going to be big."

"You don't know who might have been Bob's big investor?"

"I don't."

Cindy brightened a little. "Maybe the Judge could help you find an investor for your enterprise, Sam. I know he's done it for other people."

Sam's head snapped up, instant attention, a salesman's smile spreading across his face.

"What a great idea. We've just started this business, Judge. One partner was supposed to be providing additional capital, but he's run into some problems and he's a little short. We're looking for an investor, one to three million to build out our message center. It'll be fully equipped, state of the art, fully staffed, fully operational. It's guaranteed thirty percent on your money and a continuing equity stake in our business."

"I'm not sure I know of any..."

Sam interrupted. "Don't make a decision yet, Judge. Come see our center in the morning. Let me show you what it's about first. You'll be impressed."

Sam gave the Judge a gooey smile, all teeth, like an adolescent girl looking to be asked to her first dance.

"Okay," muttered the Judge, figuring he had to start somewhere looking for Bob's killer. He turned back to Cindy.

"Cindy, tell me about your daughter, Jackie. How old is she now?"

"Twenty-eight, Judge. Had Robbie when she was almost sixteen. Way too young. I tried to talk her out of it. But she had some flower-child idea it would be wonderful to have a baby. She dropped out of school and had Robbie. I've been helping ever since."

"How is it Jackie's missing, Cindy?

"We had a big fight about two weeks before Bob disappeared, Judge. I called her out on her drugs. The last year Jackie's started smoking weed, dropping pills. Showed no interest in Robbie. It's like she just withdrew from us. Left me to deal with Robbie, help him with his homework, show interest in his school, interface with him, give him attention. In her head I think she'd just abandoned her son. Anyway, we had a big fight. I told her she couldn't do drugs in front of Robbie anymore. Couldn't do drugs in my house anymore. Jackie got quite snotty. Packed her things and marched out."

"Where'd she go?"

"She went straight to her dad, of course. He hired her as his executive assistant at The Spire, to help with bookkeeping and with the subcontractors while he tried to finish construction. He gave her a unit there to live in next to his."

"So, she's not really missing?"

"No, she's really missing. The night Bob disappeared; Jackie disappeared too. Didn't call here, no forwarding address, nothing. Just… poof. Gone. No one's heard from her since. Not me, not Robbie, not any of her friends."

"She have a boyfriend, Cindy?"

"Not that we know of."

Cindy went to a framed picture on the piano, slid the picture out from the frame, and handed it to the Judge. "Taken about four months ago."

The Judge recognized Jackie, but she looked different from the last time he'd seen her perhaps eighteen months before. No more the young woman next door type in holey jeans and college sweatshirt. In the picture she wore a spaghetti-strap dress, emerald-green, cut low to disclose a significant décolleté. Her hair was done up in a sophisticated swirl above her head and she had cherry lips and Cleopatra style mascara which came out beyond her eyes at each corner to give a slightly Asian cast. She looked younger than her twenty-eight years, but somehow worldly-wise. Not at all the refreshing young woman the Judge remembered. The Judge tucked the picture in to his side pocket.

"Do you think the people who killed Bob went after her too?"

"Christ, I hope not, Judge. But I don't know. I just don't know."

"She's out catting around," said Sam, deciding to rejoin the conversation.

"You don't know that Sam," snapped Cindy.

"How else would she be supporting herself, Cindy? She's got no education, no skills, no experience… except in drugs and fucking around. You've coddled her all her life. It's time she stood on her own two feet, even if she lists a little to starboard given all the drugs she taken." Sam chuckled at his own joke.

"That's not fair, Sam."

"It's perfectly fair. She should come take her bastard son and get out of our hair. You've been an enabler all your life, Cindy."

The Judge stood up, making an NFL time out sign with his hands.

"Love to keep score for you two," he said. "But I've got other things to do."

He propelled his bulk toward the door, reached it, and quickly let himself out, ignoring the rising tones of the voices behind him.

The Judge pulled away from the thirsty tree and gunned his car around the downhill curves leaving the

Henderson Ridge, sliding the wheels slightly, angry, taking it out on his car.

Life was so unfair. He would find who did this to Bob and he'd settle the score. He'd find Jackie, see what was up with her. He felt the worst for Robbie. A twelve-year-old boy with a dead grandfather, a lost druggie mother, a grandmother warring with her boyfriend of the month, and a Godfather who'd been next to useless.

CHAPTER 6
MONDAY
7:30 P.M.

The Judge parked in The Spire lot. The building and grounds of The Spire were vacant, all work suspended pending resolution of the bankruptcy. The Judge used the key Bob had given him to open the main door and entered the lobby. It was quiet and empty like an ancient church, particularly with The Spire's corner tower reaching into the sky and visible through the open center courtyard.

The lobby's glass walls looked out on the exterior, and back through the inner courtyard garden and pools visible behind the check-in desk. Every interior surface that wasn't glass looking out to a view was a mirrored wall reflecting one's own image back. Even the ceiling was mirrored, giving the Judge some discomfort as he glanced up and saw the top of his head and its ever-growing patch of bald spreading there. The way he was going he'd soon look like Friar Tuck. Damn! He hated mirrors on ceilings. Of course, there was the time the mirror on the ceiling was in the bedroom and he was *in flagrante delicto*. That mirror had been practically smoking. He smirked at the thought.

He took the glass enclosed elevator up to the top floor and turned left into the paneled corridor, walls and floor covered in sandalwood. The wood left a slight fragrance, stirring in the air as he passed. At the end of the corridor two massive doors guarded Bob's condominium suite. This was where Bob had been living while trying to marshal The Spire through to completion. The Judge punched Bob's personal code, his birthday, into the panel beside the doors, and one door swung open.

The living room of the suite was light and airy, floor-to-ceiling windows on the opposite wall and right wall displaying vast views of the Vegas Strip, lights on now the sun was below the horizon. The walls opposite the view walls were mirrored, as was the ceiling, giving the impression the Judge was standing in a mirrored jewel box with the lid closed. The Judge always felt a little vertigo when he stepped into this room. But Bob gushed about it to anyone who'd listen. The Judge supposed that was why ice cream came in chocolate and strawberry. Different people liked different things.

But Bob's living room was disturbed. The two white rugs usually in the middle of the room were piled in a corner. The twin white leather sofas that usually faced either other at angles so they both caught the view, had been slid into another corner and rolled onto their sides. Their cushions were scattered behind them, and their exposed undersides had been ripped open to expose springs and padding. The Coffee table that usually sat between the sofas was in another corner on its side, its narrow drawers pulled out, contents scattered on the floor. Someone had done a careful search here. Only the massive bar against the left wall, all antique brass, hanging stemware and brightly labeled bottles of spirits, looked untouched.

The Judge turned right and right again, entering a short hall with a guest toilet to one side and a door at its end leading to Bob's office. The office door was closed. He swung the door open, then stood back, gaping at more destruction, this time of cyclone proportions. Half-open drawers and cupboards, papers and notebooks scattered across the floor, another sofa and a chair turned on their sides, bottom fabric torn away. Across the floor, across the table desk with its teak frame and glass top, across the shelves and open doors of the teak bureau behind it, and over the two chairs facing the desk, correspondence, accounting records, reports, drawings and plans of The Spire sprawled in all directions.

Bob's favorite picture, a serigraph by LeRoy Neiman, *Roulette II*, had been ripped from the wall and thrown against the desk, it's glass shattering to shards around the floor. The wall where the picture had hung now gaped a large hole where Bob's wall safe had once sat. The small safe itself was on its side behind the desk, its combination dial face smashed open, its open door hanging from one hinge. It was empty. A sledgehammer and large chisel lay nearby. Someone had come prepared.

The Judge walked back to the living room and across to the small side car kitchen. Here the scent of rotting food tainted the air. The kitchen was much like the office, in tatters. Boxes and cans of food pulled off the shelves and strewn on the floor, the refrigerator standing open, food mostly dried out now and piled at its base, the ice compartment empty.

The Judge returned to the living room and walked down the corridor leading to the guest bathroom. Open doors to either side displayed the master bedroom to the left and a second small guest room to the right. Mattresses were tipped off beds. Half-pulled-out empty drawers and emptied closets leered at the Judge across floors hidden by clothes thrown every which way. The bathroom was the same, the floor covered with bottles and containers swept out of mirrored cupboards and cabinets.

Someone had searched Bob's suite with a frenzy. The Judge wondered if they'd found what they were looking for. The way every cranny and crevice of the penthouse was ravaged, he suspected they hadn't.

The Judge walked back to Bob's office and sat down in Bob's chair, surveying the desktop and the floor's rubble. Surprisingly, the leather mat on the desktop had not been disturbed, just buried with debris. The Judge used his arm to brush the mess off the desk to the floor. None of it was of interest.

The Judge was looking for something else, and he spotted it over in a corner, half open, leaning against the wall. It was a three-ring notebook with a labeled sheet in the clear plastic on its front: THE SPIRE: FINANCIAL STATEMENTS. The Judge got down on his knees to pore over the notebook. It looked intact; no pages torn out. As he glanced back at the desk, he noted a folded paper hidden under the desk mat, visible only from the underside of the desk glass.

He picked up the binder and returned to the desk. He slid his hand under the desk mat and pulled out a folded letter. It had originally been crumpled, perhaps in anger, then smoothed out, folded twice, and shoved under the desk mat. The Judge unfolded the letter and spread it out on the desk:

You lied to us, Bob, you son of a bitch. You assured us you'd have enough money with the raise of eleven million dollars in The Spire Investors LLC syndication to complete The Spire Project and open its doors to sales. You've miserably failed. Now the project is in bankruptcy and our investment is lost.

You'd best watch your back, my ex-friend; someone is going to stick a knife into it. You're going to bleed out all over the sidewalk, and I'm going to be there to jeer at you and watch you die. It's about the only satisfaction I have left now you've destroyed our future.

Forrest Langley

The Judge folded the letter and tried to slide it back under the mat. The paper caught against something. The Judge lifted the pad off the desk and, sure enough, there was a second small piece of paper there, folded over and taped to the glass. The paper had some sort of website address on it, but it wasn't a www address. The Judge stuck this paper into his pocket.

Then he turned his attention to the binder. First, he turned to the tab marked *Charter Documents* and paged through to the back of the *Articles of Limited Liability Company* document, stopping at the list of investors there.

He ran his finger down the list to Forrest Langley and jotted down Langley's address and telephone number on the back of a scrap of paper. Then he took a cell phone shot of the whole list.

Next, he opened the tab marked *Financials*. The financial statements were filed chronologically with the most recent financials on top; handwritten in pencil on green accounting paper in Bob's scrawl. The top set was dated the day before Bob disappeared. The Judge spent ten minutes studying the financials, and particularly the *Source and Application of Funds Statement from Inception*, and the current *Balance Sheet*.

The financials reflected how Bob had put every penny he had into The Spire at the start to buy the land and obtain permits. He'd then raised over eleven million privately from investors in his syndication, using the money as his equity contribution in tandem with a construction loan he took out build The Spire. The original budget was 38 million, all in.

But the cost overruns on the project to date had already extended to an additional twelve million, and the project still didn't have its occupancy permit. Some units were still missing bathrooms and kitchens.

According to the handwritten notes in the margins, the twelve million had been covered by two infusions, the first for cash of five million by wire, the second for seven million paid mostly in bitcoin wired into a Spire Coinbase account. A note indicated a small portion of the second loan had been delivered in US currency. The source of this additional money wasn't clear from the ledger. A notation beside five million in new money read 'SC'. Beside the second, later infusion of seven million there was only a small doodle. It looked like a spider in a web.

The issue in some sense was moot now with the project in a Chapter 11 Bankruptcy proceeding, heading for a bankruptcy receiver. All equity holders and debt would be wiped out as the secured construction loan lender foreclosed and dumped the project onto the market for a quick sale for pennies on the dollar. The wipeout would include the new capital raised, whoever the source, and the syndication investors. There looked to be one million out of the later seven million still unexpended, at least as of the day before Bob disappeared. The trustee would no doubt find a way to consume most of that in fees if the funds were still around.

If either source of the additional capital infusions were loans from the Vegas Mob, they wouldn't take kindly to their loss. Nor would an angry investor who'd risked his life savings in the syndication. The Judge wondered if the bankruptcy filing, signaling the death of The Spire Project, sealed Bob's one-way ticket to the middle of the desert.

The Judge left the records in Bob's office, made his way back down to the lobby and left the building. He drove to the Meridian Condominium Complex on Flamingo, one block and a half away, where for some years he'd kept a small one-bedroom condo for meeting Nevada clients. The Judge was sagging as he pulled in and waved at the security guard to operate the gate. It had been a long day, a long drive, and an emotional journey, particularly viewing what was left of Bob Hanson on that steel slider. And then facing Bob's Ex, and Bob's grandson, Robbie.

He wondered what it would be like to no longer exist. Supposed it would be like nothing… just nothing.

The Judge poured himself a single malt over ice and wandered aimlessly around his condo for a while. The unit was furnished with used furniture from The Venetian, newer stuff but with all the gold edging and carving that was the hotel's hallmark. A collection of antique-colored lithographs from Venice patterned the walls, Venice, Italy being one of the Judge's favorite haunts. Scattered amongst the pictures hung a collection of Mardi Gras masks from the Carnival in Venice, New Orleans and Rio.

He smiled at the thought of the ruckus he participated in during multiple Mardi Gras parties around the world in his younger days. Days when he'd had more energy and was certain he would live forever. Where had those days gone? And where had his certainty? He was feeling vulnerable tonight.

The unit had its own private outdoor balcony, three stories up, looking over the clubhouse and pool. Now it was dark a kaleidoscope of color cascaded in from the blazing Strip and the Giant Wheel two blocks away.

He called Katy but had to leave a message, remembering she was at her Wiggins dinner party. Thank God he didn't have to be there. He poured himself some more Scotch, Laphroaig PX Cask single malt, his favorite, watched a little news on TV, and finally went to sleep in the big queen bed with its romantically carved bedframe that had been the toast of The Venetian Bridal Suite.

CHAPTER 7
TUESDAY
10:00 A.M.

The Judge had foolishly pulled the bedroom blackout drapes closed before he drifted off. He awoke to dark of night, even though the bedside clock showed almost ten. He threw open the blackouts and was immediately sorry. The bright desert glare of morning stabbed deep into his eyes. He covered his eyes with his hand and ducked away, groaning.

He showered, shaved, and grabbed a cup of Starbucks in the Hughes Center behind the Meridian. He called the office of the bankruptcy attorney Bob had hired and made an appointment to meet at 1:30 that afternoon. Then he pulled out the scrap of paper with Forrest Langley's telephone number on it. This was the angry investor who had threatened Bob's life. He called Langley and requested a brief meeting to discuss The Spire. Langley growled, "Sure," and hung up.

Thirty minutes later the Judge pulled up to an iron-gated entry leading to a big house set behind a partial screen of bay laurel trees. The house didn't look the sort owned by a guy financially on his last legs. The house and grounds were plush.

The Judge pushed the button set into a massive concrete pillar supporting its front gate and the eight-foot white-washed wall which appeared to encircle the property. There was a whirring noise over his head. He looked up to see a robotic camera adjusting itself to get a better view of him, its single eye pushing down and forward at him like some prehistoric spider about to spring.

There was a crackle in the speaker set in the wall, and then a disembodied voice came on.

"Yes?"

"I'm the Judge, here to see Mr. Langley. I made an appointment."

"Okay," said crackle-voice.

A buzzer sounded and the gate began a slow creepy opening, as though waking from a dusty sleep. The Judge piled back into his car and drove through, swinging around the trees and onto a cobblestone surface in front of a colonial style house. The Judge parked beside an aging Chevy that was missing paint and sported balding tires. Whitewashed and sitting proud, the house looked like a miniature Tara from *Gone with the Wind*. Its white clapboard siding clashed with the bright orange notice, taped next to its door, announcing a foreclosure and auction of the house, grounds and furnishings in five days.

So, it was true. Forrest Langley was broke.

As the Judge stepped up onto the green-painted porch, the front door opened, and a man lounged against the frame. Late sixties and emaciated, dark splotches under his eyes and whisps of white hair scrambled across an almost bald pate, he peered at the Judge with angry eyes.

"I already talked to police. I don't know anything about that bastard's death, 'cept it served him right. Hope he suffered for hours."

"Bob Hanson?"

"Of course, Bob Hanson. The most corrupt real estate syndicator there ever was. That's why you came to talk, isn't it? Cause I threatened him?"

"Yes. I found your note in his files. It was very threatening.

"Yeah, well the police didn't mention my note. But it was no secret. I threatened to kill Hanson. He deserved to die. Only sorry someone beat me to it."

"Can you explain a little more about what happened? I'm trying to get a picture of it all."

"Who are you exactly?"

I'm an investigator, looking into Hanson's death for his family. I won't take long."

"Sure. Come on in. Want a drink? I'm having Scotch on the rocks myself. Keeps me going about this time of morning."

The Judge was ushered down a long hall and into a living room, stepping around boxes stacked here and there, some already sealed, some open and partially filled. Forrest introduced Laura Langley, his wife, a small birdlike woman, late sixties, who looked equally stressed. She briefly brushed her hand across the Judge's and then perched on the edge of a green brocade sofa. The Judge settled on a matching sofa across from her.

Forrest sat down next to his wife, who took his hand and put it in her lap to hold.

"You invested in Bob Hanson's Syndication, is that right? Asked the Judge."

Forrest growled, "The rat told me it was as sure thing. I couldn't lose."

Laura Langley brought a small pink hanky out of her sleeve and started to dab at one eye.

"We're in a cash bind now, Judge," Forrest said. "I was counting on a return of cash from my Spire investment. Now I'm losing the house, the furniture, everything. The cars are already gone. I bought that old clunker out there from Car Max. Hanson lied to me straight up. Said I couldn't lose money. Said the project was already mostly built, would be finished quickly, had the units already eighty percent pre-sold. He lied and lied and lied. If I'd had any liquid cash left, I'd have hired a hitman myself."

"But you didn't?"

"Hire a hitman? No. And I didn't have anything to do with his death, unless evil wishes count."

"How much money did you lose, if I can ask?"

"Two million."

"What sort of work did you do before you retired?"

"I had a string of pawn shops here in Vegas."

"That must be a great business in this town."

"It used to be. Till the Mob moved in. First, they wanted rent every week. Then they decided it was too lucrative a business to let honest people operate. So, they started taking over, setting up their own shops to split the market and initiating a program to force us smaller shops out. First it was threats, then 'accidental' fires, followed by a rash of break-ins. Where that didn't work on some of us, they used violence. I sold out. Took my cash and retired. Figuring I was set for life. Boy, how stupid was that?"

"You don't realize how transitory life is, Mr. Judge, till you start losing stuff," Laura Langley muttered in a low whiskey voice. "I love this house. We've been here for twenty years. We raised our children here. So many wonderful memories. I thought I'd die here. Now it's gone. It doesn't belong to us anymore. Wiped away by one foolish thirty-second decision, a signature on a stupid subscription form."

"Where will you go?"

"We're going to move in with our son for a bit, get our feet grounded while I liquidate some offshore assets, decide what to do next," said Forrest. "And I guess I might go back to work."

"I wish you wouldn't, dear," said Laura in a small voice. "We've got Social Security and some savings. We can still have a reasonable lifestyle. You don't need to go back. I don't want to lose you." Laura's last words caught in her throat. She brought a small ivory hanky from her sleeve to press against her mouth. Seeking control.

"What sort of work would you do now?" asked the Judge.

"After I sold the business, I did specialized jobs for people. Kind of a contract specialist. It was interesting work. Each case different. I still have a good reputation in my field."

Laura stared at her feet; hanky pressed harder now.

"Were the other investors equally angry?"

"Of course."

"You think one of them might have killed Hanson?"

"You mean given him a nice jaunty ride out into the desert? One way, no charge?"

"Yes."

"I don't know. There was another guy, vocal like me. A short little guy. Stood up and yelled at Hanson at the investors' meeting. Said Hanson was dead meat."

"Do you remember his name?"

"Someone called him Shakely or Shorty, or something like that. I never actually met him. But he seemed as angry as I was. Younger guy, forties. Looked lower class."

"How so?"

"I don't know. Guess the way he dressed, cheap sport shirt, beat up jeans. Had a five o'clock shadow. Kind of a swarthy complexion. Looked Italian. And a mean smirk after he spoke."

"No accent?"

"No. He was a local."

"Have you seen this girl before?" The Judge pulled the picture of Bob's daughter, Jackie, from his coat and passed it over.

"Sure. She's the Asshole's young assistant. She was there the last two meetings of investors, recording the session, taking notes, passing out materials. Pranced around in a skirt way too young for her and way too short, nice legs though. She even answered some of the questions. Told the same lies Hanson told."

"Have you seen her recently?"

"Yeah. Saw her late last week hanging at the bar in Bally's. Trolling for men." There was a sneer in Langley's voice.

Laura Langley suddenly came alive. "What were you doing in that place?"

"Just a business meeting, honey."

"Yeah, I'll bet. You were gambling again, weren't you, Forrest? You stupid prick."

"Shut up, Laura. Go back to your sulk."

"Was the girl with anybody?"

"Not right away, but then some dude showed up and introduced himself. You know, like he had an appointment. They went off together, arm in arm, heading for the elevator bank. She was pretty good looking for a rent-a-girl, still young and fresh."

The Judge nodded a thanks, rose, was escorted to the door and deposited again on the front porch. He walked slowly across the driveway to his car, wondering what it was that didn't quite ring true about Forrest Langley.

CHAPTER 8
TUESDAY
11:00 A.M.

As the Judge left the Langley's' he considered the various people he knew in Vegas who might help answer the twin questions: Who killed Bob? And where was Bob's daughter Jackie?

A name came to mind immediately. A person who used to say he had the pulse on everything going in Vegas. But was he still active? And would he help? It was worth a try. He checked his watch. It wasn't noon yet. If the guy were still around, he'd be at his place of choice for morning business.

The Judge took Interstate15 past the Strip and old Las Vegas, swung through the loop onto Interstate 515 East, and immediately got off on Las Vegas Boulevard. He turned left three blocks later onto East Freemont and rode it to the historic Fergusons Motel. He pulled into its parking lot and parked beside Mothership Coffee Roasters. Mothership, a mid-century modern with wood and marble bar glistening through white framed windows, looked like the lobby of a swank hotel from the Fifties. In the far corner seat against the window, staring out at the parking lot, was the man the Judge was looking for. His office had been this corner table at Mothership Coffee Roasters for over fifteen years.

Early sixties, with a full head of stark silver hair framing a face tanned by the sun and smoothed by uplifts and lasers, Angelo Rosolino, called the Silver Fox by many, sat sipping a cup of joe as he watched the Judge climb out of his car. Angelo nodded almost imperceptibly at him through the window, indicating he recognized the Judge and deduced the Judge was coming to see him. Then Angelo turned and said something to the large man sitting across from him in the booth. A man who had the face and nose of a retired boxer. The man quickly got up, surprisingly light on his feet, and disappeared into the back of the coffee shop to give Angelo privacy.

The Silver Fox was influential in Las Vegas. He was a capo in the Chicago Mob. He also had special ties with the Philadelphia crime family, the Cleveland crime family, the Buffalo crime family, the Los Angeles crime family, the New Orleans crime family, the Milwaukee crime family, the Trafficante crime family, the DeCavalcante crime family, the Bufalino crime family, and the Patriarca crime family. And special alliances with many Italian criminal organizations in Canada, Sicily, and mainland Italy. Rumor was he'd also been involved as a young man with alleged CIA plots to assassinate certain Cuban leaders. He'd settled in Las Vegas years before under direction from the Chicago Mob to act as special liaison for Chicago with the Las Vegas and Hollywood families. Angelo was a powerful guy.

Before he'd become a judge and was still practicing law, Angelo had asked the Judge to represent him in a DUI in California. The Judge had no idea who referred him but needed the business to pay the rent. And every defendant is entitled to the best defense. The Judge had used some fancy footwork around the unreliability of breathalyzers to persuade a jury to let Angelo off. And a bond of sorts had been established between the men.

"Judge!" Angelo said, showing a set of perfect white teeth and squinting his eyes in a friendly fashion, not getting up but extending a well-manicured bronze hand. "So nice to see you after so long. You don't come, you don't call, you don't write, I thought you'd forgotten your old friend Angelo."

"How could I forget you, Angelo? You're larger than life."

Angelo smiled, whispered, "So some have complained. What brings you to my humble coffee shop? And so late this morning?"

"A case, Angelo."

"Of course... of course. I knew that. With you, Judge, it's always a case."

"I was hoping I could call in a favor on this case, Angelo."

"Oh... well... there are favors, Judge... and then there are *Favors*. Which kind do you need?"

"Just a little information if you have it. A little direction on where to look for answers regarding two people, both friends."

"Oh, Judge. Why ask me? I'm just an Italian senior here in Vegas trying to enjoy the last of my time in the sun. But if I know something, of course I will tell you. Shoot. Who do you want to hear about?"

"First, about Bob Hanson, Angelo. The developer of The Spire Project."

"The project out at Flamingo and Kova? The one that's failed?"

"Yes."

"Hanson's the one that died in desert, Judge?"

"Yes."

"Wasn't that a suicide?"

"A what? A suicide? No. Where'd that come from, Angelo? Someone dropped him off thirty miles from any road in the middle of the desert for Christ sakes!"

"Oh. Sorry. So, what about him?"

"He was a special friend of mine. I'm looking into his murder. I understand he may have taken out a couple of hard money loans with some folks who perhaps run in your circles, Angelo. Folks who weren't too happy when the project was placed into a bankruptcy proceeding."

"Yes, I heard that too, Judge. Heard it was Shorty Calkin and his crew over at the Buoys and Gulls Casino. Loaned the guy around five million. Soft dollars."

"By soft, you mean not reported?"

"Just an expression, Judge. I didn't say the dollars were unreported." Anglo gave the Judge a bland smile. "But then again, wouldn't surprise me. I hear all sorts of rumors, Judge. Kinda my business."

"So, this Shorty made the loan?"

"What I heard. Guess Shorty was assured his dough would get The Spire an occupancy permit. But it never happened. The project never opened; just crashed and burned. What with vigorish and all, probably six million dropped down the toilet. I heard Shorty's a little sore."

"Sore enough to give Bob Hanson a one-way ride into the desert?"

"I don't know. No rumors on the street about that. But frankly I doubt it, Judge."

"Why so?"

"Well, things are done differently now. Not like the old days when a delinquent borrower would just disappear. Now when someone owes us money, we kind of see ourselves as bankers. Last thing we want to do is rub somebody out. How we going to get paid then? Bankers want their debtors to keep working. And so do we. You owe us a lot of money you can't repay…. What with the vig and all, you essentially belong to us. You work for us. We collect what we can as long as you're working. We never forget. Each month we have a handout to collect a little something, to remind you. And who knows, you may get lucky again, and then we get it all paid back."

"So, you don't think Shorty's a candidate for the murder?"

"Well, you never know about people, Judge. Maybe Shorty's more old fashioned in how he runs his business. I don't know. Perhaps you should talk to Shorty, see what he says."

"Where do I find Shorty?"

"He offices upstairs in his Buoys and Gulls Casino. But be careful waltzing in on Shorty, Judge. He's a mean grumpy little guy. Takes pleasure in hurting people. Even in my trade he's known as a borderline psycho."

"I'm going to find who's responsible, Angelo. Bob Hanson was like a brother. He didn't deserve what he got, no matter how much money he owed."

"Suit yourself, Judge. You're the same old bull-headed guy we've come to love and respect; you never change, or some might say you never learn. But understand, I can't protect you. I've got no influence with Shorty. As long as he stays inside his reservation he can do what he wants. You understand?"

"I do, Angelo. And thanks for the lead."

"You said there was a second person, Judge?"

"Yes. Bob Hanson's daughter, Jackie Hanson, twenty-eight but looks young twenties, has gone missing. Stormed out of her mom's house and never came back."

"You check the morgue, the police?"

"Yes. Nothing."

"You think Shorty might have taken it out on Bob's daughter, Judge?"

"I don't know. Is this Shorty vindictive, Angelo?"

"Yeah, can be. But this Jackie's twenty-eight. Must be time to leave the nest. Maybe she just decided to sever ties and strike out for herself."

"I need to find her, see which it is. Make sure she's okay."

"She have any money, Judge? Able to snag any of The Spire's construction money?"

"I don't think so."

"How long she been gone?"

"A little over two weeks. Disappeared same time her dad did."

"A boyfriend?"

"Her family says no."

Angelo sat back in his seat. Watching the Judge now with smiling eyes. Finally, he spoke. "You know the deal in this town, Judge. Twenty-eight, looks younger, out on her own for two weeks, no boyfriend, no family support, no money."

"Lay it out for me Angelo."

"Best case she snagged a job as a waitress. More likely she's sustaining herself either selling drugs or selling herself. These girls have a different view than our generation, Judge. They're educated, lots of options. Figure they're entitled to share their bodies just like guys, and better yet for money. No shame, no disgrace. Just equality with males. You got a picture of this Jackie?"

The Judge produced Jackie's picture from his pocket.

"Pretty girl. She'll get by. But there may be personal costs to her spirit, lots of wear and tear. Costs she may not appreciate till later. I'd check on Vegas escort sites, see if you find her. Email me her picture if you like. I can ask around."

"You ever heard of a guy named Sam Compton?"

"Why?"

"He's the new boyfriend of Bob Hanson's ex-wife. Just wondered."

"Yeah, I know him, Judge. Samuel Compton. Has a partner and just started a cold-call operation out on Interstate 15."

"What sort of reputation does he have, Angelo?"

"Not good. Addicted gambler. Every time he gets a little money ahead he blows it at the sports book. Owes a lot of people in this town. Not huge sums, never had the credit for that. But twenty bookies owed five thousand each, it adds up. Guy's always desperate for money. He should leave Vegas, get as far away from his addiction as he can."

"Sounds like he's not the best choice for a boyfriend."

"If this Ex has any money, he'll soon be through it. Then on to the next patsy. Also, rumor has it he's into young girls; treats them pretty rough too. That's just a rumor, Judge. Don't know if it's true. You think that's why the daughter left?"

"I don't know, Angelo. But thanks for the background. This helps a lot. One final question."

"Yes sir?"

"It's just a rumor, but my friend Hanson may have gone to the 'Dark Web' for additional construction money."

"The what?"

"The Dark Web, Angelo. There was a notation beside a seven-million-dollar loan to The Spire project, made on Hanson's books.

"What'd it say?"

"Well, it didn't really say anything. Just a doodle of a spider in a web."

"You know what it meant, Judge?"

"I'm not sure. But his ex-wife said he'd gotten a loan off the Dark Web. So, I'm thinking the spider and web maybe's a reference to that."

"I don't know this Web stuff, Judge. In my day we relied on four-party telephone lines, code words, and private meeting in cars driven to remote locations. I'm amazed how far the world as turned since my active days in business."

"I don't know much about it either, Angelo. My impression is the Dark Web's a place used by South American drug lords, international swindlers, intelligence agencies, and third-world leaders who go to bail money out of their country. Along with perhaps a zillion Chinese trying to get assets out from under Xi Jinping's thumb.

"Sounds like lots of tough criminals, Judge. All very unforgiving. I'd stay away from this black web if I were you."

CHAPTER 9
TUESDAY
11:30 A.M.

The Judge pulled into the parking lot in front of Buoys and Gulls Casino, a smallish establishment occupying the corner of St Louis and 60th, a kind of a no-man's land between the Strip and Downtown Las Vegas. Like other casinos, there were no windows, nothing to disturb the alternate reality created inside for gamblers slavishly throwing chips at gaming tables and pushing credit cards into slots.

That didn't mean the exterior was blank. Neon signs with flashing bulbs and rotating displays on electronic billboards on all sides proclaimed the best odds in town, sexy-clad hostesses, cutthroat prices on well drinks, and an all you can eat buffet for five dollars prepared by the finest French Chef. And in the tall letters on each side wall, the words *EASY CREDIT* blasted out to the world in neon pink paint.

By height of the building, the Judge could tell there was a second floor. The Judge entered the small cavern that was the casino, green carpet, faded rose walls, and a ceiling dominated by a mixture of spotlights, cameras and two-way mirrors. The usual slots lighted up several aisles with their circus lights, periodically belching nocturnal noises as coins clattered into their trays. No electronic slots here.

The cocktail hostesses were indeed scantily clad, but old enough to be the Judge's mother. They had none of the polish seen on older airline flight attendants. They just looked undernourished and tired. The Judge supposed he'd be tired too if he were running around in fishnet and heels all day, fending off gropers and caging tips.

The place looked about a quarter full, a mixture of tourists and locals, some crowding around three crap tables and two blackjack tables at the back, others pumping slots, using their special English on the handles in the hope of a payday.

The Judge turned to the security guard posted by the door and whispered, "I'm here to see Shorty."

The guard looked at the Judge suspiciously, noting his Rolex and the bulge in his pocket that was his wallet, then shrugged and pointed to a nondescript door behind one of the active crap tables. "Buzz the door. They'll decide upstairs if Shorty wants to see you."

The Judge ambled over to the door and pushed a button in its frame. A small camera lit up beside the door while the Judge was eyeballed, then there was a second buzzer and the door clicked open. The Judge mounted worn carpeted steps to a small upper lobby decked out in faded red carpet and pink wallpaper. He was met by a burly guy who was packing.

"Why do you need to see Shorty?"

"Angelo suggested Shorty might be able to help me."

The man brought his cell phone to his ear and spoke softly, then waved the Judge on, pointing to double doors on the other side of the small lobby. The

Judge pushed against one of the doors and it smoothly swung open to expose a spacious office carpeted in luxurious green pile. Thirty screens covered one wall displaying multiple live views of each gambling table, the slots, the bar with its register, the cashier, and the external entrance to the building. Three security people unfixed their eyes from screens to nod as the Judge passed, and one pointed to another door at the other end of the room, half open.

Inside, a small man sat behind a large mahogany desk, the bulk of his desk emphasizing his small stature. Late forties, he had a big head, big ears, a large nose and a lined pocked face, reminding the Judge of the face of the moon. Flat black eyes regarded the Judge without interest, thin lips twisted in what was a pretend smile. He didn't get up but waved the Judge to a nearby chair. As the Judge sat down, he realized the chair was lower than normal and the desk slightly raised, giving Shorty a four-inch advantage. It didn't help. Sitting down, the Judge was still taller.

"So, how's the Silver Fox?" Shorty asked in a cigarette-damaged voice. "Is he well? And who exactly are you?"

The Judge gave his name, explaining that most people called him Judge.

"What can I do for the Fox?"

"Angelo said perhaps you could help me. I'm looking into the death of Bob Hanson, the developer of The Spire."

"Heard about the guy. Stupid fuck. Screwed somebody over and got a one-way trip to the desert. Bet it improved his tan." Shorty snickered. "What's this Hanson guy to you, Judge?"

"He was my closest friend. We go back to college days; we were like brothers."

"So what? He's dead. Why are you asking about him now? Ain't going to bring him back."

"Want to find the persons who did this. Took him for the ride. And the person who ordered it. See there's an accounting for what was done."

"Oh, you're here for revenge, Judge. A smart ass looking for revenge. Not so smart, friend. See, revenge can be an expensive luxury. Particularly in this town…. May find yourself taking a similar ride into the desert. You always been a foolish fuck like this?" Shorty's eyes pinned the Judge. Dark pools of animosity tinged with a tad of humor.

"Yeah, Shorty. I've always been like this. And I will find who did it. Who ordered it? Perhaps it was a ride taken under your orders? I hear you lent money to Hanson's Spire Project."

Shorty's face changed then, his head coming up, a half snarl forming on his lips, his flat eyes alive with fire, nostrils flaring.

"You God damn right I loaned the bastard money. Five mil plus. Assured me he could finish his stupid project with it; lied through his teeth. Took my money, spent my money on God knows what, now the project's in foreclosure, he's dead and I'm out of pocket big time. The Fox knows all this. He got his cut. Why'd he send you here?"

"When did you loan Hanson the money?"

"I don't have to tell you nothing, sailor. Maybe you should get out of my office."

65

"The more I hear about you, Shorty, and now I meet you, you're starting to look like a prime suspect in Hanson's death."

Shorty rose from his seat, his face contorted, trying to control his anger. He took a couple of deep breaths, visibly calmed himself, and eased back down into his chair.

"Okay, asshole. Here's all I know. About six months ago, when it looked like there'd be a small shortfall under the project construction loan, Hanson came to me. Asked for a hard money loan, big interest and a big spiff at the end. I'm in that business. I do hard money loans. I listened to his pitch. And loaned him the money. Stupid me."

"And it's never been repaid?"

"What do you think? Turned out there was nothing small about the shortfall! Hanson's small hole became a huge gaping canyon that swallowed the whole God Damn project."

"Did you get security for the loan?"

"Sure. A bullshit second trust deed, worthless."

"Did you try to collect?"

"I did. As soon as I learned of the bankruptcy, I sent someone to have a heart to heart with Hanson. But by then the flake was hard to find."

"Did you order him a ride into the desert?"

"Wasn't me. If I'd caught up with him, I might have. But I didn't. He ducked my guys for a week, then up and disappeared. Next thing I know the law's hauling his carcass in from the desert floor. Couldn't have happened to a nicer guy. But it wasn't me, dickhead. Fact is, I heard maybe he killed himself."

"You mean he deliberately walked himself thirty miles into the desert and then collapsed?"

"Yeah. Maybe. I don't know and I don't give a fuck. Either way my money's gone."

"I'm also looking for Hanson's daughter, name's Jackie. She's also gone missing."

"Wow, you're a regular missing person bureau ain't you, Judge?"

"The family's asked me to track her down. Angelo thought you might have an idea how to reach her."

"Good old Angelo. Nice of him to volunteer my time, the senile old bastard. Ought to stay in his rocker, watch his football games, stay out of other people's faces. The Silver Fox ain't relevant anymore; people keep telling him... but he don't seem to get the message."

"I'd consider it a special favor for me if you have any thoughts where Jackie might be found."

"Oh, well now. You can talk real pretty when you when you want something, can't you Judge?"

"So, you won't help?"

Shorty shrugged. "What the fuck. You got a picture?"

"Yeah." The Judge passed it over.

"Nice looking broad, young, nice ass. Bet she's a good mount. How long she been gone?"

"About two and a half weeks."

"Take her cell phone with her?"

"Yes. Not answering it."

"Hot girl like this... Vegas is an easy town to get by in, have a lot of fun. Into drugs?"

"Perhaps."

"Her face looks familiar. There's a website on the Dark Web, 'Curtain Call'. Might try that. It's a new site."

"You use the Dark Web, Shorty?"

"Yeah, progressive people do... Where you been, Judge? All the serious action now's on the Dark Web. Particularly for escorts. This new generation of young women, overeducated, underemployed, like to spread their ass around. Get paid well for it. You might find her there. After all, a girl's got to make a living." Shorty cackled, his crooked teeth showing, yellow-stained and sharp.

The Judge kept a bland smile, restraining himself from reaching across the desk and lifting the little thug up by his throat.

Perhaps sensing his peril, Shorty pushed a small button beside his desk drawer and instantly two large guys were there.

"This guy's just leaving."

The Judge stood and with a man on either side, was escorted through the surveillance room, across the small lobby, down the stairs, and out on to the casino floor. It was a quick bum's rush. The Judge wondered why he made Shorty so nervous.

CHAPTER 10
TUESDAY
2:00 P.M.

The Judge was sipping a Tanqueray and tonic out on his small balcony at the condo, watching the light wind spread a dusty grey cast across the profile of the Strip three blocks away. There was Bally's, and Caesars, the Flamingo and, off to the right, The Venetian. The huge circumference of the High Roller inched its circle against the light blue sky like some giant ribbon, trapped forever to its center core. He supposed we were all trapped like that, to something.

His cell went off in the kitchen, etching the strains of 'Danny Boy' across the living room behind him. He made a dash for it and pressed the answer button at the last second.

"Hello."

"Hi Judge, it's Robbie."

"Robbie! How are you? So good to have you call."

"I called 'cause they won't tell me what's going on."

"Who?"

"Grandma. Her friend, Sam. I thought you'd tell me for real, Judge."

"Okay, Robbie. I'll try."

"Grandpa Bob is dead, isn't he?"

"Yes, Robbie."

"Someone killed him in the desert?"

"Yes."

There was silence on the cell for about twenty seconds.

"Do you know who?"

"No, but I'm working to find out."

"Do you know why they killed Grandpa?"

"No, Robbie. Not yet."

"Is Mom dead too?"

"No, Robbie. I think she's still here in Las Vegas."

"Do you know where?"

"No, Robbie, I don't. But I'm working on that too."

"Is Mom ever coming back?"

"That's a tougher question, Robbie. I don't know the answer yet."

"She doesn't love me anymore, does she?"

"I'm sure she loves you a lot, Robbie. She's just needed a little vacation I think."

"From me?"

"Perhaps. And from your Grandma, Robbie."

"Yes. Grandma gets real uptight sometimes. You going to find Mom, Judge?"

"I'm trying."

"When you find her. Tell her I love her, will you, Judge."

"Of course, Robbie."

"And that I really miss her."

"I will."

There was a little noise at the other end of the phone then, like the faint chirp of a distressed bird. Then the line went dead.

The Judge dialed the boy back immediately.

"Hey Robbie."

"Yeah." His voice betrayed a sniffle. He'd been crying.

"Why don't I come by on Saturday and take you to lunch? Just you and me."

There was silence for fifteen seconds, then, "You'd do that? You'd really take me to lunch?"

"Yes."

"Just you and me?"

"Yes."

"Okay, what time?"

"It'll be Saturday. No school, but you've got to get the okay from your grandmother. Have her call me."

"Okay. What time?"

"Twelve noon."

"Okay. I'll be waiting."

"Be sure to have your grandmother call me and okay it."

"Okay."

"See you Saturday, Robbie." The Judge hung up.

CHAPTER 11
TUESDAY
2:15 P.M.

The Judge returned to his balcony with his cell and called Barry Marsh, his police detective contact. "Can we grab some coffee sometime today and talk for a few minutes, Barry?"

"Where you now, Judge?"

"At my condo, the Meridian."

"I'm nearby. Want to do it now?"

"Sure." They settled on the Starbucks in the Hughes Business Park behind the Meridian.

Fifteen minutes later the Judge sat down at a quiet table with Barry at the back of the Starbucks patio.

"I need some help, Barry. Tell me about the 'Dark Web'?"

Barry looked startled. He sat back in his chair and thought about his answer.

"Well, Judge. That's an interesting question. Perhaps the more difficult question is, what is it not? You can find anything you want on the Dark Web."

"Like what?"

"It's a collection of hidden internet sites only accessible by a specialized web browser. Keeps internet activity anonymous and private. Some use it to evade government censorship, like in China. But it is also used for all sorts of illegal activity."

"So it's just basically the internet, Barry?"

"Not quite, Judge. It's very different."

"How so?"

"Picture an iceberg, Judge."

"An iceberg?"

"Yes. Or a submerged pyramid if you like."

"Okay."

"The internet is like your iceberg. It's huge, with millions of web pages, databases, and servers that run twenty-four hours a day."

"Yes."

"So, the small tip of the iceberg showing above the water level is the visible Internet. That's the internet you're used to using, Judge."

"Yeah. It's pretty cool."

"But it accounts for only about five percent of the total web, or of the mass of our iceberg, Judge. It contains sites that can be found using search engines like Google, Firefox and Yahoo. Websites are usually labeled with registry operators like dot-com and dot-org and can be easily located with popular search engines. But this is only the tip of our iceberg that's above water, Judge."

"Okay, so everything below the water line on our iceberg is the Dark Web."

"Not exactly. Let's call everything below the water line the 'Deep Web'…. Not the 'Dark Web', but the 'Deep Web'."

"Okay, Barry."

"This Deep Web accounts for approximately ninety percent of all websites. Your big search engines can only 'catch' websites close to the surface at our iceberg's tip. Everything else, from academic journals to private databases and more illicit content, is out of reach. But the bulk of this Deep Web material is legal and safe. It includes public and private databases that are not connected to other areas of the web and can only be searched within the database itself. It includes internal networks for enterprises, governments, and educational facilities used to communicate and control aspects within their organizations on a private basis. Everything from blog posts in-review, to pending web page redesigns, to the pages you access when you bank online, are part of the Deep Web. These pose no threat to your computer. Most of these pages are kept hidden from the open web to protect user information and privacy."

"Then what is the Dark Web?'

"The area at the very bottom of our iceberg is called the Dark Web, Judge. Venturing further down into this deeper area of our iceberg brings more danger. The Dark Web refers to sites that are not indexed and are only accessible via specialized anonymous web browsers. You'll find pirated sites, politically radical forums, and sites displaying disturbingly violent content."

"And it's different from the regular web I'm familiar with."

"Yes. In the Dark Web there is no webpage indexing by surface web search engines. Google and other popular search tools can't discover or display results for pages within the Dark Web. There are virtual traffic tunnels via a randomized network infrastructure. The Dark Web sites may be linked to criminal intent, illegal content, or 'trading' sites where users can purchase illicit goods or services. Illegal cyber activity can be much more extreme and threatening."

"So, how hard is it to get on the Dark Web?"

"Originally the Dark Web was solely the province of hackers, cybercriminals, and law enforcement officers. However multi-hop browsers like TOR, and even fully anonymous operating systems like TAILS have now made it possible for anyone to dive deep into the Dark Web."

"Even a teenager or a child?"

"Who knows more about technology, you, or a teenager?"

"Point taken. What exactly is TOR, Barry?"

"TOR stands for 'The Onion Routing Project', Judge. It's a network browser which provides users access to visit websites with the 'onion' registry operator. This browser was a service originally developed in the latter part of the Nineties by the United States Naval Research Laboratory to hide spy communications over the internet. But the browser has been repurposed and made public so that anyone can freely download it. TOR is just a web browser like Google Chrome or Firefox. Except, that instead of taking the most direct route between your computer and the deep parts of the Dark Web, the TOR browser uses a random path of encrypted servers known as 'nodes'. This allows users to connect to the Dark Web without fear their actions will be tracked or their browser history exposed. Sites on the Dark Web use TOR or similar software to remain anonymous. You can't find out who's running them or where they're being hosted."

"Is it illegal to go on the Dark Web?"

"No. Many uses are perfectly legal, and many users tout the value of the Dark Web. It gives its users anonymity and virtually untraceable services and sites. Because of this, it has attracted many parties who would otherwise be endangered by revealing their identities online. Abuse and persecution victims, whistleblowers, and political dissidents have been frequent users of these hidden sites. Some simply don't want their government agencies or even internet service providers, ISPs, to know what they're looking at online. Others have little choice and must hide to avoid political persecution. Users in countries with strict access and user laws are often prevented from accessing public sites. Their only option is to use TOR clients and virtual private networks, VPNs. For government critics and other outspoken advocates who fear backlash if their real identities are discovered, and for those who have endured harm at the hands of others and don't want their attackers to discover their conversations about their abuse, the Dark Web serves an important function."

"But it also gives users the ability to take illegal actions? Like copying pirated movies and music, say?"

Barry smiled. "Not so much anymore, Judge. There's very little enforcement of copyrights over the net. It's all civil liability, not criminal. So, these days you can go pretty much anywhere on the regular internet and copy your pirated movies. But..."

"But...?"

"But more serious illegal activity is rampant on the Dark Web. Criminals and malicious hackers always prefer to operate in the shadows. Cyberattacks and trafficking activities that the participants know will be incriminating are taken to the Dark Web. You can use TOR to share illegal pornography, engage in cyber terrorism, and order illegal drugs. You can loan shark desperate borrowers, set up trafficking for sex rings, and sell illegal arms. You can even contract for a murder, or in the case of a head of state, an assassination."

"Sounds like it's dangerous to surf the Dark Web."

"It can be. Malware is fully alive across the Dark Web. It is even offered in certain portals to give bad actors the tools for cyberattacks. But malware also lingers all across the Dark Web to infect unsuspecting users, just like it does on the rest of the Web. There are many other scams as well. Operators may take advantage of the Dark Web's reputation to trick users out of large sums of money. Some users on the Dark Web implement phishing scams to steal your identity or personal information for extortion."

"For sale to others?"

"Yes. All types of personal data can be distributed online at a profit over the Dark Web. Passwords, physical addresses, bank account numbers, and Social Security numbers circulate there all the time.

Malicious actors can use these to harm your credit, engage in financial theft, and breach your other online accounts. Leaks of personal data can also lead to damage to your reputation via social fraud.

And there's another risk to consider. Many TOR-based sites have been taken over by police authorities across the globe. There is a danger of becoming a government target for simply visiting a Dark Web site. Illegal drug marketplaces like the Silk Road have been hijacked for police surveillance in the past. By utilizing custom software to infiltrate and analyze activity, this has allowed law enforcement officials to discover user identities of patrons and bystanders alike. Even if you never make a purchase, you could be watched and incriminate yourself, or ruin your reputation when you seek a new position somewhere later in life.

Infiltrations can also put you at risk. Evading government restrictions to explore new political ideologies can be an imprisonable offense in some countries. China uses what is known as the 'Great Firewall' to limit access to popular sites for this exact reason. The risk of being a visitor to this content could lead to you being placed on a watchlist or immediately being targeted for prosecution and a jail sentence."

"Thanks, Barry. I think I understand more. I'm not sure how this fits into my friend's death, but it's a piece of the puzzle."

CHAPTER 12
TUESDAY
3:30 P.M.

The Judge pulled up in front of one of the large office towers in Hughes Center behind his condo. He rode a silver elevator with a glass front, shooting him up to the eighteenth floor like a compressed-air missile in an old department store tube. The doors opened noiselessly and deposited him in the middle of the lobby of Bromley & Smite, Bankruptcy Lawyers.

He'd recommended another firm to Bob, but someone else had recommended this firm and Bob had chosen it. It was an expensive firm with political connections throughout the state of Nevada, buttressed by heavy campaign contributions to the governor, the senators, the state legislature, local city councils, and of course the state judges who ran for reelection every six years. Everything was about connections in Nevada.

The firm's lobby was very clubby. Heavily upholstered leather couches in dark brown matched paneled walls in walnut. Hunting scenes in greens and reds from old England hung on the lobby walls, and one side was all glass, looking out to the Strip four blocks away.

The Judge announced himself to the receptionist, a dishwater blond, perhaps mid-fifties like the Judge, with a lined face of old leather from too much desert. She had a low grated voice to match, reminding the Judge of the Vegas Go to the Races TV commercial with the female voice over: *"Go, baby. Go."*

Four minutes later Darrel Hurtz rounded the corner into the lobby from the warren of offices behind, looking nervous.

"Judge. What a surprise when you called. A visit out of the blue. How are you?" He extended his hand to give the Judge a shake and then nervously withdrew it, unconsciously rubbing his hands together in a cleansing motion.

"Bob's dead.... You heard?"

"Yes, I know," said the Judge.

"Ah, yes. A travesty. Poor man. Everything seemed to be going wrong for him, and now this." Hurtz gestured the Judge into a small office to the left of the lobby, all glass on three sides, and carefully closed the door, sealing them into the small glass coffin.

"What's the status of the bankruptcy, Darrel?"

"Well, Judge. We filed as you know to stop the construction lender from foreclosing. And that worked temporarily. But now the construction lender has filed a serious motion for a release of the stay to allow the foreclosure to proceed."

"Will the lender succeed?"

"I'm afraid so, Judge. Particularly now that Bob, Mr. Hanson, is deceased."

"I thought Bob had negotiated an extension on the maturity date for the construction loan. Giving himself additional time to satisfy the Building Department and get his occupancy permit?"

"So Mr. Hanson said, Judge. So he said. But he could never produce a lender-executed Extension Agreement to that effect. And when I asked the construction lender people about it, they denied that an agreement was ever executed. Without an executed document there's no way the court's going side against the lender. We're dead in the water on that issue."

"How does an Extension Agreement just evaporate?"

"Bob couldn't find it. He said someone stole it. He was incensed. Claimed crooked forces in Vegas were trying to screw him into the ground. Conspiring to steal his Spire Project.

"Why has the County Building Department given the project such a hard time, Darrel? They lost the file several times, or so they claimed, delaying the processing for weeks. And then they denied all occupancy permits until every damn unit is finished. They could have granted occupancy on the finished units. The common areas were all finished long ago. And Bob could have raised some quick cash by sale of the finished units if they'd let him."

"It was within their discretion to require all units be completed."

"And they exercised it to grind Bob's project into the ground."

"I wouldn't put it that way."

"No. I expect you wouldn't."

"Look, Judge. This isn't your town. We do things a little different here than you do in L.A. This town is all about relationships, and getting along, and mutual back scratching."

"And Bob Hanson was an outsider."

"Okay. Yes. He was an outsider. He bull-shitted his way into this project, snatched the parcel out from under some big interests who thought they had a deal to put a new casino there. I'm not surprised he found little sympathy when he ran out of money and came looking, hat in hand, for accommodation on the occupancy permits and an extension on the construction loan."

"What was your last conversation with Bob like? What did Bob say?"

"He was yelling about stuff. Just like you are now, Judge. Claiming there was a conspiracy to steal The Spire out from under him. The bank, the subs, the hard money lenders I guess he borrowed from, the Building Department, the bankruptcy judge. Ridiculous."

"He was angry?"

"Yes."

"I can see why."

"Stormed out of my office with blood in his eye."

"When was this?"

"Let's see. We met just before the matter came up for a hearing, Judge Two weeks ago last Monday."

"Just before Bob disappeared."

"Eh…yes. I guess that's so."

"Who were the big interests, Darrel?"

"What?"

"You said Bob snatched the parcel out from under some big interests. Who were the big interests?"

"I don't know."

"You don't know, or you're not saying?"

"It was only a rumor. Nothing confirmed. And like I said, this town runs on relationships."

"Do you or your law firm represent some of these big interests on other matters, Darrel?"

"I can't disclose this law firm's clients, Judge."

"Are you afraid of these big interests?"

Darrel's lips tightened into a thin line and his eyes blazed.

"See no evil, hear no evil, speak no evil, right Darrel?"

"That's me." Darrel gave the Judge a tight smile.

"But you were Bob's lawyer. You were supposed to be on his side. And certainly disclose if there were any conflict of interest."

Darrel's head snapped up, his eyes turning to flint. The Judge sensed he'd crossed a hidden line.

"We've got nothing more to talk about Judge." Darrel spun on his heel and stalked out of the glass bubble room, disappearing with quick steps back into the warren of offices behind the lobby.

As the Judge crawled back into his car five minutes later, his cell went off strumming the sounds of 'Danny Boy' a cappella, as it was supposed to. On the other end was the deep voice of Sam Compton, Cindy's flavor of the month boyfriend.

"Hi Judge. Cindy said you could introduce some investors to me. You need to come see our messenger center, Bud. It's a great deal looking for capital. An opportunity to coin money."

"I remember, Sam. Tell me again what you need the capital for?"

"Right now my partner and I have to split with our money partner, even though we do all the work. He takes sixty percent of the cash flow and leaves us to cover all the expenses and split what's left between us. If we can get our own investor who will accept a more reasonable, but still generous return on his capital, we can set up our operation and cut out this loan shark partner."

"You said it was a messaging business, Sam. But you didn't explain exactly what the business was doing, or how it was different from a cold call room."

"Well, it's kind of a sensitive business."

"I'm listening."

"It involves an entirely new approach."

"Still listening?"

"It's set up on the Dark Web."

"Really?" The Judge was suddenly all attention. "What's your business do, exactly, Sam?"

"Well, you might say it's a whole new way of doing a cold call room over the Web. And the cash flow is awesome."

"I wouldn't mind hearing more. Particularly about the Dark Web."

"Let me show you the current operation, Judge. And you can meet my partner. He's so good he could sell air conditioners to Eskimos."

"When?"

"How about tomorrow morning. I'll pick you up about seven a.m. and we'll go see the business in operation. You won't be disappointed."

"All right."

CHAPTER 13
THURSDAY
7:00 A.M.

Sam was right on time the next morning, pulling up in a brand-new black Chevy SUV. The Judge crawled in, loving the scent of a new car. An hour later Sam and the Judge pulled up in front of Sam's business office. It was a small warehouse some twenty miles out Interstate 15. An old dusty stucco structure from the outside, nondescript white with peeling paint. The kind of place you'd drive by and never see, never stop. You hardly noticed the small, shiny satellite dish at the back of the roof.

Sam drove around the back of the building, out of sight from the road, and parked next to perhaps a dozen cars: Mercedes, Cadillacs, Porsches, a couple of Audis, all top of the line, all new or recent vintage. They didn't go with the exterior of the building. It had the aura of a secret big-stakes poker game.

They pushed through double glass doors taped with brown paper across the glass for privacy and were met with a blast of air conditioning. The operators didn't stint on air.

A blond secretary sat at a small desk sans privacy panel in the center of the reception area. She wore a fern green suit, open at the stop to display a generous décolletage. She was sitting with one leg under her on her office chair, the bottom of her dress open to show a flash of matching green panties and long legs that went down forever. Matching toenails peeked out from the top of the open-toed sandal at the end of the one shapely leg. She looked bored.

"Hi, Sharry," said Sam. "How's tricks?"

She gave Sam a death smile, the kind that makes you want to crawl in a hole. Then she shifted her gaze to the Judge, running an approving eye across his wide shoulders, then up to his penetrating blue eyes. "Who's your friend, Sam? You running around with sports models now?"

The Judge stood a little straighter despite himself. Sam produced a sour half smile, then waved the fingers of his right hand around in a circle. "Buzz us in, Sharry. I don't have time for your rep pa tee this morning."

Sharry obligingly pushed a button on the underside of her desk and the door behind her buzzed and then unstuck itself from its frame, opening a crack inward.

Sam walked over, pushed the door open and walked in. The Judge followed. It was a long oblong industrial space, no windows, no other exit. Two doors on the back wall were marked His and Hers, divided by a water cooler and a small counter with a coffee machine. Two rows of tables ran up the length of the room, on either side of a center walk space. Five tables in each row. Each table had four stations containing a chair, a computer, a telephone, and a box filled with three-by-five cards of various colors. The stations were three quarters filled with a motley assortment of people, two-thirds guys, of all ages, sizes and dress.

Most people were leaning over their computers, half-heartedly searching or typing. A few were speaking in low, drab tones into headset they wore. Some had coffee mugs in hand, others had cigarettes. Some people just sat staring blankly out into space, or slumped over their station, not moving, perhaps asleep. Large blower fans in the ceiling sucked smoke and odors up and out with a low hum, replacing it with crisp cold conditioned air. Everyone wore coats or sweaters. It was very cold. The Judge wondered if he might be on the face of the moon.

There was a lethargic feel in the room, as though people hadn't really started their work. But there was also an underlying air of expectation, as though something was going to pop. And pop it did.

The door flew open behind the Judge and a young man walked in, mid-twenties, black, stocky, buff, with a crew cut and large brown eyes that flashed around the room like a searchlight. His black silk slacks and black cashmere turtleneck might have pegged him as a model, particularly given the gold chain around his neck and the Franck Muller watch on his wrist. He exuded an energy hard to define but instantly felt, filling the room with his presence.

"All right," he said in a deep voice, "Sit your asses up and let's get to work, ladies."

Everyone sat up straighter, those on the phones ending their calls quickly, those sleeping startled awake and now alert. Everyone seemed to move to the edge of their seats. The room was suddenly filled with tension.

"So, each of you...who you working for here?"

"ME!" The voices rang out in unison, like a well drilled chorus.

"Who gets the money you make here?"

"ME!"

"Who's going to spend it?"

"ME!"

He looked around the room.

"Is it going to allow you to eat? Allow a loved one to eat? Make life better for a mother.... or maybe buy that new car? Raise your hand when you have focused in your mind why you're working here today."

Thirty arms shot up.

"Good. Good. But there's no money yet. Right? You've got to squeeze it out of that damn computer and close around it. Am I right?"

"YES!"

"It's either you... or the guy at the other end of that computer... Who's going to win?"

"ME!"

The response was thunderous now.

"You guys need to sound better than that... confident... energetic. Let's hear that again. Who's going to win?"

"ME!" They jumped to their feet as they yelled this time, their hands raising in the air like thirty referees clustered at a goal post. The room crackled with electricity.

"Are you excited?"

"YES!"

"Are you energetic?"

"YES!"

"Are we going to have fun today?" Mr. Turtleneck was shouting now.

"YES!"

"We going to laugh and joke with our prospects?"

"YES!"

"We going to be sure they're having FUN too… FUN talking to us?"

"YES!"

"Why's that?"

"Because we're great people."

"I can't hear you…."

"Because we're great people!"

"I still can't here you!"

"BECAUSE WE'RE GREAT PEOPLE!"

"And do we have good products to sell?"

"YES!" The room was in a frenzy.

Mr. Turtleneck put a foot on a chair and catapulted up to stand on one of the tables.

"The best products?"

"YES!"

"And how are we going to help our prospects on the other end of that computer?"

"We're going to eliminate their pain."

"That's right. And how are we going to do that?" Mr. Turtleneck was strutting up and down the table, looking each rep in the eye, his voice full-throated and wide. "We're going to ask about their situation," he continued. "Ask about their struggles, their life concerns, their big problems. We going to chat them up. Listen to their stress. Make them laugh a little. Find out what bothers them the most today. We're going to burrow in real deep." He paused for twenty seconds; everyone seemed to be counting the beat.

"Then we're going to do what?"

"CLOSE THEM!" Screeched thirty voices, rising to their feet again, waving their hands above their heads.

"Okay. Let's get to work!"

The reps dived back into their chairs and started typing furiously at their computers, email after email, notice after notice, query after query, offer after offer, hook after hook, crashing out across the Dark Web like a giant tsunami. The level of activity was up two thousand percent from before Mr. Turtleneck walked in.

Turtleneck jumped down from the desk and came over to meet the Judge.

"Judge, meet Jerry Brown. Jerry, meet the Judge," said Sam. "This is the guy I was talking to you about, Jerry. He's got some large money backers that might want to spring for a new computer room operation we'd set up just for ourselves."

Jerry's eyes focused on the Judge, almost staring through him. "You a real judge, Judge?"

"Once upon a time, a very long time ago. But I got fired from the job."

"Sorry.... You like what you see, Mr. Judge?"

"Impressive. What are they selling?"

"This week? The Blue Team is selling newly discovered young master artists. We promote a spread of five or ten paintings, different artists, if one doesn't make it big, another will. I'm a believer in diversity when you invest." The Judge got a row of white teeth in a wide smile that somehow didn't quite reach Jerry's eyes.

"Are these established artists with reputations, followings in galleries, written up in the literature?" asked the Judge.

"Not yet. They're all too young for that. But they'll get there. It would be a wonderful investment for you."

"What's it cost for your spread of paintings?"

"Fifteen thousand for a five-picture spread, twenty-eight for a ten-piece spread. But I can give you a ten percent discount since you're here and you're Sam's friend."

"Tempting, Jerry, but I don't have any free wall space."

"We can store them for you for a small monthly sum until they hit big, and you turn them over." Here were all the teeth again. This time Jerry's eyes were dancing to... probably the smell of money.

"Maybe next time, Jerry. Not right now."

"Your loss, Judge. Next week we'll be on to something else."

"Are you making misleading statements about the pedigree and value of the paintings?"

"Hey, Judge. We're selling here. This isn't a Boy Scout camp."

"Can't you get in trouble with the SEC? Isn't it like an investment contract or something?"

"Naw. This isn't a security. Besides our campaigns are exclusively over the Dark Web. Anonyms, untraceable." More teeth.

"You said the Blue Team. Is there another Team working here today?

"You don't miss much, Judge. Yes, we have a Blue Team and a Red Team. The Blue team is directed at selling our paintings to seniors over the web this week. The Red Team has a different mission."

"What is the Red Team selling, Jerry?"

"We're doing various prescription drugs."

"Like what?"

"Like Vicodin for example. They come in a twenty-pill blister pack. Off label from Pakistan. Would you like a sample, Judge?"

"No thanks. Aren't they illegal without a prescription?"

"You connected with law enforcement, Judge?" Jerry's eyes narrowed suspiciously.

"No, Jerry."

"Anyway, doesn't matter, it's all in the contracts we use. Buyer represents he has a valid prescription. If he's lying, it's his problem. Again, this is the Dark Web, entirely anonymous. We're like Teflon, Judge, nothing sticks except the cash."

"Who's your target market for prescription drugs, Jerry?"

"Young people."

"You sell to teens?"

"I didn't say that. Our customers are people who check the box that says they're twenty-one or older. They're a great market. You'd be surprised how much disposable cash they have, particularly if we label and ship it for them as school supplies, books, art projects."

"Not many young people have a prescription for Vicodin."

"How do you know? Maybe they do. We'll sell to anybody, Judge. We don't discriminate, just as long as they have a credit card. Prescription drug prices are so high these days, we're performing a public service."

"But you said you're marketing specifically to… young people?"

"Yes. Well, see, our partner has algorithms. He searches Snapchat, TikTok, Instagram, WeChat, Discord, Telegram, Signal, whatever else is new and coming. Sifts through both the Dark Web and the regular net looking for young people, and those who have lists of young people for sale. Once he has a hit, into our contact base they go. Then we'll chat them up, explain what the drug does, how popular it is. We'll tout celebrities and the younger net influencers who like to show off their drugs online. We'll show pirated clips of actors smoking or holding packages of pills or whatever we can get. We're into building demand here, Judge. And every kid we sell who has a positive experience will come back, again and again, for a lifetime, and will introduce us to his friends. We're building for the future. It's a wonderful business."

"Kids? You're selling this to kids?"

There was that smile again. "It's an expression, a matter of perspective. Your age, you probably look at me and think I'm a kid."

The Judge kept a tight smile on his face, hiding the queasy feeling he had in the pit of his stomach at the realization of what these guys were doing.

Jerry Brown ploughed on, "So, Sam says you might have some capital to help us expand."

"It's possible. Are you the owner of this operation, Jerry?"

"Sam and I each own twenty percent. Our silent partner owns the balance. That's why we're looking to set up our own operation. We're doing all the work, taking all the risk... well, I don't really mean risk. But you know. Anyway, we need to own our own business; along with a handful of carefully chosen investor partners of course. Like your people, Judge. People with vision."

"Who's your silent partner, Jerry?"

Jerry smiled, pausing for a full ten beats. "Nobody really knows. But if I did, I wouldn't tell you. It'd be my death sentence. And likely yours too."

"Has this silent partner been around very long?"

"About two years now. Came in with lots of capital to play on the Dark Web. Anything that goes down over the Dark Web, he's doing some of it. But we just started with him, opened our doors here about ninety days ago." Jerry laughed. "You think you can find capital so Sam and I can open our own operation, Judge?"

"If you dump your partner, how do you get your contact leads?"

"Everything's available for a price over the Dark Web, Judge."

"How much would you need?"

"About one-point-five mil. Peanuts, really. We give your people a note. And a big block of stock in the new company, non-voting of course. Sam and I will retain control. And I can get you a twenty percent spiff on the money you introduce. What's not to like?"

"How much can my people make?"

"It will blow your mind, Judge. With a one-point-five million investment, when we're up and rolling, I can turn that into a half million a month... a month, Judge. All gravy for your investors. In perpetuity. That's six million a year for their share."

"What about reporting it?"

"That's up to them. Obviously, they can't be specific about the nature of the business. I'm not providing no ten-ninety-nines."

"And what will you be selling, Jerry?"

"Various campaigns like here. Usual stuff. Various drugs, artwork, escort services, penny stocks, digital coins, collectibles, computer equipment, rare stones and diamonds, other valuable items, whatever's hot."

More teeth. The Judge wondered if Jerry's mother had been a crocodile.

"I'll think about it, Jerry. Maybe make a preliminary call to one or two of my sources, see if there's interest. Can't guarantee anything right now, but your twenty percent fee is enticing."

"Great, Judge. But don't think too long. I've got the word out to other sources. There'll be lots of interest. This is the opportunity of a lifetime."

They shook hands and the Judge followed Sam back into the reception and out in to the dry, dusty day where heat slammed the Judge like a blow torch.

CHAPTER 14
THURSDAY
9:30 A.M.

Sam spent the thirty-minute car ride back to the Judge's condo bending his ear on how wonderful the new business would be. After being dropped-off, the Judge called the Clarkson County Building Department, snagging an appointment with the head of the Department at 11:30.

Then he enjoyed a solitary brunch at Bardot Brasserie, a place created to mimic a café on the Champs-Élysées of the 1920s; always fun.

He arrived at the Building Department thirty minutes early and spent time on the City's public access computer examining the record for the occupancy permit filed by Bob Hanson on behalf of The Spire. It wasn't a pretty record. He'd just finished when his name was called. He was escorted into the office of Reginald Jones, Chief of the County Building Department.

Reginald Jones was black, dark black, with large eyes that displayed the whites around his pupils, and matching teeth all white and smiley. He had the look of a career bureaucrat, smart and crafty, able to navigate between shifting administrations and changing policies without losing a beat.

After verifying the Judge's identity, he settled back in his chair, cautious and alert, leaving it to the Judge to open the conversation.

"I'm privately investigating the death of Bob Hanson out in the desert three weeks ago, Mr. Jones."

"I've heard rumors to that effect Judge. It was a very unfortunate occurrence. And now his project, what was it... the Squire or something... is in bankruptcy and appears to be lost."

The Judge could almost feel Jones licking his chops in anticipation of a foreclosure sale by the construction lender of Bob's project.

"At any rate, Judge, I'm not sure why you want to talk to us about his untimely demise. I understand it might have been a suicide. Such unfortunate occurrences always stir up a lot of sentiment I know."

"There is a lot of sentiment to stir up, Mr. Jones. For instance, your Building Department has not been very helpful in getting The Spire approved for occupancy."

"We have a job to do, Judge, and we do it well. We have to protect the County and the buyers of timeshares such as were to be offered in The Spire Project. We are very efficient with such matters."

"Yes, well, I was just examining the record of your department on the Spire application. It seems you unfortunately lost the Spire file several times. That's hardly a model of efficiency."

Jones sat bolt upright in his chair. He'd not been prepared for the Judge's salvo.

"We have a lot of new people coming aboard. So, we perhaps aren't as efficient as you'd like us to be, Judge. But we do the best we can." Jones didn't seem convinced by his own retort.

The Judge said, "I understand there were certain powerful interests here in town who thought they had a deal to buy the parcel The Spire sits on and develop another casino on the ground. The feeling was that Hanson, an outsider from L.A., unfairly swooped in and stole the ground out from under them, leaving considerable ill will in his wake. Is that what you've heard as well?"

"Oh, I know nothing about that, sir. I never get involved in politics."

"No. I suppose you don't, Mr. Jones. Yet your department managed to lose just The Spire's file, not other people's project files, only Hanson's file, on fourteen separate occasions. I estimate that alone delayed The Spire Project about four months overall, what with the delays in finding the lost file, and bringing it up to date so inspections could be continued and approvals signed off on."

"Well, occasionally mistakes do happen, Judge." Jones spread his hands palms up, as though praying to the Lord.

"Fourteen times smells more to me like political corruption and greed, Jones. Hanson swooped in and stole this ground from locals. So, certain interests here in Vegas retaliated, bringing political pressure on the Building Department to stall the project and bring it to its knees."

Jones opened his mouth, but no words came. He was too busy hyper-ventilating. He looked like a large carp gasping for air.

Finally, he got out a low hiss, "Get out of my office. Speak to the City Attorney if you have complaints."

The Judge rose and left. He'd heard enough to validate his suspicions.

CHAPTER 15
THURSDAY
1:00 P.M.

After a brief nap back at his condo, the Judge decided it was time to see where his friend had died. He rented a four-wheel-drive jeep, plugged into its navigation unit the coordinates Detective Barry Marsh had given him, and rattled off far to the east of Vegas. He turned off the highway to a side road after 45 minutes and turned again down a smaller side spur after a half hour. Finally, he turned onto a dirt track leading out into the middle of nowhere, just desert.

He ate dust for an hour and a half, shifting gears and coaxing the jeep over the more rugged spots in what was little more than a goat track. The desert was flat for a long way, with bits of dried shrub here and there amongst numerous four-wheeler tracks crisscrossing the dry plateau. Then it started to rise, gradually but perceptually, and soon he'd run out of evidence of the four-wheelers. He was slogging on his own up the track as it crisscrossed one of several slopes, gaining elevation. He stopped and looked back once, measuring how far he'd come. The skyline of Vegas stood out in the distance, looking closer than it was in the dry desert air.

It gave false hope civilization was within reach. But it was some thirty-odd miles away.

Finally, he came over a slight rise and saw at the bottom of the indentation ahead, four white stakes strung with yellow tape to form a rectangular box. This was where they'd found the body, where Bob had spent his last moments. It was a sad, barren little indentation that didn't even have a view of the distant city skyline. What a miserable place to die.

He supposed there wasn't really a good place to die.

He stopped the jeep and got out, leaning against the simmering hood, brooding at the nine-by-twelve cordoned-off space. He climbed to the rise behind the stakes, the last hill Bob would have come over, his last view of the Vegas skyline. Then he brought out the small compass he'd bought and measured his position. He was due west of the center of the Vegas.

The Judge turned and started to walk in the opposite direction, east, on a perpendicular away from the skyline, guided by his compass. His guess was Bob would have made a beeline for the Vegas skyline. What other hope did he have? And by going backward on the same line the Judge would be backtracking on Bob's trail. He couldn't be certain. As Barry had said, there were no marks in the shifting sand. Only shell patterns made from the sweeping wind that scorched the earth like a blowtorch.

The Judge could picture Bob's journey, a halting journey by here, steps heavy in the soft sand. Perhaps staggering, tripping, falling, even crawling, desperately trying to stay alive. Shadowed by ever-present turkey buzzards overhead, ever waiting, ever patient, silent, certain of their prey. The Judge forced down the bile raising in his throat.

The Judge made each foot lift out of the sticky sand, one foot after another, hard work, traversing the dune that slowly rose to the east. Finally, he crested it and half walked, half slid down its steeper back side, down to a dry arroyo at its base, and up again to chaparral that grew out of packed barren ground on the other side. His mouth was dry, his nose filled with dust. He was unsure how far he could go.

He surveyed the brush, spotted a narrow animal path off to the left and followed it, his pants trying to hook on to the thorny branches that reached out for him along the narrow trail.

He felt the burning sand under his feet, the blazing sun on the back of this neck, the perspiration running down the inside of his shirt. He covered perhaps four blocks; it seemed like twenty. Then he gave up, reversing his course, marching back along the narrow trail, down toward the arroyo again and the indentations of his earlier steps up the dune beyond.

The sun blinked over him, farther along in its flight across the sky. Something passed between him and the sun. A large bird, circling. Christ. The turkey buzzard! He was being stalked from the air. He ignored the creature, a descendant of the giant pterosaur that roamed the skies when the world was new. It would have to find dinner elsewhere. If it came close, he would kill it... for Bob.

There was split second of flash from beside the brush ahead, metal and glass reflecting the sun for just an instant. He stopped, held a small thorny branch aside with his foot, and saw something partly buried in the sand. It looked like the dusty top of a silver cell phone. He stooped and pulled it out of the sand. It looked new. Dead of course, but it had to be Bob's. It'd be useless out here; no service, but he dusted it off and slipped it into his back pocket. Perhaps it would unlock a secret or two about what happened in this God-forsaken place.

There was nothing else to find. Bob had not written a message in the sand as to who had done this to him; or maybe he had, and it had blown away. Time and tide wait for no man, and neither does the desert wind. If there'd been a message, it had disappeared into the clutch of secrets the desert keeps dear.

He finally reached the jeep, weary, feeling like a balloon someone had pricked to let out its air. He consumed a bottle of the water he'd brought. Then he backed the jeep around in the sand, worried he might get stuck, and headed back the way he'd come.

Back to so-called civilization.

CHAPTER 16
THURSDAY
8:00 P.M.

The Judge put his key into the door of his condo. The desert was on his neck, in his underwear, even in his socks. After he showered, he looked at Bob's cell phone, sitting, charging now on the bathroom counter. It was sucking up charge and almost seemed to be beckoning to him.

He could wait no longer. He yanked the charger cord from the cell phone and held the power button down on the side. Graphic and random letters flickered across the screen in a kaleidoscope of colors, then the images righted themselves and asked for a code. The Judge punched in Bob's birthday. A welcome screen appeared, and then the cell was on. Damn, it actually was Bob's cell phone.

The Judge hit the call button and then the recent calls button. Seven numbers spit out on to the screen, all dated the day Bob had gone missing. Apparently earlier calls had been erased. The Judge grabbed his pen and paper and jotted down numbers and their times and length. None of the numbers were identified with a name.

He moved to messages. The most recent message started, *Jackie*, and then stopped. The Judge suspected the cell had run out of juice at that point. He opened the next message down.

"This is Grandpa, Robbie. Afraid it's my time to go now. I won't be seeing you again. But I love you very much. You've given an old man a tremendous amount of joy. Think of your old Grandpa from time to time as you go through your life, and the good times we've had together when you were so very young. All my Love."

The next message down was to the Judge. The one he likely tried to send after the Judge failed to answer Bob's desperate call. Reading it brought the same lump to his throat. A day late and a dollar short after his friend had disappeared.

"Christ, Judge. Pick up your damn phone. I've dug a real hole for myself on my Spire Project. This guy I went to doesn't play around. I think his people are after me now. I can't think of any way out. I need your advice. One of your Hail Mary solutions that always saves the day. God, I need to talk to you buddy. Call me as soon as you see this."

The Judge felt miserable all over again. He'd really let Bob down. And Bob had tumbled down a rabbit hole, never to be seen again. Snuffed out. Feasted on by turkey vultures. The lines of the Judge's mouth tightened. He was going to nail the bastard responsible if it was the last thing he did.

CHAPTER 17
FRIDAY
9:00 A.M.

The Judge sat at the edge of the pool at the Meridian with his toes in the water, and watched two older teens, a boy and a girl, frolic around the pool. The morning was already hot, but it would get worse. There was a wind, but it was right off the desert, hot and dry.

The teenagers were at the flirting stage, giggling and touching and getting close, daringly close, exploring their personal boundaries, not yet lovers if the Judge were to guess, but soon. Inexperienced, curious, driven on by an exchange of pheromones. God, the Judge wished he were young again.

Sex was old hat for him now. Something you booked with your wife in advance, like the theater. A ritualistic dance they performed once every other week on the assumption the other had a strong interest or need. Was that maturity... wisdom... practicality...? Or merely a sign you were rusting from the inside out, growing old by the minute? He sighed.

His cell phone went off beside him on the edge of the pool with a wolf whistle. He'd have to re-set the damn ring tone... again. The teenage girl whirled, thinking the whistle was for her, flushed, disappointment sliding across her face as she realized it hadn't been a whistle for her.

"Hello. This is the Judge."

"Hi, Judge. It's your friend, Angelo."

"Hello, friend. What's up?"

"Still looking to find who killed your guy, Hanson?"

"I am, Angelo."

"There's one of Hanson's investors, Landon, or Lincoln or something, used to run a pawn shop string here in town."

"Forrest Langley. Yes, I know him."

"Well, seems Langley got into his sauce at that Arts District Bar last night, the Velveteen Rabbit. Too much to drink. Shooting his mouth off. About how he took care of the scumbag that ran the Spire fraud. 'I gave the bastard his just deserts,' is what I heard he said. And better yet, through another source I heard an Uber driver saw Langley drive into the Spire parking lot the night your friend seems to have gone missing. Thought you might want to know."

"Thanks so much, Angelo. That's very interesting. I'll follow up."

"I'd be careful of the guy, Judge. He's a hardheaded old cuss, mean as a junkyard dog. Used to run collections for some of our boys in the old days. Gather yourself plenty of witnesses and a quick way out if you talk to him."

The line clicked dead.

CHAPTER 18
FRIDAY
12 P.M.

The Judge had difficulty finding Forrest Langley. He was gone from his foreclosed house. His son's address wasn't discoverable. Finally, the Judge gave up and called Angelo for help. Angelo didn't answer, so the Judge left a message. Thirty minutes later Angelo called back.

"Angelo here, Judge. Langley's now got himself a big spread up in the hills above Summerland. Looks to me he's not as broke as he claimed. But be careful if you talk to him, Judge. A leopard doesn't change its markings, and neither does a snake."

The Judge jotted down the address. Forty-five minutes later he was in front of Forrest Langley's new digs. The lot wasn't near the size of Langley's former estate, no gardens, no circular driveway. But then this wasn't flat desert land. This was a pristine lot on the rim edge of the Summerland Mountains, hanging over the plane below, providing a fantastic view across the desert, out over Summerland sprawl and all the way to McCarran Airport and the Strip. And the house... the house, well.... Words failed. The ultra-modern structure was all glass and steel, with windows on all sides, like an aquarium. Mrs. Langley met the Judge at the front door and insisted on giving him a tour.

Approximately 10,000 square feet, cantilevered off the edge of the mountain, hanging out into space, with an infinity pool at its edge with a glass bottom so one could practically swim over the lights far below. Six garages to accommodate the antique car collection, a separate sauna, Jacuzzi, tennis courts, a long wide terrace, and a chef's kitchen that spared no expense. Seven bedrooms, formal living room, family room with player piano, library, gym, sports room with a big-screen TV and a pool table... the Judge couldn't think of anything Langley had forgotten.

"I guess this isn't your son's house, Mrs. Langley."

"Well, no. Forrest is very discreet about what he says and what he has. I still miss our old home, but Forrest says it's safer for us up here."

Forrest Langley was in his office, one of the rooms strung along the cliff and the view in the half-moon floor plan. The office had blond pine paneling, an open ceiling with wooden beams, a skylight with tinted glass and adjustable shades. And contrasting with the modern, Italian hunting scenes from the 18th century framed the rear wall.

"I thought you were broke." said the Judge.

"Well, you know.... Fortunately, an offshore Nevis company has hired me on as special consultant. They had just built the house, and in negotiating with them over the terms of my contract, they offered this place for us to live. Beautiful, isn't it? But of course, I don't own it. We're only guests here."

"Yes. Well, it's astonishing how quickly your situation changed. An offshore corporation I take it you own?"

Langley smiled. "That falls under 'none of your business', Judge. Any luck on finding who dumped your asshole friend out on the desert?"

"Progress, Langley. Lots of progress. In fact, you've suddenly come back into view as a person of interest in my investigation."

"Me? How so? Why me?"

"I understand you were at a bar last night, bragging you were the one who took care of the Spire scumbag."

"You have good sources, Judge. But they misheard. What I said was I was glad somebody took care of the Spire scumbag. I didn't say I did it."

"There's more, Langley. You were seen going into The Spire the night Bob Hanson went missing. Forgot to mention that didn't you...?"

Langley looked stunned.

"Well?"

"Yeah, I guess I was there briefly. So what?"

"What were you doing there?"

"I went to threaten Hanson a little. Shake him up. See if there was any way to get my money back. But I missed him. He'd already gone."

"So you say."

"So I say. I pounded on his door for a while. But the lights were off. He was long gone."

"Anyone see you leave, solo, without Hanson?"

"Hell, I didn't think anyone saw me come. No. No one saw me leave."

"What time did you arrive, and what time did you leave?

"I arrived about ten forty-five. Left fifteen minutes later.

"And the gig about being broke. That was just an act?"

"Well, you know…"

"No, I don't know."

"I try to maintain a low profile. This country is ravenous for taxes. With a bounty system for turning people in. I keep my finances to myself. But I'm still angry at your fraudulent friend, Hanson. Took my money, lied to me, to all the investors. Lost my money through fraud. He got what he deserved."

"Judging by your rig on this mountain, it was a small loss for you."

"Judge, if you're like me and you started poor, came up hard, doesn't matter how much is involved. A nickel, a dime, a dollar, a million, someone steals from you, you feel it. It's emotional. You get angry. Your fight mechanism kicks in."

"Would you have killed Hanson if you'd caught up with him?"

"Who knows. Maybe I've done such things in the past, maybe I haven't. Not saying. Now, I think we're done here Judge. Get out of my house and leave me alone. Don't ever come back."

"One more question."

"Did anyone ever tell you Judge you have the personality of a dental drill?"

"You ever heard of a kingpin on the Dark Web here in Vegas who's into, loan sharking, maybe other illegal stuff that can make a buck?"

"Yeah, I've heard there's somebody like that."

"Know who he is?"

"No. Heard some people call him the 'Spider.'"

"Got any ideas who he could be?"

"I wouldn't know. There is a guy, just off the Strip, who's savvy with computers. Might have those skills. Very into the net. Started small but he keeps getting bigger and bigger. Pretty ruthless. Wouldn't want to get up close to that guy."

"What's his name?"

"You didn't hear it from me."

"That's right. I didn't hear it from you. Who's the guy?"

"I don't know his name, but his casino's called the Boys and Girls, or something like that."

The next screen was filled with financial and personal information for the Judge to complete. But there was also a question box.

The Judge typed in the question box: *What is the name of your company?*

The reply was quick. *You must be joking. This is the Dark Web.*

How will I get the money?

Wired from an anonymous Cayman Islands bank account to your account, in bitcoin.

How will I repay the loan?

Wire the money back to our anonymous account.

What if the project doesn't work out and I can't repay the loan immediately?

That's not an option.

I don't understand.

You're getting dark money from the Dark Web. If you want the loan, it must be promptly repaid according to its terms. If it's not timely repaid, your life is forfeit.

You mean my life is the security?

You got it, pal. You want the loan or not? I've got others waiting to apply.

Is it your money I'm borrowing?

Yes. And I am the collector on the debt, one way or another. Feet down… or feet first.

How is that legal?

It's not, fool. You want the money or not?

Can I think about it?

The screen suddenly froze. A small spider with a red dot on its belly crabbed halfway across the bottom of the screen and disappeared. Then the screen went blank. The Judge had been cut off.

Jesus, this was where Bob had gotten his second seven million to carry his Spire Project forward. And he'd pledged his life.

CHAPTER 20
FRIDAY
3:15 P.M.

The Judge sat for a moment, looking at the blank screen. He wondered if this Spider guy had made the seven-million-dollar loan to Bob. Why else would Bob have retained the site address? And there was the doodle of the spider and a web in the Spire Ledger. It made sense.

Then he thought about Bob's daughter, Jackie Hanson. She'd gone missing the same time as Bob. He wondered if this Spider was connected to Jackie Hanson's disappearance. He moved out to his balcony with his laptop, opened it, and returned to the Dark Web. He typed in *Female Escort Sites Vegas*. Perhaps he could find Jackie on a Dark Web Site. Where had Shorty said to look? It was *Curtain Call*.

Curtain Call - Vegas came right up on the Dark Web. They advertised *Professional Adult Entertainers for Every Taste*.

The Judge took a deep breath and typed in the false ID name he'd used earlier, 'Martin'. The site didn't ask for a last name, but it did want a credit card number, expiration date, security code, name on the card, and address. The Judge reluctantly punched in his law firm credit card's data.

The site then ran through of list of what it called *Likes, Wants and Needs*, beginning with what race he wanted. He checked Caucasian. The next questioned asked whether he wanted large breasts or small; he selected small. He hadn't really noticed Jackie that way last time he saw her, over a year ago. It was a guess.

Heavy set or slender, tall, medium or short, prodded the site.

He checked slender and medium, guessing that Jackie looked pretty much the way he saw her a year ago in Vegas.

The questions continued, getting more specific and a little embarrassing. This site was not for the faint of heart.

It wanted to know what costumes he preferred, what form of pre-play, whether he was into dominatrix or submissive? Did he want bare back (extra, and a certificate would have to be produced first), or Trojaned?

He had to check preferred attitude: cosmopolitan, educated, chatty, squealy, quiet, shy, aggressive, lusty, inexperienced, well experienced. Did he want head first? And what positions did he like? Missionary, cowgirl, reverse cowgirl, doggie? Did he want the windward passage, or yoga positions? These had an extra charge.

It went on to ask for desired hair color, eye color, full lips or no, full hips or no, pubic hair or shaved.

Jesus, it was like ordering a sandwich at Jersey Mike's!

He wondered who the site would be sending Martin's information to and sweated now they had his real name and address from his credit card.

He could have his adult entertainer for two hours in his room, or all night and breakfast. Two hours would be more than enough time to see if she knew Jackie. He completed this last questions and hit return.

A set of pictures flashed up on the screen of beautiful girls, both a headshot and a nude body shot. It was a dazzling array of flesh. He was asked to rank his favorite three by priority and assured that at least one of his choices would likely be available for that evening, or someone very similar.

None of them were Jackie Hanson. He selected the one that looked most like Katy, his wife: blue eyes, blond hair, an angular face and slender body. She was perhaps ten years Katy's junior. He put in his condo address and telephone, having second thoughts about this approach to finding Jackie. Trouble was, he couldn't think of any other way. *Ah well*, he finally concluded. *The things we have to do to make progress on a case.* He hit enter.

A series of add-ons popped up next. He could have a second girl to go with the first at a twenty percent discount, or two additional girls at thirty percent off the two.

He could have a videographer who'd come and video the whole scene, creating his own personal porn movie.

He could buy and keep a sex toy as a souvenir or rent one; the girl would bring it along. There followed two pages of pictures. Some of the toys made the Judge think of the Marquis de Sade. Others were so obscure the Judge didn't have a clue how they'd be used. He supposed hands-on instruction was included; and smirked.

The Judge declined these opportunities to heighten his experience, only to be taken to a second upsell page which offered a variety of drugs to make his experience more unforgettable, from ecstasy to cocaine, and a selection of oils for use in play. The coconut and peach oil sounded intriguing, but the Judge passed.

He specified a time, 9:00 p.m., and his condo address, and hit the purchase button.

There was some whirring and clicking noises. And then the site advised his credit card payment had been processed; he was all set. A small black spider with a red dot on its underbelly appeared briefly at the bottom corner of the screen and crabbed half away across; then the screen went blank. Just like on the hard money loan site.

The Judge reached for his cell phone and called Angelo. The Silver Fox answered immediately.

"Hi, Angelo. A question for you."

"Of course, Judge. How can I help?"

"You ever hear of a kingpin guy on the Dark Web who works from Vegas? Someone who's big time into escorts, loan sharking; who knows what else? Call's himself 'the Spider'. Has a Spider logo on his site?"

"No, Judge. But then I don't go on your Dark Web. Too busy, too tired, probably six generations too old. But let me make some inquiries."

"Thanks, Angelo."

CHAPTER 21
FRIDAY
9:00 P.M.

At 9:00 p.m. that evening his doorbell rang, right on the dot. He opened the door and escorted in a young woman matching her picture, early twenties, with short blond hair, light blue eyes, and a Nordic cast to her cheek bones. She carried an ice-cold bottle of Korbel Extra Dry California Champagne which she handed to him and said, "I'm Margie. I hope you like what you see."

The Judge accepted the bottle and set it aside on the kitchen counter.

She was wearing a long grey raincoat, a London Fog. She threw it open to expose small bare boobs and a yellow G-String bottom that didn't quite cover the top of a V of close-cropped dark hair that belied her blond curls. She slid out of yellow stiletto pumps, shortening her height to a less intimidating five foot two.

"Can we just chat?" asked the Judge.

"Sure. We can chat about whatever you like, Martin. I'm here to serve."

She dropped her coat over a chair and sat down on his couch, patting the cushion for him to sit down beside her. The Judge gingerly did.

She eased herself closer to him, letting her hips touch his. Her smooth leg made contact with his, burning through his slacks. Then her bare foot began playing with his shoe.

"Great. You see, I'm looking for someone… for the family. And I understand she works for your organization. I'm trying to reach her. I'm hoping you can help me if you know her."

Margie looked doubtful. "I'm not supposed to talk about Curtain Call, or the other girls, Martin. It's a no-no."

"Yes, well, I really need to find her. Her name's Jackie. And I can make it worth your while."

Margie's eyes narrowed. "What does that mean?"

The Judge brought five crisp new one hundred dollar bills out of his pocket and laid them on the coffee table.

Margie's small hand went for the bills at warp speed. But the Judge's hand was quicker, covering the little pile. "I need the information first."

Margie looked at the Judge, critically now, sizing him up. "You a cop?"

"No, Margie. Kind of like a private investigator."

"A private dick, Martin. You're a private dick?"

"Yeah, I guess."

"Did you want to fuck, or just the information?"

"As beautiful as you are, Margie, right now I just want information."

Margie nodded her understanding.

"Suppose I help. You're not going to tell anyone I helped, right?"

"No, Margie. No one will know you helped me. It's private, just between you and me."

Margie leaned back against the sofa, relaxing, assessing her situation.
"Okay. How can I help?"

The Judge produced a picture of Jackie Hanson and handed it to Margie. "Know her?"

Margie studied the picture. "Yeah. I know her. Seen her around. I think she's in the Spider's other crib, The *'Crème de la Crème'*. Goes by the name of Sheila, maybe."

"Sheila what?'

"I don't know. No one uses last names."

"Where's your crib?"

"Oh no. I'm not talking about the crib."

"Okay, then who's this Spider?"

Margie's face turned white. She looked like she was going to be sick. It was more than fear. It was terror.

"I got to go now, Martin," she finally gasped. "Keep your money. You're going to get me killed. You understand. Killed… dead… no more me. You must think I'm really dumb. Just let me out of here."

"Okay, okay, Margie. No more questions. Just take the money and get a note to Sheila"

Margie looked doubtful.

"Just a personal note, from me to her."

"You stalking her or something?"

"No. I'm just an old friend of her dad's. It's worth five bills to me."

"What's in the note?"

"Just that it's about her dad, and it's urgent I speak to her."

Margie frowned, trying to think carefully through it all. Then she looked at the $500 covered by the Judge's hand.

"Okay, Martin. You'd better be on the up and up. The guy that runs the Curtain Call, he don't take any shit. He'll kill you as soon as look at you. And if the Spider gets wind of this, death could be very long and very painful. Where's the note?"

"Who runs Curtain Call?"

"Oh no. No deal. I'm out of here." Margie started to rise from the sofa.

"Okay, okay, Margie. Just take the cash and the note. Give the note to Sheila." Margie sat back down, leaning into the Judge, more relaxed now a deal was struck.

The Judge produced a pad and pen out of his pocket and wrote a note, folding it over, putting 'Sheila' on the top, and below that, 'Private'.

Margie took the note with her left hand while her right shot for the money again. It was scooped in a split second.

Just then there was a rattle at the door, as if someone was struggling with a key to get in. Margie grabbed the Judge, throwing one arm around his neck, shoving the money and note under her fanny, fear spreading across her face again.

The door stuck for a moment, then flew open.

Oh, shit!

Rolling a small carryon, Katy walked in with a "Surprise...surprise, Judge!"

CHAPTER 22
FRIDAY
10:00 P.M.

Three jaws dropped open simultaneously. The first mouth to snap shut was Katy's, her chin coming up, aqua eyes flaming. The carryon was dropped with a thud, and she marched into the room with an authority only an owner has, claiming her condo... and her husband.

Margie cowered at the onslaught, sliding her mostly naked body behind the Judge on the sofa for self-preservation, and began to squeal, "Oh no. Oh no. It's the wife. Oh my God. Oh my God."

The Judge belatedly got his hands out in front of him, palm out, and tried to say in his best boyish charm voice, "This isn't how it looks."

His voice sounded hollow, even to him. Margie snuggled in further behind his back on the sofa, her squeals reaching higher notes now.

Katy ground to a halt in front of the Judge, hands on her hips, one toe tapping angrily on the carpet.

"This is just research, Katy," offered the Judge, feeling a sweat break out on the back of his neck. Perhaps from Margie's panting down the back of his shirt.

"Research my ass! Better yet, your ass! Miss whatever-your name-is, would you take you tits off the back of my husband. Unwind yourself from behind him and get the fuck out of my condo... NOW!"

Margie squealed once more, dived out from behind the Judge and up off the sofa, dove into her coat laying across the adjoining chair, scooped up her heels, and fled for the door.

She was gone in a heartbeat, the door mechanically starting to close behind her as the Judge yelled, "Don't forget to give Sheila my note." The Judge admired how Margie's small claw held the bills and note fast, even in her panicky dash for the door.

Katy stood over the Judge, taking in some large breaths, steadying herself. Then turned and sat down on the edge of the opposing chair to the sofa, rigid, back straight as a rail, feathers clearly musted.

"Okay, Judge. Let's have it. It better be one hundred percent true, and it better be good."

The Judge explained how Jackie Hanson, Bob's daughter, had gone missing about the time Bob disappeared. How she had been working as an assistant on The Spire Project with Bob. How she perhaps knew something about Bob's demise and might be at serious risk herself. How the Judge had visited Angelo, who had directed him to Shorty, who thought he saw Jackie's face on this site... this Curtain Call site on the Dark Web.

"You mean this call girl site," interrupted Katy.

"They don't use that term anymore, but..."

"A tart is a tart, Judge. I know it, she knows it, and you know it."

"Well, so she came and took off her coat, and it turned out she wasn't wearing anything much, and I was just explaining to her I only wanted to get a note to Jackie. Didn't want her... er, services. And she was okay with that, and then you burst in."

"You mean I arrived at *MY* front door and entered *MY* condo, to find *MY* husband with a naked tart in his lap."

"Aw, Katy, it wasn't like that. We'd just finished discussing a transaction where she was going to give my note to Jackie, and she was about to leave. And she had her swimsuit on."

"That micro-G-string bikini bottom wasn't a swimsuit, Judge. You don't go anywhere near the water in that. And what was that wad of hundreds she left with?"

"Payment for undertaking this task for me. Reaching out to Jackie."

Katy's eyes narrowed. She stood then, turned, and marched down the short hall and into the bedroom, throwing on the overhead lights full and sniffing suspiciously.

The Judge gave himself a mental pat that he'd carefully made the bed this morning. Thank God they hadn't gone in there.

"Okay, Judge. I'm giving you the benefit of the doubt for the moment. But I'd better not find incriminating evidence or hear questions from the neighbors as to what was going on in here."

"On no, Katy. Nothing happened, I didn't even have a chance to give her a drink... I mean... Margie doesn't drink... I mean there's no way I would have offered her a drink."

"So, this ice-cold bottle of Korbel in the kitchen isn't yours?"

"Oh no. She brought it." He mentally kicked himself. He knew it was better to just keep his mouth shut.

"I'm taking a shower now, Judge. I want to wash the airplane off. I'll see you in bed. And you'd better not be already worn out.

The Judge gave her his best boyish smile. And this time he just kept his damn mouth shut.

CHAPTER 23
SATURDAY
12 P.M.

Robbie had spent the better part of an hour sitting on the back of the sofa next to the window, watching, waiting for the Judge's car to pull up. He knew it was way too soon. But maybe the Judge would be early. His mind was unsettled, a mass of confusion and longing. He hoped the Judge could make sense of it all.

Grandma hadn't helped. All she'd managed to say, over and over again was, "You're just like your mother."

He was starting to fidget now. It was always tough staying still. And he'd been sitting for an hour. That was how much he wanted to see the Judge.

There was a noise of a car climbing the hill below them and then it crawled into view. It was a white Mercedes alright. But then it sped up and went flying by. It wasn't the Judge.

He waited some more. The Judge was ten minutes late. Perhaps he'd forgotten, wasn't coming. Robbie's heart sank.

Then, suddenly, there it was. A second white Mercedes, quiet and well cared for, a convertible with a black top, slid up to the curve in front of the house. The Judge was here!

"I'm going now," screamed Robbie up the stairs, projecting his voice into the interior of the second floor, hoping Grandma heard, then flew for the door. He was halfway across the lawn before the Judge could get out of his car.

They drove in silence for a time. Robbie didn't know what to say, suddenly nervous.

"How are you, Robbie?" Kind blue eyes turned from the road to regard him briefly across the seat.

"Okay," he managed to get out, his heart jumping.

"It must be tough with your mom away. You're lucky to have a nice grandma."

"Yeah," he blurted. "When's my mom coming back?"

"I don't know, Robbie."

"Doesn't she love me anymore?" There, he said it. Bitterness welled up in him.

"I'm sure she loves you, Robbie. In her own way. I suspect she's not well right now. I think there are things in her head that are making her troubled. She doesn't want you to see her troubled."

"I don't mind if she's troubled when I see her."

"Of course you don't. But I suspect she's afraid she might hurt you in some way, or the people around her might hurt you. The people she works with. She's trying to protect you. She doesn't want you exposed to a life she feels compelled to live right now."

"I don't understand that."

"No. It's adult stuff. And it's tough, I know. Perhaps someday, when you're older, you'll understand better. How is school going?"

Robbie thought a second, decided not to talk about all the tardy slips he'd collected.

"Okay, I guess."

"Do you do sports and stuff? I used to play tennis."

"Naw, I just go and then leave. It's all dumb stuff they do there. I don't need it. Just boring. I don't do stuff at school."

"Do you have friends at school?"

"Oh yes. I have one friend." His words came then, in a rush. He rattled on and on. It felt so good to have someone sympathetic to talk to. He talked about school, about his dumb classes, about a special girl he liked, about the football team he was afraid to try out for. How in sports he always seemed to get hurt. About the dorky history teacher who he thought was lame.

He talked with the Judge all the way through the trip down to the Black Bear Diner. It was Robbie's favorite restaurant. The food was plentiful and suited his tastes.

He got to choose off the menu without the usual advice he got from his grandmother. He even got a second dessert.

He talked during their walk through the mall, and during a peek into Dick's Sporting Goods. The Judge bought him a Raiders hat. He chattered all the way back up the hill to home.

135

He talked about his friend, and the girl he liked, and girls in general, and about the Raiders, and about his Grandpa Bob, who he missed terribly. He talked about his dad, missing in action as he'd explain to school friends, and about high school coming up, and what he might like to do some day. He talked about the movies he liked, and the TV shows he watched, and about homework, and all the help Grandma was giving him on grammar.

He talked about how he was sad much of the time. How he missed his mom, how he didn't really understand why she didn't want to see him. How he loved his grandma, how Grandma's friend, Sam, was okay, but a little rough and had no interest in him.

It was wonderful and exhilarating. And the Judge actually listened. Listened carefully, asked questions sometimes, repeated back what he'd said sometimes. It was like he'd been starved for attention, dried out for lack of it, and then the rains had come in a torrent. It felt so good. He sniffled a little here and there but didn't cry. He was too old to cry. And it didn't help anyway. It didn't change things.

The Judge got out of the car and walked him to his door. Robbie turned around and hugged this man with the kind blue eyes. Tight. Desperately.

Then the Judge was gone, and he was alone. Tired. He hurt some place deep inside again. Didn't know what to do about it. He slowly trudged up the stairs to face his homework.

CHAPTER 24
SATURDAY
2:00 P.M.

The Judge was disturbed at how sad Robbie had looked... and sounded. But he didn't know what to do about it. He needed to find Robbie's mother. Get her back into a relationship with the boy. But how? How? How?

And he needed to identify who had ordered the hit on Bob. See that justice was done. That would be some closure for the boy. For everyone. For him too.

The Judge found himself pulling into the parking lot of Mothership Coffee Roasters, the Silver Fox's diner. He couldn't think of anywhere else to go.

His leads were thin. He'd thought Forrest Langley might be the guy he was looking for. Langley was slippery. And had lost a lot of money in The Spire venture. He certainly had motive. And opportunity, as he admitted being at The Spire the night Bob disappeared. But the Judge couldn't see him driving Bob off into the desert, investing perhaps five hours in a round trip. He looked more a meat and potatoes sort of guy who would just put a slug in your head.

Angelo was his usual ebullient self, rising from his coffee to give the Judge a hearty handshake.

"I need some help, Angelo. And I don't know where else to turn. You know this town, its people. I'm hoping you can give me some perspective."

"Sit down, sit down, Judge. Have some coffee. I find if one sits back and lets the universe come to them, rather than chasing its around, answers mysteriously appear."

"It does feel like I'm running around in circles, chasing my own tail."

"What happened with Forrest Langley, Judge? I did some more research on him myself. Five years ago, when he was in the pawn shop business, I'm told he used to moonlight as a hitman for my Italian cousins around the country. Piled up a lot of offshore money and made something of a name for himself. Do you think he killed your friend?"

"He certainly had motive, Angelo, and opportunity. And the ruthless disposition. But he just doesn't feel right. Did you find anything out about this Spider on the Dark Web?"

"Couldn't find a thing, Judge. You sure this spider isn't just some kind of urban legend? I'm doubting he really exists."

"No, Angelo. He's very real. He's all over the Dark Web. Into all sorts of illegal activities. I've been on two of his sites. One for loan sharking. One for escorts."

"My, my, Judge. You do get around. I think you have more fun than I do. Old guy like me has to get his satisfaction vicariously. Tell me more about this… eh… Spider, and about his escort services."

"That's the problem, Angelo, I don't know more. The Spider's just a little cartoon black spider with a red dot on his underside, scampering half-way across the screen on the Dark Web before his link closes."

"It's very curious, Judge. Just this morning I got a call from my colleague in Chicago. He was asking about an unauthorized guy working the Web. Here, in Vegas."

"Unauthorized in the sense that the mob wasn't getting its cut, Angelo?"

"Apparently so. I was told a lot of revenue was being siphoned away. I'm supposed to put an immediate stop to it. You think this might be the same guy, your Spider guy, Judge?"

"Maybe. Might be exactly who your Chicago friends are talking about."

"And you think this Spider had something to do with your friend… ah… Hanson's death?"

"I do. I think Bob borrowed a large amount of money from the Spider, secured by Bob's life."

"That's old style, Judge. Like I said. We don't treat borrowers like that anymore."

"It's very clear on the Spider's site. You don't default… on penalty of death."

"That's a dumb way of doing business. This Spider can't be very clever."

"Clever enough to completely hide his identity. Did your Chicago friends say anything else?"

"Not much. They think the guy is quite broad in his business. Gambling, escorts, loan sharking, moving a lot of drugs, sports book, fraudulent investments, even murder for hire, all done across this Black Web."

"You mean the Dark Web, Angelo."

"Err, yes. I guess so. Anyway, the guy's cut something like a twenty percent slice out of anticipated revenues for himself. Guys like this give us heartburn, Judge. First, and maybe foremost, they cut into revenues. And if the idiot is thinning his drugs with dangerous substances, or running a murder for hire operation, that brings unwanted public outrage and attention from the authorities. The last thing we need. We are practical, no-nonsense businessmen, Judge. We want things to be quiet and steady."

"Does Chicago want you to do something about this guy?"

"What do you think, Judge? Vegas and L.A. are incensed; asked Chicago to enlist someone trustworthy to put an immediate stop to it."

"That would be you?"

"That would be me."

"So are you looking for my Spider now too, Angelo?"

Angelo spread his hands. "I've been asked to find this guy and put a stop to it. Don't know if he's also your Spider. But if that's the case, so much the better. But where does one look? You tell me Judge. I don't know much about your Black Web, but I know the net can be operated from anywhere. Anywhere inside the U.S., or from Russia, from the Caribbean, really from anywhere in the world as long as there's good net service."

"Yes. It can. But this Spider is very local, Angelo. And if he ordered the killing of my friend, Bob Hanson, I'm going to track him down. I'm going to see that justice is administered, wherever the guy's hiding."

"Let's work together, Judge. I'll share what I learn from my inquires and you do the same. I'll bet between us we can get both of them, or perhaps just the one, if it's just one guy."

"Deal," said the Judge.

"Do you have any leads at all, Judge?"

"I have one."

"Yes?"

"Langley suggested my Vegas Spider might possibly be Shorty."

"Shorty?" Angelo snorted. "You really think it could be Shorty?"

"So far it's the best I've got."

"But Shorty is so… so… well, small time. I mean granted he does a little hard money loan business and runs a few girls through his small casino. But I don't know."

"Angelo, you're the one who said Shorty loaned Bob Hanson money on The Spire Project."

"That's what I heard. But I assumed it was a straight up deal. Second trust deed, high interest rate, generous vigorish. Not something you bet your life on."

"Suppose there was a second loan? This one over the Dark Web? A Spider loan made by Shorty where Bob bet his life as security."

"It's possible, Judge. In fact, the more I think about it, the more I think you might be on to something. Shorty has a computer degree of some sort, I think. And he's certainly a greedy little bastard. He might just be foolish enough to try to corner the illegal commerce market over your Black Web. Let me make some inquiries."

CHAPTER 25
SATURDAY
4:00 P.M.

The Judge was tired. He'd talked to a lot of people. But he felt no closer to finding Bob's killer. Nor had he located Jackie. He wondered if Margie would come through and deliver his note.

He sipped his single malt over ice on his condo balcony overlooking the club house and began to scribble notes on a yellow tablet. Katy came out draped in his bathrobe four sizes too big for her, looking like a beautiful waif. She settled in the chair beside him. She had a warm smile on her face, none of the frosty look he'd got the night before. The sex had been good. And the second time better, with shudders that bounced off the walls and rattled the roof beams. He'd apparently weaseled his way out of her wrath. He suspected his snores had helped, blending in with her purring sleep, creating the familiar. Neither one slept well when they weren't together. Old marrieds.

"Well Judge, you got it figured out? Who killed Bob?"

"They didn't exactly kill Bobby. They just dropped him off. He suffered badly out there. It would have been kinder to put a bullet in his head."

She put her hand on his arm, consoling, energy flowing into him, calming. Thank God she was here.

"What do you know for sure, Judge?"

"In the last months, Bob was working closely with his daughter, Jackie, on The Spire Project. And she disappeared when Bob did. No one's heard from her since. There are rumors she's supporting herself as a high-end escort."

"That's what that tarty woman was about."

"Yes. I think she knows Jackie. I gave her some cash to deliver a note to Jackie."

"Do you think she will?"

"Deliver the note? I don't know. You scared her pretty good when you ran her off."

"Damn right I ran her off." Katy snorted. "No one messes with my man. And shame on you for getting yourself in that compromising position."

"It was only compromising because you arrived unexpectedly."

Katy's face started to color, her blood rising.

"Or too soon, Judge? Is that what you mean? Who knows what would have happened if I'd been ten minutes later?"

The Judge quickly changed the subject.

"It turns out there were secret business interests that badly wanted the land under The Spire. Bob slid in, outfoxed them, and purchased the land away for his project. He left hard feelings behind with the powers that be in this town."

"Like who?"

"I don't know. That's the trouble. I don't know much of anything. I've just picked up fragments here and there."

"You know there were hard feelings."

"Yes. According to Darrel Hurtz, the bankruptcy lawyer. And then there was the mortgage lender, who, according to Hurtz suddenly turned combative, denying there was ever an agreement for an extension of time to pay the loan. Moving quickly to foreclose, forcing Bob to seek protection in bankruptcy."

"But there actually was an agreement to give Bob more time to pay?"

"Yes. I think so. Cindy, the ex-wife, says there was. And Bob told the bankruptcy attorney there was a legal extension. But Bob later said he couldn't find it. He claimed someone took it. Also, the city has been cutting the project no slack, insisting all the units be completed, right down to the garbage disposals in the sinks, before any unit gets an occupancy permit and can be sold. Effectively foreclosing Bob's ability to sell units and generate cash. And the Building Department has mysteriously lost the file and delayed the project, again and again and again. I think someone has applied pressure at the Building Department to slow the construction way down, squeeze Bob out."

"These same hidden interests?"

"I believe so. And there's something else. Bob borrowed an additional twelve million in two increments. First five million, and then seven million, in a desperate effort to finish The Spire. But it turned out to be not enough. The Spire still sits with no occupancy permit. The money was deposited into the project's accounts. The five million looks to be a standup hard money loan, with a junior deed of trust securing its repayment, and carries heavy interest. Some offshore lender that's hard to track. But the seven million was mostly in bitcoin, and the rest in hard cash, black money, drug money maybe, I don't know. No lien or security interest was ever recorded to secure the loan. There's no documentation, only the accounting record of the seven million deposit. I'm hoping Jackie knows where those funds came from, whether it was the same lender, and why there's no documentation of the second loan."

"Is any of the money left?"

"There was. About one million out of the second loan in bitcoin. But when Bob went missing, thel bitcoin disappeared."

"Any suspicion where these loans came from, Judge?"

"I'm thinking the Dark Web."

"If Bob was so under-water, what did he find to put up as collateral for the second loan?"

"It may have been secured by Bob's life, Katy."

"Oh."

"There are other players in this mess too."

"Like whom?"

"There's a guy named Forrest Langley. Bob raised money in an initial syndication and Langley was one of the investors. The front money was for plans, permits, fees, and some initial construction costs. This was required by the construction lender, who wanted to be sure the owner had skin in the game. Langley hates Bob. Claims Bob's syndication was fraudulent. Claims Bob misrepresented the risks of the project, suckered Langley into investing the bulk of his retirement money into a project that was sure to fail. Says he wishes he'd had the opportunity to shoot Bob in the head."

"Did Bob really do that? Take their money under false pretenses? Destroy their retirement?"

"I don't know, Katy. Bob could have. He was desperate. And Bob could sell. He could sell sand to a saguaro."

"Do you think Langley had a hand in Bob's disappearance?"

"Maybe. But then again, others had motive."

"Like who?"

"Cindy. Bob was long delinquent in his alimony, and Cindy is set to lose her house because it's in Bob's name. He took a loan out against it to obtain more money to sink into The Spire."

"I'll bet she's really angry."

"Yes. Cindy's broke and bitter."

"Well, there you go, Judge. Isn't it usually someone in the family, often the spouse or ex-spouse, who commits a murder?"

"Something like twenty-five percent of murders are committed by family members, it's true. But she'd have needed help."

"Isn't there a boyfriend?"

"Yes. A guy named Sam Compton. A real piece of work. Run's a cold calling scam out in the boondocks east of here; upgraded to selling over the Dark Web."

"Selling what?"

"Anything they can make a buck on, legal or not. Phony art investments, misstated stock offerings, 'no-chance' syndications, prescription drugs."

"Sounds like a real charmer."

"Yes. And his money partner in his operation comes from the Dark Web. Money controlled by some powerful person here in town. He won't say who."

"The Dark Web again."

"Yes."

"It all sounds complicated Judge. This may be the murder that doesn't get solved."

"I'll get to the bottom of it, Katy. I'm bringing Bob's killers, and the one who gave the orders, to justice. I'm not leaving until I do."

"I know you're very stubborn, Judge. But sometimes things just can't be figured out. Sometimes you have to just let things go."

"Not this time, Katy. But it's nice to have you here to help. To give me some perspective on this mess."

"That reminds me, Judge. I came primarily to join you of course, but also I have a date."

"A date?" The Judge's head shot up. "With who?"

"A bachelorette party date, Judge. Marie Stone's. She's getting married again. And she's invited me to her bachelorette party. I'm quite looking forward to it. But I'm afraid you going to have to have dinner alone."

"Maria Stone. Your crazy friend from Lake Arrowhead?"

"Yes."

"When's your party?"

"Tonight. Can you drop me off at it, and then pick me back up?"

"Hurump," muttered the Judge. He hated eating alone.

CHAPTER 26
SATURDAY
11:00 P.M.

The Judge checked his watch. It was a half hour before he was supposed to pick up Katy from her bachelorette party. He'd often wondered what females did at these bachelorette soirees. He'd heard rumors of course. Tales of games of taping toilet paper to make bridal gowns or negligees. A wedding ring toss, a game of romantic movie quotes. Stories of bringing in a manicurist, a yoga instructor, or even setting up a braid bar, whatever the Hell that was. There were also stories of minimum food so as to keep the bride in control and able to fit into her wedding dress until the deed was done. Things like little sandwiches with the edges all cut off, practically bare inside except for a single thin slice of cucumber or tomato. He shuddered at the thought. Katy would probably need dinner afterwards.

He decided to arrive a little early just to see what it was all about. Besides, it was Vegas the friends had picked to gather in, and the bride, Marie Stone, a close friend of Katy's, had something of an exotic reputation in the Lake Arrowhead community. The Judge wondered if it carried over to Vegas.

The bachelorette and friends had rented a party room at a casino for their function. No one was supposed to know where it was, but of course the Judge was told, as he was Katy's wheels.

He wondered at the sly smile the front door reception guy gave him when he asked for directions to the bachelorette party. He was directed to the back wall of the casino, and a heavy padded green door that stood there, closed.

The door swung open easily on well-oiled hinges, spring loaded, noiselessly closing behind him. He stepped into a small dark foyer, with a bar and coat racks on the left, twin doors marked 'Hers' and 'His' on the right, and a closed glass door dead ahead. Even though the glass door was closed, there was an insane amount of racket coming through as the door glass vibrated to a rap mashup that was painful to the ears.

Strobe lasers flashed across the other side of the glass door in purples, reds and yellows, briefly illuminating an interior of arms, hands, feet and hips as a crowd of women danced around inside. The Judge opened the glass door a crack and peeked around the glass. There was a small circular stage a foot of the dance floor in the center of the room, surrounded by women of all shapes, sizes and ages dancing around it and screaming and waving their arms about. It was what Saint Mary of Bethlehem Hospital of London must have looked like in the 1400s, known then as Bedlam

The Judge was suddenly afraid to go in. He took a deep breath, pushed the glass door all the way open and stepped into Hell. The music was even worse without the glass protection. The strobe lights initially blinded him, leaving him to thrust his hands out like a blind man so as to avoid tables, chairs, and spiraling women, all drunk, who were whirling around and pretending to dance to a noise that had no rhythm or beat. There was the scent of forty kinds of perfumes mixed with the sweat of a party that had been going for the while, assaulting his nose and leaving a rancid taste in his mouth.

As his eyes adjusted to the gloom between strobe flashes, he saw there were three young men on the small circular stage, bare chested, tight jeans, also pretending to dance to what was undanceable. They looked like super models, unnaturally tan and well oiled, with pecs he might have dreamed of back when he was twenty.

One young man was sitting on a chair, and Marie Stone, the bride to be, was straddling his lap and running her crotch up and down a bulge in his pants that looked the size of a grapefruit. The other two men were doing a bump and grind sort of dance, each forward thrust of their pelvises bringing high pitched shrieks from fifteen drunken women circling their stage.

There was fourth young man, nude except for a jockstrap and an enormous stuffed squirrel's head covering his head, attending to tables in the shadows across the other side of the room. God knew what he was doing over there, but the Judge certainly didn't... and didn't want to. The Judge quickly adverted his eyes.

One of the guests, late thirties with blond hair and blue eyes, bumped into him and clung, semi-collapsing on him in a cloud of vodka and fruit punch.

"This's Marie's last chance to fuck a hot guy," she slurred. After this it's only old Harry. Poor thing. What we give up for a little security. Christ, it makes me sick." The Judge quickly held her away, lest she get sick.

Feeling uncomfortable and out of place, he tried to look invisible as he circled the room against its walls, keeping in the shadows, looking for Katy. He finally spotted her, sitting at a table on the edge of the dance floor with a friend, animatedly yelling at her friend over the racket. She was drinking from a punch glass, and she looked to be well over her normal limit. She'd be hung over and hell on wheels in the morning. He'd have to get an early start on his day tomorrow, get out of the condo before she woke up.

As he started in Katy's direction, a large blond of gargantuan proportions crossed his path, stopped, and turned to him, her eyes focusing with some effort on his, then measuring him up and down. Mid-forties, big boobs crushed inside the elastic top of a gold sequin dress, big neck, arms, legs, hips, fanny, and jowls that'd stop a train.

"I know you," she shouted over the din in a sailor's voice that would carry in any gale. "You're the Judge." She gave the Judge her best smile... for what it was worth.

"Nice to see you," mumbled the Judge, no recognition of who the woman might be

"I'm Janet Mason, Marie's sorority sister from USC," she yelled. "I'm an engineer with the County Building Department. You're the one giving the Department heartburn." She giggled, clearly smashed.

"How is that?" asked the Judge, suddenly focused.

"You told Darrel Hurtz, the project's lawyer, that the County Building Department has been deliberately stalling on issuing an occupancy permit for The Spire. Hurtz immediately called my boss and raised Hell. Said he couldn't sweep this under the rug no more. Said if he was going down it wouldn't be alone." Janet hiccupped and shoved a meaty hand over her mouth, her eyes widening in surprise.

"You should buy me a coffee some morning. I got lots of interesting gossip about The Spire, and its nice developer, that Bob Hanson, a lovely guy. And what goes on at my department."

She giggled, then winked. Or the Judge guessed it was a wink. A sort of a funny squishing movement on one side of her face among the folds, false eyelashes and makeup as one eye momentarily closed.

"Is it unusual to deny a partial occupancy permit to the units completed?" asked the Judge.

"Fairly unusual if all the tenant improvements are in. But The Spire always gets special attention. It's political."

She reached into a ridiculously small shoulder purse given her size and produced a card she thrust at him with an unsteady hand. "Got to get 'nother drink, by for now." She gave him another smile and wobbled off.

The Judge resumed his trek, dodging female bodies swinging around in random patterns purporting to be solo dancing to the non-music.

He reached Katy and tapped the back of her shoulder. She swung around, disappointment replacing her aroused smile as she saw it was him.

"How's you likes the Lightening Up Striking Boys?" she shouted at him over the din.

"Very… surprising," was all he could manage. "Shall we go?"

"Yes, I suppose it's time. It's been a grand party." She got unsteadily to her feet, and they began maneuvering between chairs, tables and women toward the glass door, the Judge leading in full retreat.

CHAPTER 27
SUNDAY
10:00 A.M.

The Judge arrived at the Starbucks in Hughes Center behind his condo five minutes early, but Janet Mason was already there. He'd called her early and set up the meeting. She wore a tight-fitting red dress with white polka dots, cut low to display an enormous bosom. She sat with her legs crossed on the outside patio in a tucked away corner, the hem of her dress flipped over a bit to show a long stretch of leg. When she took off her dark overlarge sunglasses, the Judge could see pain in her eyes that the mascara and eyelashes couldn't quite hide. She winced at the sunlight and fumbled to get her shades back on quickly. She was mighty hungover. But she'd still showed up. The Judge had to respect that.

"Listen Judge, I can't stay long. I feel awful. Hung the Hell over. If I never see another fruit punch again it will be too soon. But I'd said I'd come and here I am. This has to be a privileged conversation, however. You can't ever repeat any of it or tell people we met. Agreed?"

"Agreed, Janet."

"I just feel sorry for Bob Hanson, and for his daughter too, Jackie. They were honest hardworking people and were entitled to be treated fairly."

"And were they?"

"Not in my opinion. Even before the application for occupancy permit was filed, Harry Jessup, the County Supervisor for our district, was in our department. He was sitting on the corner of Reginald Jones' desk, whispering to him. I don't know what all was said, but I heard enough through the open door to my office to know it was about the Spire Project.

The Supervisor was livid. Said the parcel had been stolen out from under his group by Hanson. Called Hanson an L.A. pig. Would build a piece of crap on the parcel, sell it off, and leave the county with years and years of maintenance and unpaid taxes before the structure collapsed of its own ungainly weight. He told Regie in no uncertain terms he wanted the project delayed, by whatever means necessary. He wanted all permits either denied, or delayed, slowed to a snail's crawl. "Delayed until the project fails." That's what he said. Also said Regie best take care of it personally. Or Regie might have to kiss his pension goodbye, as he might be looking for another job."

"Do you know who else was in this cabal to see that The Spire failed, Janet?"

"I'm not sure Judge. Regie, Counselman Jessup, and the attorney, Darrel Hurtz. Those three for sure. There was the name of a banker mentioned, Clyde

Armstrong. Heads a major construction lending bank in town."

"That's the banker who has claimed his bank had no executed extension agreement extending the term of the construction loan. It all begins to make sense. Do you know what the group's plan was for the parcel of land where The Spire sits?"

"Yes. They had been negotiating with the owner and another developer to buy the property and put an ice hockey stadium there. It was a big deal. They had a professional ice hockey team lined up to come to Vegas once a stadium was built. They were really mad when the property was sold at the last minute to Mr. Hanson."

"Angry enough to give him a one way ride out into the desert?"

"I don't know about that, Judge. Angry, yes. Bitter, yes. Vindictive, yes. But these are businessmen and a lawyer. I don't think they'd be murderers."

"Sometimes I'm surprised how far people will go, Janet. They let their emotions run away with them. Do things that surprise themselves and everyone else who knows them."

Janet looked doubtful.

"Anyway, thanks for this information. It's quite helpful. It's part of the mosaic I'm trying to piece together of what happened to my friend, Bob Hanson."

The Judge took a last slurp of his latte, gave Janet a professional handshake she seemed disappointed to get, and departed the patio.

CHAPTER 28
SUNDAY
11:30 A.M.

The Judge returned to his condo to find Katy still asleep. He tiptoed around the living room, not wanting her to wake. She'd be difficult until she stuffed three aspirin down to calm her head. He was succeeding too until his damn cell phone went off, belting out 'Danny Boy' acapella as it was supposed to do.

"Oh my God, kill that phone!" Katy croaked from the bedroom before covering her curls with the blanket and two pillows again. The Judge snatched the phone up and just caught the call at the end of 'from glen to glen'.

"This is Barry Marsh, Judge. Thought you might like an update on the Hanson case."

"I would, Barry. You working overtime, Detective? It's Sunday."

"The missus likes the overtime money. Anyway, based on our investigation, we've now classified Mr. Hanson's death as a suicide."

"A what? How? How can that be?"

"We found his car, three hills over from where he started his little trek. The keys were in the ignition.

Plenty of gas. Runs fine. We figure he parked there and started off, came over the hills and down into the shallow valley. Walking toward the Vegas skyline some thirty miles away. A miserable way to do yourself in if you ask me, but it takes all kinds."

"But you didn't find a note."

"No. No note. One could have been blown away after he collapsed. But he had his wallet, filled with twenty-five hundred in cash, and his credit cards. No indication of robbery. From what little we can tell from examination of the body after it was dined on by local critters, no bullet holes, no signs we could find of blunt instrument trauma, no obvious knife wounds, although admittedly the animals had done a good job of stripping off his flesh."

"Did you find his tracks from where his car was left to the location of the body?"

"Well, no. The wind and the sun obliterated all of his tracks, and even the tire tracks of the car."

"Don't you think it odd he left his car keys in the ignition?"

"Well… no. Who's going to steal the car way out there? Sides, if you're going to kill yourself, you don't need your keys, or your car, anymore. His profile fits suicide. He'd lost everything in his real estate project, destroyed his credit, too old to start again, divorced from his wife; estranged from his daughter, had an argument with his mistress."

"How do you know he was estranged from Jackie?"

"Well, Judge, the Ex said the daughter had a fight with her dad before he disappeared."

"Damn, Barry. It just doesn't fit. The man I know would never have committed suicide."

"Do we ever really know anyone, Judge? And we're always changing. Anyway, Captain says it's a suicide, so its suicide. Case closed. Thought you'd want to know.

The Judge sighed. "Yes, Barry. Thanks. I appreciate the heads-up. Have you told Cindy?"

"No. Thought maybe you could take care of the ex-wife for us, Judge. Since you know her."

The Judge sighed. "Yes. I'll talk to Cindy. But this is the first I've heard of a mistress."

"Mistress, girlfriend, a gal he was spending a lot of time with, Judge, from what we can tell."

"Who is she?"

"Elka something. Russian, I think. We haven't been able to find her. But she had a big shouting match with Hanson in the Fat Tuesday MGM Bar the night before Hanson disappeared. Bartender told us they were a couple, been in there before."

"All right, Barry. I'll break the news to Hanson's Ex."

The Judge hung up, called Cindy, and arranged for lunch an hour later.

CHAPTER 29
SUNDAY
12:30 P.M.

The Judge met Cindy at a small table on the 11th floor of the Eiffel Tower at Paris Las Vegas. The Eiffel Tower Restaurant provided elegant French cuisine, magnificent views of the Bellagio Fountains across the street, and perspective on the endless parade of humanity flowing below along the Strip sidewalk. The Town was busy.

Cindy settled into the small chair, lapping over the tiny seat a little just as did the Judge, and ordered a Scotch on the rocks, an aberlour sixteen-year, one of the few things he admired about her. She could always knock back alcohol with the best, particularly if someone else was buying.

They made small talk for a bit about the old days, the people they knew from USC, and the recent gossip. Cindy went through her Scotch like a house afire and waved her finger around in a circle for a second.

Finally, the Judge asked, "How you really doing, Cindy, really?"

"I'm doing, Judge. Bob was a fuckin' clown. I won't miss him."

The Judge looked at her sitting back in her chair now, the alcohol hitting. There was no delicate way to say it and so after her second drink he just spit it out.

"The police have decided Bob committed suicide, Cindy."

The color drained from her face. She opened her mouth, but no words came, just hyperventilation. She looked like a large trout out of water and out of oxygen.

Finally, she gasped, "They can't do that. It was murder for Christ's sake! We both know Bob wouldn't kill himself."

"I objected, but they could care less."

"Oh, shit. Shit. Shit. I'm fuckin' screwed, Judge. I'm fifty-two years old and broke. My tits have dropped, my coochie's dried up, my waist is gone, my rump is a train wreck, my knees hurt, and I'm developing jowls. I may as well follow Bob out to the desert. Without the insurance I'm screwed."

"What insurance?"

Cindy clapped a hand over her mouth and muttered "Shit" into it.

"What insurance, Cindy?"

Cindy was silent.

"What insurance, Cindy?"

Cindy sighed.

"Bob had an insurance policy I made him take out when he said he was refinancing my house 'cause he needed money for his project. I threatened him with jail for failure to pay back alimony. I made him scrounge up enough money to buy life insurance."

"How much?"

"What?"

"How much life insurance?"

Cindy looked over the Judge's shoulder out the window at the dancing fountains, spraying the air with whisps of fantasy, wrestling with what to say.

"Ten million, Judge. Bobby coughed up ninety thousand for two-years of premiums when he started The Spire. He squeezed it out of the construction loan somehow, pretended it was for a vendor or something, made me beneficiary. I was really going to court to get him arrested and he knew it. He yelled and squirmed and pleaded and cried, but I'd had enough of his bull shit."

"It's still inside the two-year period of the paid premium?"

"Yes."

"But it has an exclusion clause for suicide?"

"Of course, within the first two years. Those assholes!"

Cindy looked at the Judge now, her eyes blazing. "The police can't do this. They can't destroy my only chance for a good life. Those bastards. Those fuckin' Goddamn shit-eating cops. I won't let them. I'll sue. I'll put them all in jail. They can't do this. Someone murdered Bob. You know it, I know it, everyone knows it. God damn them to Hell."

The Judge ran through the list of facts that made the police conclude it was a suicide. The car with the keys in it over the hill in the dunes; Bob's financial troubles; his fight with his girlfriend; no indication of physical assault or trauma; his bee line march from the car straight out into the middle of the desert.

"No note, Judge. There was no note. And you know Bob. He was of sound mind. He wouldn't have killed himself. Besides, if a man wants to commit suicide, he eats a gun or something. He doesn't strand himself out in the desert where he's going to suffer. This is a full crock of shit."

Cindy threw herself hard against the back of her chair and began to cry. Tears rolled down her cheeks as she muttered, "It's just unfair, Judge. So... God damn unfair. I earned that money. I put up with Bob all these years. Didn't put him in jail when he couldn't make alimony and child support, which was most of the time. Held his fuckin' hand when he'd come back and cry on my shoulder about his latest real estate failure. Or when the latest trashy tart he'd been bonking left for greener pastures. I've singled handedly raised our daughter and paid for all her schooling. Now I'm just totally fucked."

"Slow down, Cindy. I'm still investigating. Suicide doesn't sound right to me either. I'll get to the bottom of what happened. I don't think Bob killed himself."

She looked up him then, a spark of hope in her mascara-ruined eyes, clutched at her hand purse and produced a hanky. She gave her nose a good blow. Heads turned at the tables jammed in around them. She produced a weak smile for the Judge.

"Does Sam know about the insurance?"

"Sam knows everything. He's my financial adviser."

"You have a confirmed gambling addict as your financial adviser?"

"Sam wouldn't touch my money, mostly because I don't have any. If I got the ten mil, I was going to move on without Sam."

Still the same old sentimental Cindy, thought the Judge. For her it was always about the money, or perhaps the security it assured.

"You didn't tell me there was girlfriend, Cindy. Tell me about her. I had no idea Bob was involved with someone."

"He got picked up by this little tramp. Twenty years his junior. Coulda been his daughter. She got her claws in real deep. He was supporting her on the side. Thought I didn't know."

"What's her name?"

"Elka something. Russian. I'm sure she's illegal. Looking for a quick marriage and her green card."

"How long have they been together?"

"Maybe six months. I met her once. Ran into them at a restaurant here in town. Anorexic little bitch, no tits, no ass. If she turned sideways, you'd miss her. Big nose, calculating eyes. Figured she score big with Bobby's Spire Project. Guess when you're as desperate for it as Bob was standards don't matter." Cindy sniffed.

"Know where I can find her?"

"Jackie knows. Jackie actually likes her, the little traitor. Find Jackie. She knows where the tart's pitched her tent."

"What really happened with Jackie, Cindy? Why did she leave?"

"I don't really know, Judge. I came home as she was storming out of the house with her suitcase."

"What did she say?"

"Nothing... I mean bull shit. Yellin' Sam tried to attack her, crap like that."

"You didn't believe her?"

"Hell no. Sam is the nicest guy. And loves me. He'd never touch Jackie."

"You're sure?"

"Sure I'm sure."

"But you just said you'd dump him if you got the insurance money."

"That's financial. Not because I don't like him. But you're right. He's a spender and a gambler. He ain't spending any of my money."

"Is it possible he's a chaser too?"

"Not with Jackie for Christ sakes. She's my daughter."

As their lunch arrived Cindy gave the Judge a direct stare. "I should have married you, Judge. Instead of my adolescent frat boy who never grew up."

The Judge gave her a tight smile. They both knew it could never have happened.

CHAPTER 30
SUNDAY
2:00 P.M.

The Judge waited until Katy left their condo to do some shopping, then turned to the Dark Web on his laptop. He put in the site name that Margie, the young escort girl had given him, *Crème de la Crème*. It was the site she'd said Jackie Hanson was using for business

Again, they wanted to know all about the Judge's predilections for sex, and again they wanted a credit card. He checked all the boxes using Jackie's characteristics: located in Vegas, slim, brunette, about five-foot, 28 to 30. Forty accounts came up, each with multiple pictures of each girl, mostly provocative. None of them were Jackie.

He thought about it a minute, then changed the age range to 22 to 27 and hit search again. This brought up one hundred and twenty pictures to peek and leer at. It was kind of fun. Some of the girls were not pretty, some looked tired, others looked pretty mean, and some looked like the girl next door, young and all American. Just as well Katy wasn't here. He seemed to be lingering over the pretty ones.

Number one hundred and six brought up Jackie Hanson smiling at him, claiming to be 22 and shy. She had no kids and a college degree. She looked good and could have been 22. Her stage name, if that was the proper term, was Sheila, as Margie had said. Her tag line was *The girl next door you always had a crush on!*. There were pictures of her riding a horse, dancing at a club, riding her bike at night in front of the Venetian. And of course, a couple of shots tastefully done, partially exposing small breasts.

He hit the like button, and then typed a message from Martin, his Dark Web identity.

"Martin here. In town for three days on business. You're very beautiful. Would you like to meet some time?"

Her response was immediate.

"Might be fun, Martin. I like your profile. You sound like a really cool guy. We could meet and see if there is mutual chemistry. I need a physical and emotional connection before I feel comfortable. Only way to see if that exists is to meet."

"So, lets meet."

"When?"

"How about now?"

"I'm still in bed. Kind of a lazy day for me. But we can meet later this evening if you've got a credit card you're prepared to use."

"That sounds awesome, Sheila. Let's plan on it."

A half screen showed up immediately under her picture where he was asked to put in his credit card info and make a $500 deposit. He did so.

"Thank you so much, Martin. I'm very much looking forward to our meet up. I am attending a pool party tonight at the Hendricks, a boutique hotel opposite The Rio over on Flamingo.

Come to the pool party at the back of the hotel. It's a nice public place and we'll both feel safe. If there's a connection, and I think there will be with you, we can take it from there."

"What time?"

"Ten pm. And you don't need to bring your trunks. LOL."

"Okay."

"If we hit it off, Martin, we can discuss some details and move on from there. Perhaps have dinner, champagne, end up back at your hotel room for the night and have a lot of fun. Oh, and Martin. If for any reason either of us is uncomfortable and we don't move forward, half of your deposit will be returned."

"Sounds fair. I'll see you tonight."

"You certainly will, Martin. And I will see you too, all of you! LOL. Ciao."

The Judge sat back in his chair, surprised at how easy that had been.

CHAPTER 31
SUNDAY
10:30 P.M.

The Judge was late, and he knew it. He'd forgotten about traffic on crossing the Strip, even though in distance the Hendricks was just up the street and over the freeway pass. He'd told Katy he had a meeting and wouldn't be too late. She was ordering dinner in and nursing her sore head from the night before. No use stirring her up about his true destination. He finally reached the Hendricks Hotel and reluctantly relinquished his car to the valet. He hated having other people driving his car.

He moved through the lobby, casino, and grounds as though a were a puzzle, stopping staff here and there to get directions. He ended up outside at the rear of the property, all garden and shadows, sans the floodlights that lit up everywhere else.

The entrance to the hotel swimming pool was there, surrounded by a high wall, and further screened by tall trees and shrubs. A guard house was placed at an angle in front of the pool entrance, blocking a view of the deck and pool beyond. All very, very private. Faint sounds of music drifted up from behind the guardhouse.

The Judge marched up and leaned in at its small window. A burly uniform inside looked at the Judge suspiciously, then asked his name.

"Martin."

"You on the list?"

"I don't know."

"Let's have a look, Martin." He picked up a clipboard and paged through its sheets while the Judge stood nervously, shifting his weight from one foot to the other. He hoped he wasn't going to see anybody he knew, except of course for Jackie.

"Who put you on the list, Martin?" Suspicion again.

"Sheila."

"Okay. Go on in. Have fun. Don't do anything I wouldn't do." He winked.

The Judge entered the through the gate and turned the corner to the back side of the guard house. There was an extended brick patio with tables and benches, set in nooks surrounded by trees and high foliage. At the other end was a break in landscape framed by two large palm trees and a path that bent to the left behind the outlines of a white structure.

The Judge followed the path and wound his way to the front of the white building, marked 'Changing Facilities'. On the other side was an Olympic-size pool. The music he'd heard before was now four times louder. A disc jockey in a far corner was spinning records, old 45s, shifting from one to another and melting the sounds together in a patchwork of racket. Worse even than the bachelorette party.

The pool was well lit from its bottom and sparkled in clear aqua, casting little light onto the deck around it. The Judge could make out shadowy shapes of women and men crowded together at the other end of the deck, some dancing, others talking. People were dancing in the pool too, pink chubby male bodies in boxy shapes, and sleek female bodies in smaller, more slender shapes, balanced by boobs of assorted sizes.

There was only one problem. Nobody wore swimsuits. They were all butt naked!

In the middle of the path stood a woman of Amazon proportions, blond, mid-forties, reminding the Judge of a champion weightlifter. She wore a tight yellow stretchy workout suit which covered but was too sheer and tight to hide a large chest, strong muscular legs and hips, and everything in between. She didn't look the sort he'd want to meet in a dark alley.

"You can undress in the changing room behind you," she said. "Just be sure to use the 'His', not the 'Hers'. Leave your clothes in a locker. Be sure to lock your locker and take your key. You can leave the key with me, or you can wrap the loop on it around your wrist."

"But I don't swim," said the Judge.

"We both know you're not here to swim, Bud."

"But I didn't bring my swimsuit."

She looked at him then, carefully, as though he'd just said the most stupid thing in the world. Then shrugged. "This is a 'No Clothes-No Option Pool Party', Hon. You couldn't wear your suit even if you'd brought it. No one gets past me unless they're in their birthday suit."

"But Christ, I'm an old guy. No one wants to look at my protruding belly and saggy butt."

"Rules are rules. I don't make them. I just enforce them."

"How about I leave my shorts on? They're boxers, blue polka dot on a yellow background. Really cute."

"I can't let you in that way."

The Judge sighed. "Okay, I guess I'll go in the pool then. Are there towels?"

"Sure. A stack of them in the locker room. You can get one there."

"And bring it out with me?"

"Of course."

"Draped around me, like in a sauna?"

"Look, Mister, take off your clothes, get yourself a towel, then you can join the party and do whatever the fuck you want. Okay?"

"Okay."

The Judge disappeared into the locker room and took off his clothes. He looked in the mirror at his aging body, all paunch on two spindly legs, capped by a shallow chest above his bullet head with his big nose above, and his shriveled plumbing below. He felt nausea washing over him. He hated to look at himself naked, and he hated even more to have others look at him in that condition.

After a big sigh, he emerged five minutes later, sans clothes, a white towel three sizes too small stretched across his tummy and groin, held together in a clutched left hand lest it slip down. He felt ridiculous. He could feel his face burning a bright pink.

He waded through the crowd around the pool edge, trying not to stare at the collection of boobs, dicks and vaginas surrounding him as people chatted animatedly. At least he wasn't the only guy with a large paunch. He walked carefully, trying to discourage the too-short towel from opening across his middle. He felt like an embarrassed schoolboy and wished he'd given the whole idea up.

He spotted Jackie at the other end of the crowd, giggling with two female companions, clearly having fun. She'd matured since he'd seen her a year ago, although granted he'd never seen her quite like this. She was still rail thin. As he got closer, he could see through the gloom new lines in her face and shadows under her eyes that makeup didn't quite hide, evidence of a lifestyle he didn't want to think about. He felt sorry for her.

He inserted himself in their threesome. "Hi. You're Sheila?" Jackie's professional name on the site. "I'm Martin. Your guest. You invited me online."

Jackie's face lit up in an open smile as she stepped out of her group with a "Later guys," to inspect the Judge. The Judge felt like a prize bull being appraised for what he might be worth... and might produce in income. She noted his safety-pinned towel with amusement, then looked up at his face... and froze.

"Oh, shit. It's you...the Judge!"

She instinctively brought an arm up across her chest and shoved her other hand down to cover her crotch

"We can't meet like this. You can't be here. You can't see me like this. Christ what are you doing here? What do you want?"

"Just to talk, Jackie. Just to talk."

The surprise and embarrassment in Jackie's eyes were replaced by something else now... fear. She looked around behind the Judge, scanning the crowd, then nervously grabbed the Judge's hand and started them back for the lockers.

"Fuck, we can't talk here. Too many eyes. Get dressed. Meet me outside on the little patio. To the left, at the table and bench. Stay in the shadows there." She bolted into the 'Hers' locker room.

Five minutes later the Judge sat outside on the bench, hidden in the shadows of large plants that blocked what little light came from the Vegas skyline. He wondered if Jackie would come.

Five more minutes went by. The Judge was about to give up when a small figure crept quietly over the pool path, cautiously looked around, then darted for the Judge's shadowed table. She hunkered down beside the Judge and began to softly cry.

CHAPTER 32
SUNDAY
11:15 P.M.

The Judge did his best to console her. Taking her hand and whispering it would be okay. He felt a lot more comfortable talking to her now she had clothes, though her thin silk dress, bright red and cinched at the waist with a silver belt, did little to hide her body. She was a walking advertisement for her calling.

After a while the tears stopped. She gave a big sigh, and then just sat there, staring out at the patio. Her face had the most desolate look the Judge had ever seen.

"I'm trying to find who killed your dad, Jackie. That's all. Not here to judge anybody's lifestyle or give advice."

"They'll kill you Judge. They'll kill me for talking to you. Just like they killed Daddy. And they'll kill Mom, and my Robbie, and that slug of a boyfriend of Mom's. They'll kill everyone, even the dog."

"Is that what they said, Jackie?"

"Yes. They were vividly clear."

"Who, Jackie? Who killed your dad? Who....?"

"I don't know who actually gave him the ride. But I know it was the Spider who ordered it."

"Tell me what happened. Tell me from the beginning."

"If I talk they'll kill me."

"No one will know, Jackie. I won't tell anyone we've talked."

She looked at him then. Bright blue flashed from her racoon eyes, ringed with mascara from tears. She wanted to believe him; he could see that. In fact, she wanted to talk, to get it out, to frame it in words so it was less scary. She took a deep breath.

"I guess it started when I bailed out of Mom's house. Mom was unbearable, trying to boss me around like a teenager. I'm a twenty-eight-year-old woman for Christ sakes. And then when Sam tried to force me behind Mom's back... That was it. I just left. Anyway, I moved in with Daddy at The Spire. He hired me to be his assistant."

"This was when?"

"About eight weeks before he disappeared."

"Tell me about the Project, Jackie, tell me about the financing. Do you know about that?"

"Some. The original budget, complete, was thirty-eight million. But the Building Department kept slowing us down, even frequently losing our file. And several subs substantially increased their bids. They threatened to walk off the job if Dad didn't pay more. And the interest carry on the construction loan was enormous as the project just dragged on and on without completion. Dad figured we were going to be twelve million over budget by the time the project was allowed to open its doors and sell time shares. But he was wrong. It was more."

"So, what did Bob do?"

"Before I'd arrived Dad went online and got a hard money loan for five million."

"Secured by a Second Trust Deed?"

"Yes. I think so. That kept him going."

"Who made the loan?"

"I don't know. I saw the trust deed. The beneficiary was some dummy shell in the Isle of Man."

"But you were still some seven million short."

"Yes. That's what Dad figured."

"What did Bob do?"

"He somehow got another loan over the Dark Web."

"For seven million."

"Yes. He knew the five million wasn't going to cut it."

"Secured by another junior trust deed?"

"I don't think so. Dad said it was a very dangerous loan with a short fuse, only a six-month loan. But he felt he had no choice."

"Did he say who made the seven-million-dollar loan?"

"Yes. He said it was this Spider."

"What did he say about the Spider?"

"Dad said there was a character on the Dark Web who called himself the Spider. And who specialized in making distressed loans. Turns out the asshole specializes in lots of things on the Dark Web. I'm even working for the Spider now."

"Do you know who the Spider is?"

"No. He's very careful to keep anonymous."

"Was the seven million in loan money wired in?"

"It was a funny. It was mostly in bitcoin, put into a bitcoin account Dad opened for The Spire. A small portion arrived separately, as in two hoods carrying suitcases of money."

"Tell me about that."

A shadow spread over Jackie's face, beyond fear, it was terror.

"I really don't want to talk about it."

"I need to know, Jackie."

Jackie looked around, as if the Spider could be hiding in a nearby corner. Then, "Dad said two large thugs came to his Spire unit. Each over six foot and big. Big boned, big shoulders, lots of muscle, real thugs. Dad said between them walked their supervisor, a nasty little guy in a pinstripe suit and a yellow tie. Said the little guy looked like a pimp. Unfortunately, I met them the next morning, after Dad disappeared. His description was right." Jackie shuddered.

"Can you describe this pimp-like guy, Jackie?"

"Yeah. I guess. Older, maybe early sixties, five feet, maybe less. Thin, with light brown hair, mottled skin, a big, hooked nose and bad teeth. But the worst part are his eyes. Mean slitty little eyes that look out from his face with hate toward everyone and everything."

"And back when the seven million loan was made, they delivered a part of the seven million in cash?"

"Yes. That's what Dad said. I guess it came in two separate deliveries."

"Did your dad know why it was cash?"

"No. Dad suspected it was illegal money, drugs or gambling or something. But I also think Dad wanted it that way. The subs were all quitting for lack of payment, and liening The Spire. It was getting more and more difficult. I think Dad used the cash to pay off certain of the more critical subs he needed to keep going and ignored the others. He was desperate to complete the Building Department's punch list and obtain The Spire's occupancy permit."

"Was this little guy the lender? The Spider?"

"Dad said no. This pimp guy was just another hired thug."

"Where'd the bitcoin come from?"

"According to the receipts I saw it came from some account in the Caymans."

"Was all the seven million spent too, Jackie?"

"No. At the time Dad disappeared and I left, there was still unspent money from this loan in a secret account Dad set up at a different bank. Dad didn't want the construction lender or the subs to know he still had some liquidity. Said they'd react like sharks sensing blood in the water."

"What happened with your mom, Jackie?"

"I moved out because of Sam. First, he started hitting on me all the time. The lech. I'm his girlfriend's daughter for Christ's sake. It came to a head when he attacked me in the laundry room off the garage. Forced me over the fucking dryer. Tried to put his dirty paw under my panties. I yelled and cursed and cried. Then I managed to turn a little and I slapped him across the face. That startled him and he backed off. I can still smell his pig breath!"

"Did you tell your mom?"

"I tried, but Cindy wouldn't listen. Said I was making it up. We had a fight about it, screaming at each other. Then I just left. I couldn't live there anymore."

"What about Robbie?"

"I wanted to take him, but I had no money, no one to watch him. Dad said when The Spire was complete and he had some capital out of it, he'd set me up in my own home with Robbie."

"Did you know about you dad's girlfriend?"

"Elka, sure. She's really nice. Loved my dad. Wasn't all about the money like Mom."

"You and she friends?"

"Yes."

"Know where she lives?

"Out on the Eastside. On Springdale. A condo project. Green Oasis or something."

"What happened after your dad disappeared?"

Jackie turned pale again and started to shake. She wouldn't look at the Judge. Panic was etched across her face. She swung her head around in all directions, convinced they were watched. Her breath came in ragged gasps. She started to hyperventilate.

"Jackie, you've got to level with me. I need the whole story. What happened?"

"It's hard to talk about, Judge." she said in a tiny voice, almost swallowing her words. "I'm so scared."

"Tell me Jackie."

"That next morning, the night Dad disappeared, around five a.m., the thugs Dad talked about paid me a visit."

"In your unit?"

"No. I was worried about Dad. About eleven or so I visited his apartment. I wanted to check if he was okay. But he wasn't there. I decided to wait for him to return, and I fell asleep on his sofa."

"So, Jackie, you actually met the two big guys and the little pimp guy?"

Jackie's eyes went wide, reliving it in her mind.

"They somehow knew a part of the loan money was left. Approximately one million dollars in bitcoin. They wanted the balance of the money back. They demanded I give them the ID and password to Dad's bitcoin account."

"What'd you do?"

"I explained I couldn't do that. They said not only I could, but I would. I started to argue with the little guy... and then... and then.... Oh my God, it was awful."

"Go on Jackie, what happened."

"He... he... he.... Oh, shit Judge, he pressed me against the wall and shoved a loaded revolver so far down my throat I gagged. And then cocked the trigger. I can still small the garlic and his rotting teeth, taste the gun oil on the barrel, see his mean shit little eyes…like a rat's. God, Judge, I thought I was dead."

"So, you gave him the codes?"

"Yes. What else could I do?"

"Did they leave then?"

"No. They slapped my face a few times. I was so scared. And then… and then…" Jackie started to cry again, more a whimper than cry.

"Go on, Jackie."

"The pimp guy made me stand on the sofa in Dad's condo. Then while he and his two thugs watched, he made me do a strip show and take all my clothes off. I was balancing there on the damn sofa, nude, the damn thugs making mean comments and catcalls about my body while I tried to dance to some music they put on their cell. I've never felt so vulnerable in my entire life. So alone, so utterly defenseless, so… used."

"Did they assault you?"

"Not sexually. But the pimp got me off the sofa and put me down on my knees and stood over me. He waved his gun around in my face." Jackie gave a little sob.

"Anyway, I started to cry, to wail, I guess. He slapped me hard across the face; I thought my head would come off when he hit me. Then he said, 'If you ever tell anyone what happened here, Jackie, you die… and your little boy, Robbie, dies… And your dog, and you mom, Cindy, and her boyfriend, Sam… They all die. The whole household. Got it? And you'll die in an especially painful way.' Then he laughed his mean laugh again."

"Then?"

"They said my dad owed them a lot of money. Said since my dad was gone. now I owed them the money. Said I was going to have to work it off, work for them. I shook my head. No. Then... then... the little guy took his gun out and shoved it in my mouth again. Said I could work for them, or I could die.... Which did I want? Did I acknowledge my debt, going to start servicing it with my personal services, or was I going to die? I was so scared, Judge. I just nodded okay. They put Dad's robe around me and spirited me downstairs and out into their van, took me to the Hutch."

"The Hutch?"

"That's what they call it. Like a bunny hutch. Sort of a lounge in someone's living room, filled with young girls sitting around, waiting for calls to go out as escorts with men from the website. An older lady, mid-fifties, a madam I guess, took charge of me. Gave me some of her drugs. Got me calmed down. Cleaned me up, provided me a couple of revealing outfits. Took pictures of me dressed and nude in all sorts of suggestive positions. Set me up on their web site. Explained the ground rules, what the split was, how to give a good performance, how to coax larger tips from guys, encourage them to come back. I got a little bigger cut on repeats.

They kept me high on drugs for two weeks, put me right into service, like some breeding dog or something. That little pimp guy showed up from time to time. To remind me what would happen if I didn't provide my services. Work off my debt."

"And this Hutch was owned by the Spider?"

"That was what the girls that worked there thought."

"But the Spider didn't actually show up there, or run the place?"

"No. No one knows who the Spider is. He's just this creature on the Dark Web that pulls strings like a puppeteer and makes everyone else dance to his tune."

"Can you think of anything else, Jackie?"

"No. Except, the thugs thoroughly searched my dad's unit, tore everything apart, looking for something."

"Did they find what they were looking for?"

"I don't think so. They were very angry after they got through. The pimp guy was muttering that the Spider was going to be very, very unhappy. He looked real worried."

"Anything else?"

"No. That's all I know, Judge. I've felt trapped for weeks. A cycle of partying and sleeping and sex and drugs. They provide lots of drugs. I've been in a kind of perpetual daze, not sure what's happening much of the time. I guess that's a blessing."

"Why didn't you call the police?"

"Judge don't be stupid. This is Vegas. The Mob runs this town and does whatever it wants. They own the police."

The Judge nodded his understanding. Your mom wants you back, Jackie."

"I can't go back there. Not with that creepy prick Sam there. Anyway, it's like there's no air in her house, I can't breathe. And she's always on my ass about everything. It's no good for me there."

"What about Robbie, Jackie? He wants his mom back."

"I'm no good being a mother, Judge. It's better for Robbie if he stays with Mom. He was a mistake in the backseat of a Chevy one night when I was fifteen. I never should have kept him. Should have terminated. Cindy bullied me into going full term. I never should have listened. Anyway, Robbie's better off where he is, and safer too."

"So, what do I tell Cindy?"

Jackie produced a sad smile. "Don't tell Mom anything, Judge. It is what it is. I make a good living and have fun sometimes. Course other times it's rough."

"You've been seriously traumatized, Jackie. How about this? I arrange for some one-on-one professional counseling for you. My nickel. Someone who can help. Will you go if I set it up? For your dad?'

Jackie reached over and placed a hand on the Judge's arm. "I'll think about it," she whispered. "I'll think about it."

She got up then and slid back into the shadows, quickly making her way to the path and back to the pool party.

CHAPTER 33
SUNDAY
11:30 P.M.

As the Judge got up from the bench, he sensed movement to his left. He sat back down and peered into the shadow across the patio. A small shape emerged. A man. A very small man, dressed in distressed jeans and a Prabal Gurung khaki shirt. He wore a baseball hat, the brim shading his face as he crossed the patio to stand over the seated Judge, casually tossing a small caliber gun back and forth between his hands. Only his nose protruded from under his hat to catch the light. It was big and hooked.

"What's the matter, fellow? You didn't like Sheila?"

"I guess I wasn't in the mood," said the Judge.

"She put you off in any way? I'll have a word with her if she said something not attractive."

"No. She was very friendly. Very genuine. I'm just tired from all my contract negotiations." The Judge found it difficult to take his eyes off the pistol flopping between Mr. Hat's hands.

"You spent a lot of time talking to her. What'd you talk about?"

"Nothing much."

"You pay her?"

"Ahh, no. But we didn't do anything."

"That's where you're wrong, my man. You booked her time. Frank, isn't it, Frank Martin. You booked her time, Frank, so as she couldn't see someone else. See, it's a lost opportunity cost. And Sheila's time belongs to me. She owes me a bundle, and I'm sort of her agent. I keep an eye on her. Anyway, you gotta pay for the lost time. It's five hundred. For her time."

"But we didn't do anything."

"Like I said, you talked to Sheila a while here on the bench. Poured your heart out to momma, did we? Gotta pay for that, son. It's the way it works. You don't want any trouble, do you?"

"No trouble," said the Judge, reaching for his wallet.

"That's five hundred for her time you booked, and another hundred for me, sort of a collections fee. Cause I could see you were about to run off. Not pay your debts. That's a no-no in this town."

The Judge stood up, fumbled out his wallet with shaking hands, tried to fish out six one-hundred-dollar bills. As they came out, two fell from his shaking grip and fluttered to the ground. Mr. Hat's eyes followed the bills to the ground like a shark, his gun hand dropping to his side, focused on the money.

The Judge wrapped his wallet around his knuckles and stepped forward as he threw the punch, rotating his shoulder and throwing all the weight of his body behind the momentum of his swing as he'd been taught.

There was a satisfactory crunch as the Judge's fist connected with Mr. Hat's nose. He could feel cartilage and bone collapse under the blow. Mr. Hat screamed, dropped the gun, fell on all fours, and threw his head back, trying to stanch the blood pouring down his throat, choking him.

The Judge picked up the fallen gun and put it in his coat pocket. Then he leaned down and plucked Mr. Hat's wallet from his back pocket, noted his name and address on the driver's license inside, Arney Gunn, and dropped it besides the fallen man.

The Judge used his foot to tip the little man over on to his back where he lingered, like an overturned beetle, arms and legs up in a defensive position. The hatred in the mean little eyes changed to panic now.

The Judge planted his foot on the man's throat as he looked with some satisfaction at the ruined nose.

"Who provided the money for The Spire loan, Arney?"

"What?"

"You heard me. Whose money was it?"

"I don't know nothing 'bout that."

"Don't lie to me. I know you were there. You were the delivery boy for the money sometimes. Whose money was it?"

"I don't know what you're talking about."

The Judge pressed a little on the man's throat with his shoe.

The man tried to scream, but all he produced was a gurgle. The Judge released the pressure a little.

"Okay, okay. I was there."

"Whose money was it?"

"The Spider's."

"Who's the Spider?"

"I don't know... I don't know. Nobody knows. It's all handled over the Dark Web. All anonymously. Like you said, I was just a sometimes delivery boy."

"Who gave you orders?"

"The Spider."

"How?"

"Over the Dark Web. Emails."

"You never met your Spider?"

"No."

"But you must have some idea who he is, or where he is."

"Vegas somewhere. That's all I know. He seems to know everything that's going on here."

"Where did you pick up the money to deliver to Hanson? You and your two thugs.?"

"I don't know."

The Judge pressed his foot a little more on the neck. There was another satisfying gurgle attempting to be a scream. The Judge lifted his foot some.

"Tell me now or you're dead." There was a snarl in the Judge's voice.

"Okay... okay... don't... don't...Got email instructions."

"Where'd the money come from?"

The Judge added more pressure again with his foot.

Another panicky gurgle of "No-no, don't do that no more." The man coughed, blood spattering the Judge's shoe.

"We picked up suitcases from an Uber driver. Delivered them. All I know."

"Who's we?"

"Two big guys. Muscle. Work for me. They don't know nothin' either. We just delivered a straight up loan."

"There was nothing straight up about it and we both know it. It was rigged from the start. Someone bought off the Building Department, so they became very unaccommodating, bought off the construction lender so suddenly the deal for an extension of time to repay the loan disappeared."

"I don't know nothin' 'bout that."

"You sure?"

Mr. Hat nodded his head as best he could under the circumstances.

"Who at the Building Department?"

"I don't know. God, I swear. I don't know."

"You got the unspent bitcoin back, right?"

"Yeah. I mean we got the account and the password and forwarded it on."

"Why?"

"Instructions. The loan was past due. Borrower not cooperating. Put the Project in bankruptcy. The Spider said he wanted whatever money was left in the project."

"Where did you send the bitcoin?"

"I don't know, somewhere offshore. I got an email telling me."

"Where's the email?"

"I dumped it from my computer, burned my printout, like I was told."

"Which bank was it supposed to get wired to?"

"I don't know. I don't remember."

"Try."

"Some bank in the Caymans. Isla Cayman or something. I don't know."

The Judge relaxed his foot a little.

"Did you kill Robert Hanson?"

"No."

"Did you give him a ride out into the middle of the desert? Drop him off?"

"No. Nothing to do with that."

"Who did?"

"I don't know."

"Who's the Spider?"

"I don't know."

"And what about Jackie? She calls herself Sheila now."

"I don't know nothin'."

The Judge started to add pressure with his foot.

"Wait, wait. I'll tell."

"Go ahead."

"The Spider told me to put her down after she gave us the codes for the account that had the unspent bitcoin."

"But you didn't."

"No. She doesn't know anything. I figured she's an asset, may as well put her to work. I scared her good, so's she wouldn't say anything about us."

"You and your two thugs?"

"Yes. And I keep an eye on her."

"Did you arrange for her to join this escort service?"

"Yes. I set it up. I get a percentage. It's a good life. Easy money. She's good at it."

"Does the Spider know you didn't put her down?"

Fear spread across the man's face again.

"No... no. Don't tell him. He mustn't know. He'll kill me, you, her, all of us in a heartbeat."

"Okay, friend. You're to stay away from Jackie... Sheila, understand? I don't want to hear you've been around her again. Understand?"
The little man nodded desperately.

"You tell them at the Bunny Hutch her slate's clean. She doesn't owe anyone anything. She's free to leave. Got that?"

The little man nodded his understanding.

"And keep the money. It was well worth my satisfaction".

The Judge removed his foot, turned, and stalked away. He crossed the patio, out the guard gate, and started to enter back into the casino. Then he stopped and spun around.

CHAPTER 34
SUNDAY
11:45 P.M.

The Judge marched back through the gate to the patio, and on to the path, waving casually at the guard. He brushed aside the Amazon lady and her stern chattering about how he had to take his clothes off, and planted himself outside the door to the 'Hers' changing room. Thirty seconds later Jackie pranced out, trying to look fresh and happy, the running mascara scraped away from her eyes, her hair pulled back in a ponytail, wearing nothing at all.

Her eyes widened as the Judge stepped in front of her, blocking her path.

"We're leaving now, Jackie. Go throw your clothes back on." It was his judicial voice he'd so effectively used to give stern orders from the bench. A low growl of a voice with gravel in it. The kind that brooked no interference. Her eyes widened further. She spun around and retreated into the changing room. Two minutes later she was back, fully dressed, submissive, ready to obey his next command.

"Let's go. There's someone I want you to meet."

She followed him out the gate, hiding behind his bulk. But she stopped suddenly and stepped around him, looking with shock at Arney Gunn still sitting on the ground, his knees up, holding the ruins of his nose, trying to stanch the blood flow.

He looked at her with bloodshot eyes, defeat written across his face.

"You're never going to touch her again, isn't that right, Arney?" the Judge asked.

Arney nodded.

"I can't hear you!" snapped the Judge.

"No, sir. Never touch her again," gurgled Arney.

"You're going to stop shadowing her. From now on, no contact, ever! You just leave her be."

"Yes, sir. No contact ever."

"What's going to happen if you contact her again?" asked the Judge.

"You'll kick the shit out of me, again."

"No." The Judge took Arney's small gun out of his pocket and leaned down, shoving it into Arney's mouth. "I'll kill you." He pressed it further in, just long enough to hear Arney choke. Arney owed Jackie that much. Then he removed the gun from Arney's mouth and used it to tap Arney's broken nose. Arney screamed.

"Do you understand the terms of our agreement?"

"Yes, sir. You'll kill me." Arney's face was a mixture of loathing and fear. The Judge could see fear win out.

"Okay. Get the fuck out of here." Arney rolled over on all fours, unsteadily got to his feet, and limped off through a side exit from the patio.

"Come on, Jackie. We have some more things to talk about. And I can't leave you with this pool crowd."

The Judge and Jackie got their cars from valet and the Judge followed her back to her studio apartment, a small hole in the wall place on the outskirts of Downtown Vegas.

She changed into jeans and a sweater and made tea, rattling her china with unsteady hands. They settled in across a tiny table squeezed into her kitchen over steaming cups of Earl Grey.

"Do you really want to continue in this escort life, Jackie?" asked the Judge.

"No, Judge. No, I don't. I mean the money's good, fifteen thousand or so a month, one-eighty a year straight up, no taxes. But it's not real. Up all night, sleeping in till one in the afternoon. Alternatingly donning this mask of coquettishness, moving your body to attract, oohing and ahing on the size of their dicks, telling the same lie about how big they are, over and over. Making all the staged high-pitched groans and yelps, then pretending to come five times in a half hour.

Some of the men are cruel. Some are physical, they just wear you out. Others smell like pigs. And some... some just... I don't know, they want you, they need you, but they hate themselves at the same time, and they hate you for making them need you. There's no empathy. They make you feel so cheap, so used. Like you're a commodity they consume and then discard with distaste.

I suppose that's why the drugs feel so good. They help you forget."

"We'll get you some help, Jackie. Get you into a treatment program. Find some money to help you go back to school, finish that degree. Accounting, wasn't it?"

"Yes. I'd like to do that. I'd like to raise my son again. Like to wake up in the morning not in a drug induced haze. Like to feel real again. Alive. Settled."

She reached across the table and patted the Judge's hand. "Help me, Judge."

"I will, Jackie. I will."

The conversation paused then, each lost in their own thoughts, Jackie's small hand still on top of the Judge's.

Finally, the Judge said, "Let's talk a little about your dad, Jackie, and The Spire Project."

"My poor dad." Jackie let all her air out in a whoosh. "He didn't deserve that, didn't deserve to die... and not like that. He was just trying to make his project work, fighting against enormous odds to build something beautiful. Tilting at the windmills like he always did."

"How's The Spire look with its twelve-mil additional investment? Can you get it to sales and cash flow?"

"The Spire could still pencil out big time, Judge. If we could get that one million the Spider took back, get out of bankruptcy court, and obtain our occupancy permit to sell some of the units. There was lots of profit there. It would have been an enormous whale for my dad if only he could've generated some liquidity from sales."

"And Bob told the lawyer he'd negotiated a six-month extension on the maturity date of the construction loan. Is that right? Did he?"

"He did. He told me all about it. But someone got into our files and stole the executed Loan Modification and Extension Agreement, and all the copies."

"And then the lender reneged?"

"Yes."

"They must have known you no longer had the executed extension. Someone from their group made sure it disappeared."

"I'll bet you're right. I hadn't thought of it that way."

"What happened next?"

"The construction lender served a notice of default, set a date for foreclosure on the project. Dad had no choice. He put the project into a Chapter Eleven reorganization with the debtor in possession. But it all went to shit anyway, Judge. The subs walked off. The building department lost the file again. The bankruptcy law firm started demanding a huge retainer to continue. And that's all I know."

Jackie gave the Judge a weak smile.

Okay, Jackie. That gives me a good picture of what happened. It helps a lot. Why don't you get some rest? We'll talk tomorrow. And I'll have a referral for a drug rehab program.

The Judge stood, gave Bob's daughter a hug, and left, moving slowly now. He was tired. It was one in the morning. And he would be in trouble with Katy for not calling.

CHAPTER 35
MONDAY
7:00 A.M.

The Judge sat in his favorite chair on their little balcony and watched the light creep up and across the desert floor from behind their condo, gradually lighting the back sides of Bally's and the Flamingo Hotel. His mind had been churning all night with the possibilities of who might have given the order to kill Bob, making lasting sleep difficult. He nursed a cup of hot coffee in both hands, appreciating the heat in the early desert temperature. It would be a scorcher later, of course.

Katy appeared suddenly on the balcony and settled into the chair next to him, up extraordinarily early for her. She was dressed in a favorite silk robe she kept in Vegas, bright yellow with embroidered rosebuds everywhere. With tousled hair, applying her small hands to rub sleep from both eyes, she looked positively ravishing.

But she was stirred up. He could sense it. The Judge braced himself, sensing they were going to have "The Conversation". Katy was worried, mostly about him, and wanted to drag him back to Los Angeles where she perceived it was safe.

He wasn't going to go. Out of respect for her he'd listen, pretend to consider her reasoning. Of course, he knew that she knew that his mind was made up and the issue was closed. But she loved him dearly and she had to try. And he loved her dearly and had to listen. It came with the territory when you married a bull-headed male. He smiled at the thought.

"Judge, it's time to go back to Los Angeles and give up this foolish quest. The police have determined Bob committed suicide. So, there's nobody to catch."

"You believe Bobby committed suicide, Katy?"

"Well… I didn't know him like you did. But we're all strangers to each other in one way or another. We all have secrets, Judge. Sides of our personality we don't show to other people."

"Even us?"

"Yes. Even us."

"I knew Bob well, Katy. He was always a fighter. He'd never give up. And besides, any self-respecting male who decides to commit suicide doesn't walk off into the desert and die of heat exhaustion and exposure. He uses his gun, or maybe jumps off a bridge. No matter how hard the police push their suicide theory, it just doesn't wash."

"But Judge, you've not been able to identify this spider character of yours, even if he exists. You've gotten nowhere in your investigation. You don't know who took Bob out to the desert if that's how it happened. And you don't know who gave the order. And you don't know why. Haven't all your leads turned into dead ends? There's nowhere else to go."

"I have one strong lead. This guy Shorty. The owner of the Buoys and Gulls Casino."

"Judge, there are some pretty tough characters in Vegas who can be dangerous. Why don't we go back to L.A., and you can dabble in the case some more from there?"

"We both know I'm not dabbling here, Katy. I owe it to Bob, and to Jackie, to get to the bottom of what happened. It's just going to take a little more time. Why don't you go back to L.A.? I'll catch up with you after I'm done here."

"And leave you here to pursue your clandestine meetings with tarty women? No way, Judge. If you're staying, I'm staying." Katy stood, folding her arms across her chest, and marched back into the condo to replenish her coffee.

A half-hour later the Judge sat with his feet in the jacuzzi by the Meridian pool and wiggled his feet, enjoying the morning sun. The town was awake now. There was the clatter of a garbage truck emptying the weekend's trash from the dumpsters, and the roar of traffic out on Flamingo Road was beginning to pick up. Monday morning, people had to go to work, tourists had to go coffee their sore heads and plan their exploits for the day. Vegas was a busy town.

A stranger, a portly man, well fed, with a big stomach on short legs, ambled across the pool deck toward the Judge. He wore an antique Tommy Bahama shirt, tan golf shorts over open loafers, and no socks. He flashed the Judge a quick smile, as though they were long lost friends, and pulled a chair over by the jacuzzi to sit behind the Judge.

"Nice morning," he said.

The Judge nodded, muttered "yeah," irritated his peace and quiet had been invaded.

"Guess you have a place here in the Meridian," offered the stranger.

"Yeah."

"I'm just a guest, Judge."

The Judge's head swung around, suddenly alert.

"Do I know you?"

"Don't think we've ever met. But I know about you. Something of an amateur detective I understand."

"Occasionally. Who are you, exactly?"

"I'm Harry Jessup, one of the Supervisors for Clarkson County, Nevada."

"A local politician?"

"Guess that's what you'd call me. We don't have statesmen at my level of politics."

"You want to talk to me?"

"Yes."

"What about?"

"Well, it's a little delicate."

"Okay."

"Let's use the third person. Let me give you a suppose... a hypothetical."

"Okay."

"Suppose there was smart amateur detective nosing around our town, stirring up dirt, maybe making some fact-less allegations about our Building

Department, our government employees, even perhaps a bankruptcy attorney."

"Suppose there was?"

"Those sorts of baseless allegations could give our city and county a bad name. Discourage people from moving here, creating a business, or even having confidence in our civic institutions and employees."

"Maybe the allegations in your hypothetical case aren't baseless."

"Oh, I'm positive they are. It may look like smoke, but it's only desert dust. There is no fire here. No secret conspiracy to destroy a project and steal it. The facts, viewed objectively, won't support it."

"Okay. Suppose that were the case?"

"Well, don't you see... allegations like that, made in public forums, can do a lot of damage to our community, even though they're nothing more than groundless allegations."

"Where is this going, Mr. Jessup?"

"Well. Looking at things from another angle.... Our county has a need from time to time to seek legal advice on matters of Federal law, particularly on matters of Federal Securities Law. I understand you do Securities Law."

"I do."

"In fact, you're a national expert in this area of Securities Law, I understand."

"Some have called me that."

Davis MacDonald

"So, I was thinking maybe Clarkson County could hire your services for a year, to consult with us on municipal securities law matters from time to time."

"Do you really have much of a need for such advice?"

"Well, you never know, Judge. Never know when out of the blue you have to seek Securities Law Counsel about public matters here in Clarkson County. And of course, we'd expect to pay a retainer up front for your standby availability. I mean if we had a contract with you."

"How much of a retainer?"

"Well, I'm not exactly sure, Judge. I'd have to give it some thought. But I was tentatively thinking in the ballpark of at least six figures, plus your hourly rate of course for advice on specific matters."

"I see." The Judge held his anger and kept a bland expression on his face.

"Of course, we'd expect all conflict-of-interest issues would be removed."

"Like?"

"Well, you know. Contending there is a conspiracy to destroy a real estate project in our fair county, for instance. We couldn't have that."

"You mean The Spire."

"Well, I don't want to be specific. But just generally we'd expect you to hold up the integrity of our county and its people."

"Tell you what, Mr. Jessup, let me think about it."

"Oh, great, great. No pressure from our side. Sleep on it and then give me a call. I'll put my card here on the chair."

Jessup tucked a blue and white business card into the plastic weave of his chair, stood, and strode away toward the pool gate.

The Judge was perplexed. On the one hand, he seemed to have no legally conclusive proof of the conspiracy against Bob and The Spire. On the other, someone was worried enough to try and bribe him to quit looking and go away. Interesting.

CHAPTER 36
MONDAY
11:00 A.M.

The front tree looked thirsty as ever as the Judge walked up to Cindy Hanson's porch, grabbed the large brass knocker, and gave the chocolate door a serious knock. Cindy opened on the second knock, sleep still in eyes, her shapely body wrapped in a bright kimono of lime and violet leaves on a pale blue background that stretched to her ankles.

"Judge? Sorry, I was sleeping in. I substituted in on the late shift as a dealer on a blackjack table for the Rio last night. I'm trying to earn enough money to get my mortgage out of default. But I'm getting too old to do blackjacking, Judge. My feet ache from standing in heels all night. And I'm so sick of coaxing tips out of the damn players, all men, all interested in getting into my pants. It's a shit world."

"Can I come in, Cindy?"

"Of course."

She swung the door wide, gestured toward the living room, muttered something about coffee, and padded off toward the kitchen. The Judge heard the rattle of cups and glass, the glug of a water bottle being emptied, the groan of a microwave, the grind of a grinder, more water sounds, and then the coffee press plunged to its hilt.

Three minutes later Cindy swished into the living room, a partially full milk bottle under one arm, steaming mugs of black coffee in each hand. The aroma of fresh ground and brewed coffee filled the room with a pleasant smell.

They sat opposite each other on the leather sofas, sipping their joe, Cindy periodically pushing back a blond curl that insisted on breaking free to partially obscure one eye.

"What's up, Judge? What's happened?"

"I've found Jackie. Talked to her."

"Oh, thank God. She's okay? Is she coming home?"

"She's okay. Not coming home just yet, but perhaps soon. She's going to need some significant emotional support. She's been severely traumatized. Has a drug addiction issue, and she's angry."

"Not much new there, Judge. That's about how she was when she left."

"What about the unwanted sexual advances Sam was making, Cindy?"

"I don't believe that happened for a second." Cindy's voice rose several octaves.

"Whether it did or not, Jackie thinks it happened. Anyway, she wants to see her son. Where is Robbie?"

"Oh, shit. I forgot to get him up. He must be upstairs. Sleeping in again. That's not like him. He'll have missed his first class. I'll have to write another God damn fake note."

"Can I say hello?"

"Of course." Cindy went to the bottom of the stairs. "Robbie! Robbie! Come on down. The Judge is here and wants to say hello. Then I've got to get you to school, buster. How come you didn't wake me up? Did you forget to set your alarm again?"

There was no answer.

"Why don't you go up and roust him out of bed, Judge? He'd like that. Third door on the left."

"Okay." The Judge bounded up the stairs, looking at his watch, calculating how much time he could spend with the boy. He moved down the whitewashed hall and pushed open the last door on the left.

He knocked softly on the door. Then he turned the knob and partially opened the door, peeking into the dark room where the shades were drawn against the morning light.

Something didn't look right. Robbie was there all right. But not in his bed. He was curled up on the floor, fetus like, in soft blue flannel pajamas with the Mars Rover patterned across them. He wasn't moving. His face was grey, even in the shadowed light, his eyes unfocused. The Judge stepped in, set down his coffee cup, and leaned down to give the boy a little shake, wake him up. He withdrew his hand sharply. Robbie was cold…. So cold.

He rolled Robbie over on his back, the boy's legs and arms sprawling, unresponsive. The Judge leaned down and felt his neck for a pulse. There was hardly any.

The Judge stiffened, giving an involuntary cry. "Oh, shit...Oh, shit."

He ran to the door, knocking over his coffee cup, and screamed down the hall to Cindy. "Cindy... Cindy, come quick. Robbie's in trouble. He's unconscious!"

CHAPTER 37
MONDAY
11:15 A.M.

"Cindy! Cindy! Come.... Hurry!" the Judge screamed again.

Cindy rushed in seconds later, took one look, and sank to her knees in the plush carpet beside the prone boy, gently bringing his head to her lap, shock on her face.

"No. No. Oh no. Not Robbie. Not Robbie.... No," she moaned.

The Judge reached around to take Robbie's hand. It was ice cold. His eyes were open but glazed. Lime tinted saliva plastered his small chin, reaching up and encrusting his lips.

The Judge fumbled his cell phone out and dialed 9-1-1, praying they'd be quick. When the operator answered he replied, "Drug overdose suspected," and rattled off the address.

Cindy went to pieces then. A long high keening wail came from her, the kind that comes from a mom, or a grandma, who's just lost a child. It cut through the Judge's heart like a knife.

Sam came running in, bare chested in tattered pajama bottoms, a pistol in his hand. Ready to fight, whatever the threat. He slid to a stop at Robbie's feet, the gun dropping to his side, shock spreading across his face.

The Judge helped Cindy gently move Robbie to a sitting position on the floor, his back braced against the bed. Cindy sat beside him, holding his head, which kept wanting to flop to the side. Sam sat in a nearby chair, twisting his hands together in distress, an expression of uncertainty as to what to do replacing shock.

The Judge stumped his way down the stairs, tired now beyond all reckoning. He threw open the front door and went out past the thirsty tree to his car, leaned on the its side, and waited to flag down the rescue truck he prayed would be there in seconds.

Three minutes later the rescue truck arrived with a screech of tires and flashing red lights, no siren. This was a residential neighborhood. Two men in thick-padded overalls clunked into the house at the Judge's urging, lugging boxes and their backpacks, looking efficient. Minutes later an ambulance pulled up and two white-coated young men ran in, toting a collapsible stretcher between them.

Then they all came out of the house, making a sad little parade. The two white coats first, pushing the stretcher in which Robbie was strapped, an oxygen mask covering his still grey face, an IV in his arm.

They were followed by Cindy at the foot of the stretcher, tears streaming down her cheeks, her breath coming in short painful gasps.

Then the two firemen, slow now, tired, probably close to the end of their shift, professionally somber looks pasted on their faces.

And finally, Sam, looking disoriented, uncertain, following the tide. Robbie was loaded into the ambulance and Cindy scrambled in beside him, the doors eased closed, and the ambulance sped away, the rescue truck behind it, both sets of red lights flashing. Sam had dashed to the garage, and now sped away after them in a new Porsche, bright yellow, reminding the Judge of a taxi.

The Judge wandered back into the house and up the stairs, back to Robbie's room. He stood in the doorway and studied each detail of the room. Then he stepped in and stooped to retrieve a small paint brush tipped with lime-green paint on the floor near where Robbie had lain. He walked over to the small desk where Robbie's computer sat. In front of it a paint kit was open, displaying six colorful small pots of pain inside a foldable plastic tray. Beside it sat a plastic model of an ancient Japanese warrior, perhaps six inches tall, its pieces glued together, its leggings painted the same pink color.

There was a small parcel post box on the desk, unwrapped and open, about the size of the paint kit. It was addressed to Robbie Hanson at the house's address and further marked with stenciled letters: School Supplies.

He started to put the brush down on the desk, then stopped and brought the brush to his nose. There was the scent of lime and sweet. And something else, a hint of something floral, but also metallic and chemical-like. Familiar, but what? He put it to his nose again.

Shit, it smelled like cocaine!

He picked up the paint box and dabbed his little finger into each of its six colored pots and brought his finger each time to his nose. They each smelled like candy, flavored to match their color, and each had an underlying hint of coke. He turned the box over and looked at the information embedded in the plastic bottom: *Imported by HB Enterprises, Dominica,* and in tiny print below that, *product of Columbia.*

Shit. Someone was shipping coke-loaded paint sets to kids by parcel post. And it may have killed Robbie.

The Judge turned to Robbie's laptop on his desk. The machine was closed. He tucked it under his arm and slowly retraced his steps down the stairs, out the front door, checking to be sure it locked, and across the white rock front yard past the thirsty tree. He started up his car and headed for the hospital, trying to level his emotions, alternating among shock, sorrow, anger and guilt.

He was going to get whoever was behind this distribution of drugs to kids. His first thought was the Spider.

He dialed Barry Marsh as he drove, explaining what had happened and asking if they could meet at the hospital. The Detective said he would come.

CHAPTER 38
MONDAY
12:15 P.M.

St. George Hospital was awash with traffic and the ER lobby was packed. The Judge waded through the throng looking for Cindy and Sam, then gave up and went to the desk to ask. He was directed down a hall and around a corner to a small waiting room for families with loved ones in the ICU. The furniture was all brightly colored in the little waiting room, yellows and bright greens. As if bright colors could make you feel better while you stewed in this unhappy little room and your loved one went under the knife.

Cindy was huddled against Sam in a corner, sniffling into a damp handkerchief.

"Any word?" asked the Judge.

"They say they don't know yet." Cindy said in a tiny voice, swallowing her words, slumping back into her chair, tears starting to flow again.

Sam was quiet, almost sullen, slouched down on a sofa, looking like a man who wanted to be anywhere but here.

"I am going to try to find out who sold drugs to Robbie, Cindy. Do you have a password for his laptop?"

"There was a parent password when we first set it up for him. I wrote it down somewhere. I'm pretty sure I can find it. If I do, I'll text you."

The Judge settled in an overstuff leather chair of puke yellow.

About twenty minutes later a doctor came to the door, stripping off his face mask and looking woebegone. "Your grandson is in a coma and can't breathe on his own. We have him on life support, but it doesn't look good."

"Oh my God. No.... No!" wailed Cindy.

"What's the prognosis?" asked the Judge, suddenly cold all the way down in his bones.

"Sometimes they come out of these drug-induced comas. Sometimes they even come out without brain damage or paralysis. But it's not looking good. We need to hear from his mother. She would be the one to authorize removal of life support if it's decided that's what needs to be done."

Sam took Cindy in his arms and tried to comfort her. The Judge stepped out into the hallway and called Jackie's number. There was no answer. He was about to try again when his cell rang in his hand, doing its impression of Dragnet, indicating a message head been received.

It was a message from Barry Marsh, saying he was downstairs in the cafeteria having coffee. The Judge excused himself and headed for the elevator.

Marsh was sitting in the far corner of the hospital cafeteria with his back to the wall, just as the Judge liked to sit. They both understood the lesson of Wild Bill Hickock, shot in the back the one time he accepted a seat at the poker table with his back to the door. The Judge slid into the seat to Marsh's right, which also had a wall.

"How's the boy?" Barry asked.

"It doesn't look good. He's in a coma and on life support."

"I'm sorry, Judge."

"Robbie was playing in his room with a set of watercolor paints, Barry. But they had the taste of cocaine."

"I can believe it. They ship drugs out from the Dark Web disguised in all sorts of products and wrappings, using Parcel Post."

"But selling drugs to teenagers, Barry. Jesus. I thought that happened only in poor parts of town, down the alley somewhere near the local ghetto school."

"It's an epidemic going on in our young people, Judge, right under the nose of parents. The parents just don't see it, or pretend not to."

"What's driving it, Barry?"

"That's a difficult question to answer, Judge. Part of the problem is the content in the social media we have today. Many celebrities and web influencers consistently post pictures of themselves drinking and getting high on a variety of platforms. And that influences young people who view their postings. This kind of content normalizes and glamorizes dangerous behavior. Experimenting with illegal drugs, popping prescription pills, binge drinking. It makes teens wrongly believe it's appropriate, romantic, macho, for them to do these things. The whole society is riddled with this ambivalence about drug use, legal and illegal."

"And on the Dark Web?"

"Yes, then along comes the Dark Web. The drug dealers have been quick to seize the opportunity for sale of their products across the Dark Web. Many have left the streets, trading their designated street corner or side alley for an online ID. They use social media platforms on the internet, and Dark Web platforms, to target anyone who wants illegal drugs. And they often focus on the younger set, from ten and up.

Some seventy percent of our populace is on social media. Internet apps have replaced phones as the way we communicate and buy. The drug trade has adapted like everyone else. Selling illegal drugs over the internet is convenient and fast. And it's much easier to avoid law enforcement. Almost any drug in existence, both illegal and prescription, can be purchased from dealers on the Dark Web. Data suggests almost forty percent of the revenue from drug sales on the Dark Web is from marijuana. The next most popular drugs, making up about thirty percent of sales, are stimulants like cocaine and amphetamines. Following closely behind are ecstasy-type drugs at around twenty percent."

"Where do these kids get the money to buy drugs?"

"That's the other disturbing thing, Judge. Dealers are using the web to focus on more affluent teens who have spending money. Affluent teens have their own computers and know how to access the Dark Web.

Prices can be reduced when the dealer doesn't need a downline of neighborhood distributors and can sell direct to his end user. And any currency is acceptable, including bitcoin. In fact, the United States leads the world in the crypto market-share of drugs being sold on the Dark Web, followed by the UK and Australia.

And the product is packaged and labeled as something else, schoolbooks, exercise equipment, stationary, vitamins, a paint set for art as in your case. Parents cheerfully fork over a credit card without a clue to what their child is really buying."

"But how does someone like Robbie become involved in this, Barry?"

"It can happen in countless ways. Dealers are sophisticated in using the web. They use algorithms to build social media platforms, and emojis, code words, and hashtags to get the word out about their wares. They may use something as simple as *'420 friendly'*, slang for marijuana, or hashtags like *'#MDMA.'* The maple leaf is the universal symbol for drugs, a diamond or snowflake represents cocaine, a capsule for MDMA, and a needle indicates heroin is available.

Drugs are often paid for using exchange apps like Facebook Messenger, Venmo, Apple, or Android Pay. The Dark Web dealers deliver their wares almost exclusively through snail mail. They rarely, if ever, meet in person. Packages come directly to a young person's home disguised as something else. But always with a fictional return address that can't be tracked.

And these dealers can be dangerous, even though they never meet their client. They might just rip you off and you never receive your merchandise. Worse, manufacture of the drugs may involve no quality control. They may be improperly manufactured, or contain too much product, or be laced with fentanyl, leading to unintended overdose and death. Drugs may be cut with other cheaper materials which may be poisonous, leading to adverse reactions and bodily damage.

Or the dealer might be an undercover police officer, leading to arrest for the illegal purchase of drugs, severe penalties, and a criminal record. The young affluent kids don't consider these risks. They live a sheltered existence in rich homes. They don't have a clue what they're getting into."

"How do we stop it, Barry?"

"I don't know, Judge. What our young do is a reflection of what our adult society is doing. And influencers make it look cool and adult. It's a cultural war we face as much as anything."

"With very sad results."

"Yes. I'm so sorry about the boy."

"I'm his Godfather, Barry. But I assumed the mantle without a thought about what responsibilities should come with the honor."

"I'm not even sure what a modern-day Godfather's role is, Judge."

"It's still supposed to be someone chosen to take an interest in the child's upbringing and personal development, to offer mentorship and guidance, and an alternative adult forum to the parents when sometimes needed. I've failed miserably."

"There's no way you could have known this would happen, Judge."

"I'm not sure that's right, Barry. How do we catch this guy that sold drugs to Robbie?"

"I'll be frank, Judge. It's damn near impossible. We'll never track him down."

"Is this the Spider's doing, Barry? This Vegas Spider I've been hearing about who's into everything illegal on the Dark Web?"

"He's probably the biggest purveyor of drugs in this town, Judge. But you'll never find him. He's buried so deep no one can reach him. You may as well try to catch the wind. You'll just chase your tail if you try."

The Judge's head shot up. "You're wrong, Barry. Somehow, I'm going to find the bastard and squash him, along with his people who took my buddy for a ride into the desert."

"Good luck on that, Judge. I'm sorry, but it'll never happen."

The Judge thanked Barry for his help and bolted back upstairs to see if there were further developments in Robbie's condition. There weren't.

CHAPTER 39
MONDAY
3:00 P.M.

The Green Oasis Condominium Project was on the Eastside in a blue-collar area. The building was small, maybe twenty units, but well kept. It sported a small pool and a jacuzzi. It looked to have been built originally as a motel, then converted into condominiums.

There was no lock on the gate. The Judge walked through the pool area past a swarthy guy in the pool leaning on its edge, talking on a video cell call set on a stand two feet from the water. The day was old, the sun still hot, and the oppressive heat clung to the Judge like a blanket.

He found unit fifteen and pushed the doorbell. A combination of large and small bells sounded off inside in music sounding suspiciously like the Bells of St. Mary's. Ostentatious for such a small little unit. But if it gave the owner pleasure, so much the better.

He waited. No answer. He pushed the bell again, longer. More bells. The Judge was quite enjoying the bells. It was like a new toy. But still nothing else happened. He was about to push the button a third time when he noticed the spy hole in the door was no longer blank. There had been a flash of blue eye pasted against it on the inside for a couple of seconds. There was a rattle of a latch and the door slowly rotated open two inches, enough for the eye to get a better look.

"I'm the Judge, Bob Hanson's best friend," said the Judge in his best boyish imitation of 'Aw Shucks'.

A second blue eye appeared as the gap widened slightly. The Judge felt himself scanned with razor attention. There was a big sigh. Then the door swung further open to reveal a beautiful woman, mid-thirties with long blond hair, chiseled Nordic features, inquisitive light blue eyes, and a generous mouth without lipstick.

Her eyes appraised the Judge with interest and good will. She was small chested, small hipped, and generally long and sleek, moving through space like a swimmer though water, smooth and languid. Bob always did have great taste in woman, except of course for Cindy. The woman wore a white silk kimono over not much at all; she instinctively pulled it tighter as the Judge admired her figure.

"They call me the Judge. I was a long-time close friend of Bobby."

The name jarred pain momentarily across her eyes, quickly covered. She took a big breath, steeling herself. "I'm Elka. Bob spoke about you a lot. Come in. Would you like coffee?"

"Yes, please."

The Judge sat on the very small worn softa in the very small apartment. It was set against one wall, its back to a long window that would have looked out toward the pool if the blinds had been open. But they weren't. It made the unit dark, and perhaps a bit cooler. The opposite wall had the entry door and a TV on a rolling stand. The walls were painted a light green, matching a dilapidated looking carpet in the middle of the little room showing bare threads. There were no pictures on the walls. A door to the right led to a small galley kitchen and a short hall to the left suggested a small bedroom and bathroom were hidden there. The place felt a little desperate.

Elka immediately disappeared into the galley kitchen to the rattle of pots, pans and faucet, and then the hum of a microwave. She reappeared with two steaming cups of coffee, balancing a little china creamer between the cups, supported underneath with her two fingers. The creamer had the look of a Victorian antique, chipped a bit, but clearly loved.

The Judge arose to take the creamer lest it slip. She handed him a cup and they sat down together on the little sofa, positioning themselves in its opposite corners, as wide a channel as possible between them.

"You were going with Bob I understand?"

"Yes."

"How did you find out about what happened?"

"The police called. I guess there was a card or something in his wallet. Then a few days later an attorney called. Said I was one of Bob's heirs. Guess there's only the car to sell. The police won't release it yet."

"Are you from here?"

"Sweden. But I intend to stay. I'm on a student visa to study business."

"How'd you meet Bob?"

"The usual. At a bar. We met one night, and I went home with him. He insisted I stay with him the next morning. After we met, we were never apart for more than three days at a time. It's been a year and a half. We were inseparable." There was a little catch in her throat.

"You loved him."

"Yes. And he loved me." She smiled briefly, looked down at her stomach. "I'm carrying our child."

"It doesn't show yet."

"No. But soon."

"You don't think he killed himself. Committed suicide."

"No. That's ridiculous. We were going to get married. Planning for our child."

"What will you do now?"

"Bob paid up the rent on this place for a year. He couldn't afford much, but said I at least had a place to go if I needed space. I guess I'll stay here, have our baby, apply for citizenship. One more semester and I get my Bachelor's in Business Administration at Nevada State College."

"Do you work now?"

"I'm not supposed to. Student visa. But on the weekends and between classes I sell homes and condos. I have a friend who has a real estate brokers' office and helps me."

"How was Bob the last time you saw him. Elka?"

She bit her tongue, sucked in long breath. "I was probably the last friend to see him alive. He seemed really stressed. Things hadn't been going well for several weeks."

"At The Spire?"

"Yes. Bob had run through the new loan money he'd raised, and there were still unpaid, angry subs. The investors were livid. Many units were still unfinished, and the Building Department wouldn't budge on the issuance of an occupancy permit. Bob had just put the project into a bankruptcy to stop the construction lender from foreclosing. A debtor in possession or something. It was one big mess."

"You were at The Spire that night? The night Bob disappeared?"

"Yes."

"Did you notice anything unusual?"

"Oh boy, yes. There was a hell of a fight."

"With you?"

"Oh no. I stayed in the guest bedroom, stayed out of it. But I heard everything."

"What happened?"

"The ex-wife and her boyfriend came to visit Bob."

"Cindy and Sam?"

"Yes. There was a lot of shouting and accusations flying around. They were all really angry."

"What was it about?"

"Something about insurance. I didn't really understand it all. Bob of course was desperate for money. I guess he wanted to cancel some life insurance policy and get the large upfront premium refunded back to him. He'd sent in some form."

"And Cindy and Sam were unhappy about that?"

"Boy, I'll say. They were threatening Bob with jail, lawsuits, all sorts of stuff. I think Sam was on the verge of getting physical. He sounded like a real bully. But Cindy managed to calm Sam down some. Then they left."

"They left without Bob?"

"Of course. I was there. Bob came back to the guest bedroom, apologized for my having to listen to all that. But he didn't tell me what it was about."

"Do you recall what time Cindy and Sam left The Spire?"

"Just before ten p.m."

"When did you leave, Elka?"

"Right after that. About ten-thirty. Bob walked me down to my car. I had to come back here to do some paperwork on one of my real estate closings."

"Was Bob going anywhere after you left?"

"Yes. He said someone was picking him up in front for a business meeting."

"At ten-thirty at night?"

"Yes."

"Do you know who was picking Bob up?"

"I think it was one of his lenders. He said one of them was really pissed he'd put the project into a bankruptcy. My impression was it had been a short-term loan, and now the loan was due."

"Did he say anything else about his meeting?"

"Yes, as a matter of fact. I don't what he met. It was very strange. He said, 'Don't worry honey. I'm going to grab a certain arachnid by his leather balls and give them a good squeeze.' Then he laughed."

"Do you know who made that last loan to Bob?"

"No. I asked once, but he said it was safer if I didn't know. I assumed there was a tax reason or something. It wasn't my business."

"Did you see any papers about the loan?"

"No."

"Did you see Bob meet with anyone out of the ordinary or different?"

Elka's brow furrowed for a second. "There was a strange little guy that came around a couple of times with two goons in tow."

"Goons?"

"Really big, heavy, fat guys that looked really dumb."

"Muscle."

"Yes. I guess that's what they call it in the movies."

"What was the little guy like?"

"Short, hard looking, pock-marked face. Walked like he was a foot taller than he really was. I didn't like him."

"Did you have an argument in a bar or something with Bob a week or so before he disappeared, Elka?"

"You know about that?" Elka's eyes widened in surprise.

"Vegas is really a small town in a lot of respects. Gossip travels around. What happened?"

"It was just a small tiff. Bob was under a lot of stress. We went out for dinner and had a little too much to drink. I wasn't drinking of course."

"And."

"Bob was facing up to the possibility of losing everything. Was worried he wouldn't be able to support me and a new child. He raised the possibility of... you know, getting rid of it. He just wanted to see what I thought. It wasn't a suggestion or an order or anything."

"And you got mad?"

"I got emotional. Took it the wrong way. Yelled I was having our baby come hell or high water. I guess I kind of stormed out. He followed me out the car and calmed me down. Explained he wanted our baby as much as I did." Elka gave the Judge a sad smile.

The Judge nodded, thanked Elka and stood.

"Here is my card, Elka. If you need any legal advice, or perhaps help with the estate, I'm available to help. I'm mostly in L.A., but only a cell phone call away. And I know The Spire Project well. I have all the charter documents and real estate records for it."

He gave her a formal handshake and stalked out, even more determined to bring the Spider down.

CHAPTER 40
MONDAY
4:30 P.M.

The Judge sat on the sofa in his condo and pulled over Robbie's laptop. He typed in the password Cindy had texted him. The computer booted up and opened to its home screen. He opened the TOR badge he found there. He watched as the computer connected to the Dark Web.

This was the wild west of the internet where gangs could sell their pills and drugs to naive teens with little risk. The Dark Web was sending out a sort of sickness. A sickness silently invading homes across the country, sending its tentacles out from the computer screen to wrap around the minds of unsuspecting children in their bedrooms. Snaring teenagers and even younger kids who thought they were all grown up now and would live forever.

And all the while parents sat blissfully unaware downstairs in their living rooms, thinking their kids were working on homework.

The Judge tapped on *settings*, then *library*, then on *history*. A list of Robbie's visits was there, and one site caught the Judge's eye. Not because of its name, a jumble of miscellaneous letters, but because of the small emblem beside the site's address, a tiny black spider. The site had been visited often during the last three weeks. The Judge clicked on the address, and it opened to the last page at the site visited.

The Judge sat back in his chair and stared. The page had the design and feel of an Amazon page, its easy intuitive controls and familiar arrangement and graphics making it feel safe and comfortable. All except the title, blaring from the top of the page: CONSUMABLES DELIVERED IN DISGUISED DISPENSERS.

Below was a listing of all the ways you could order drugs in wrappings that hid their true nature. There were pictures on the left side of the page displaying options; packaged as gum, as candy, as M&Ms, as bubblegum, as cigarettes, as toothpaste, as diet soda, as soap, as antacid tablets, as multivitamins, as colored pencils, as watercolor paints like the one Robbie had, and perhaps another thirty options.

The Judge tapped home, and then products. The list was extensive, with some the Judge had never heard of. Among "Major Drug Categories" the following were listed, along with their 'Street' or Slang names:

-Bath Salts (Bloom, Cloud Nine, Ivory Wave, Lunar Wave, Plant Food, Scarface, Vanilla Sky, White Lightning)

-Cocaine (Blow, Bump, C, Candy, Charlie, Coke, Crack, Flake, Rock, Snow, Toot)

-Flakka (Gravel)

-Heroin (Brown Sugar, China White, Dope, H, Horse, Junk, Skag, Skunk, Smack, White Horse)

-Krokodil (Crocodil)

-LSD (Acid, Blotter, Doses, Hits, Microdots, Sugar Cubes, Tabs, Trips, Windowpanes)

-MDMA (Ecstasy, Molly)

-Marijuana (Blunt, Boom, Bud, Dope, Ganja, Grass, Green, Hash, Hashish, Hemp, Herb, Joint, Mary Jane, Pot, Reefer, Skunk, Smoke, Trees, Weed)

-Methamphetamine (Chalk, Crank, Crystal meth, Ice)

-Mushrooms (Boomers, Little Smoke, Magic Mushrooms, Shrooms.)

-Salvia (Diviner's Sage, Magic Mint, Maria Pastora, Sage of the Seers, Sally-D)

-Spice (Black Mamba, Bliss, Bombay Blue, Fake weed, Fire, Genie, K2, Moon Rocks, Skunk, Smacked, Yucatan, Zohai)

A similar section listed prescription drugs available, 'No prescription required', including Cymbalta, Klonopin, OxyContin, Percocet, Prozac, Valium, Vicodin, Wellbutrin, Xanax, and Zoloft.

There were photos of each product, and a dropdown for each giving reviews, pricing, and payment instructions. Some products were on sale under special promotions and for others you could purchase a small sample inexpensively.

Payment made in bitcoin earned a discount, so there were careful step by step instructions on how to create your bitcoin account and transfer funds. But credit cards were accepted, and money orders or cash could be sent in as well to an offshore P.O. Box in the Cayman

Islands. Once your funds cleared you could spend your credit.

Products would be shipped by parcel post in nondescript packaging, with bogus company labels indicating the pretend packaging contained whatever you wanted: school supplies, art supplies, cleaning supplies, video games, and many more.

The Judge picked one of the fifty strains of marijuana, said to be good for sleep, and signed up to try an inexpensive sample. He was asked for his credit card, which he supplied. He specified nondescript packaging and gave his Malaga Cove address. That was it. No questions about his age, whether he had a prescription, or whether it was legal in his state. Katy would have a cow when it arrived. He smirked at the thought. But then his face turned grim again.

This was where Robbie's paint set had come from. A paint set that perhaps had killed him.

He hit the x to close the site. Again, there was the tiny black spider with the red-spot underbelly prancing halfway across the bottom of the screen.

He turned to his cell and dialed Cindy's number.

CHAPTER 41
TUESDAY
7:30 P.M.

The Here Kitty Kitty Vice Den, a speakeasy, was hard to find unless you knew where to look. You had to make your way to Resorts World, then find the Famous Foods Street Eats, a food hall with sixteen stalls spanning dumplings and lechon to fried chicken and Filipino barbecue to hot chicken sandwiches from Marcus Samuelsson. Then you had to locate Ms. Meow's Mamak Stall, a small retail store filled with Asian snacks, games, and drinks typically found in Mamak stalls in Singapore and Malaysia. Behind a shelf lined with lucky cat sculptures was a non-descript door that was the entrance to Here Kitty Kitty.

The place was small, or perhaps you'd say intimate. A brick wall ran down one side with the bar laid against it, two bartenders working furiously to liquify the crowd. Colored lights strung across the ceiling gave the place, and everyone in it, a dark purple hew. Standing at the bar, the Judge decided to forgo his beloved single-malt Scotch in favor of a Pink Kitty, a concoction of Roku gin and white peach with sparkling white peach sake.

Cindy was already there and had ordered a Mix & Matcha, Haku vodka with coconut lemongrass Nigori sake and matcha syrup. Her drink arrived first and started to disappear in large gulps even before she turned from the bar to find them a table in the popular joint.

As the Judge swung around to follow her from the bar, trying not to slosh his Pink Kitty topped to the gills in a hand-cut crystal glass, a young man with his back to the bar suddenly turned, banging into the Judge and spilling a good measure of his drink down the side of the Judge's beige slacks.

"Shit!" snapped the Judge, "Would you watch it?"

The Judge look down the front of his slacks. *Damn it.* He looked like he'd pissed his pants. *Shit, shit, shit.*

The young man, a snowbird by his look, wearing a loud ski sweater beneath a fat ruddy face, looked embarrassed. "Oh, I'm so sorry sir."

The 'sir' made it even worse. The Judge hated to be called 'sir'. A reminder of his advancing years by this whippersnapper who had all the time in the world. But the guy seemed sincere.

"Let me get you another drink. It's one of those Pink Kittens or something isn't it? They're good. Had them before. It's my fault. Go find a seat. I'll bring your replacement drink over. You'll even be a little ahead. You've got half a drink there." The Judge was given a big dumb smile.

"Yeah okay," muttered the Judge, turning to follow Cindy toward the open table she'd spotted, loathing all young people, and particularly this one. An inconsiderate idiot.

They settled at a small table across from each other in a back corner of the bar.

"I've dumped Sam, Judge. It was time. He was just hanging around so he could help spend my insurance money. When that all fizzled what with this crazy suicide theory the police are selling, I suspect he couldn't wait to leave. When I confronted him with what Jackie told you about how he'd attacked her, we had an enormous fight. So, I threw him out. Guess I'm in the market for a new boyfriend. Ever think about a little something on the side?"

She gazed speculatively at the Judge over her glass after lapping down another large slug of her drink.

"No. No, Cindy. I'm happily married and don't need any extracurricular activities. How is Robbie doing?"

"It's pretty hopeless, Judge. The doctor says after the first twenty-four hours, if they haven't come back, they rarely do. It's just so sad, seeing his little frame hooked up to all that life support crap, stretching the poor body to do things it doesn't want to do any more… like breathe." Cindy stifled a small sob.

"Jackie's back, sat there with Robbie all day. Reads to him, Comic's for Christ's sakes. Batman, and Doctor Strange. Stuff he was never interested in. She even holds particularly lurid panels up to his blank eyes to show him the action, the POWs and the WAMMIEs, as though he could see.

It's so awful. If it were me, I'd let him go. Like the doctors recommend. What's the point of making him suffer like this? But Jackie's the mother. She has to make the call. And she won't. It's like she's frozen in time. Blames herself. Blames me. Even blames you Judge. Cause you're the Godfather.

At some point the insurance runs out. Then he'll have to be unplugged. There'll be no choice. Only twelve years old, Judge. Life is so fucking unfair. So... so... so... random."

The Judge reached across the table to take her hand, at a loss for words.

Cindy took a last slurp of her drink and flagged a waiter for another as the young snowbird guy eased a new drink in front of the Judge and apologized again. Then the Judge and Cindy sat in silence, contemplating life and all its vicissitudes.

"So, Judge, can you persuade the police Bob didn't commit suicide?" she asked, turning back to business with an effort. "Can you prove Bob was murdered, Judge?"

"I'm not sure, Cindy. But I'm trying. I'm wondering if someone is exerting pressure on the police from the top, or outside the department maybe, to smooth this whole thing over as a suicide."

"Wouldn't put it past them, Judge. There're all crooked cops. It's this town. It makes everybody a little desperate, a little dishonest. I'm owed that insurance money. It was going to be my ticket out of here."

"There's another question I have to ask, Cindy."

"Go ahead."

"Did you do it?"

"What?"

"Did you and Sam take Bob for that ride?"

"No. of course not Judge. How could you think such a thing?" Cindy's eyes got big and round as her head snapped up, indignation across her face.

"You and Sam were there that night. The night Bob disappeared. Weren't you?"

"Who told you that?"

"Weren't you?"

"Yes," Cindy said inaudibly, swallowing her words.

"I can't hear you."

"Yes, God damnit. Sam and I were there. We'd got a notice about stuff. So, we went to The Spire to talk to Bob."

"And you had a big fight. Lots of arguing, even shouting."

"It was unpleasant."

"What was it about?"

Cindy sighed. "It was nothing."

"Nothing over what, Cindy. Level with me."

"Oh, you know, financial stuff."

"What?"

"The damn insurance policy, okay? The damn policy."

"What was the issue?"

"Bob was desperate for cash for his stupid Spire. I guess he was broke, surprise, surprise. Still struggling to fix things that were never going to be fixed. The Spire was lost, and Sam and I knew it. But Bob. Bob, God damn him. He just soldiers on, forever, even when there's no hope."

"And?"

"He wanted to cash out my insurance policy early. Take about fifty grand back as a refund on the premium for terminating early. Put it into The Spire."

"So why didn't he?"

"He'd tried. But the insurance company said the beneficiary had to approve."

"That was you?"

"That was me. I said no to him. I said no over and over and over again. Unless he wanted to give me the money. Bob was desperate. He might have hit me if Sam hadn't been there."

"Come on Cindy, did Bob ever hit you?"

"Well... no. No. Of course not. Anyway, that was what the fight was about. Bob said he'd go to court if he had to. It was his money. He could cancel the policy if he wanted. The court would back him up. Sam finally told him to fuck off."

"And then you left?"

"Yes. Bob was okay when we left. Just angry. Sputtering, red in the face, but okay."

"You'd didn't drag him off to a car, give him a ride into the desert? You and Sam?"

"God no. How could you even think that Judge?"

"I had to ask. Why didn't you tell me you were there?"

"Well, I guess it didn't look good."

"You mean it gave you another motive to want Bob dead."

"I suppose."

"Did you tell the police?"

"No. How'd you find out, Judge?"

"Elka."

"That bitch. That cold-blooded conniving little bitch. She ought to be gassed!"

"She was there, in the guest bedroom. You woke her up with the commotion."

"You can't believe anything she says, Judge. She's just a one issue tart. Green Card, Green Card, Green Card. Maybe she had something to do with what happened to Bob. Have you asked her?"

"Elka's pregnant with Bob's child, Cindy."

"Oh my God." Cindy drained her drink, then made a visible effort to calm herself.

"What time did you and Sam leave?"

"About ten. I never saw Bob again after that. Kind of a sad parting with an old friend I'd spent the best years of my life with. But that was Bob. His real estate projects dominated his life, making him a poor husband, a poor dad, and a poor friend."

The Judge nodded his understanding of her view, idly wondering what was wrong with his stomach after sipping his second Kitty. He suddenly had an ache. Perhaps it was the 'Braised beef noodle soup' he'd stuffed into his mouth out in the dining hall before meeting Cindy.

241

"You don't look so well, Judge. Perhaps we'd better get you back to your condo. You're turning bright red. I took an Uber over, I can drive."

"I think you'd better, Cindy. You're right. I'm feeling a bit unsteady. I wonder if there was a problem with the food I had before we met."

The Judge fished out his wallet and produced his credit card, which was immediately swooped up. Eight minutes later they walked out to the parking lot, the Judge not feeling better, in fact a tad worse.

"I still think I can drive, Cindy."

"I don't know, Judge. You're looking a little wobbly. Let's have me drive us back to your condo. I'll Uber home from there."

The Judge sighed. He hated not being in control. "Okay, I guess. Yes, you drive."

The Judge slumped into the passenger seat and watched the lights of the Strip slide by, somehow more blurred than usual tonight. As Cindy maneuvered the car through the last two blocks of traffic, the Judge muttered, "Just park it in guest parking, don't worry about the garage," and then closed his eyes for a second, or maybe it was a minute, or maybe....

He vaguely heard a male voice, the condo security guy he supposed, say, "I'll take him from here." The voice seemed somehow familiar, but he couldn't quite place it. He tried to open his eyes, but they seemed to be permanently shuttered for some reason. He vaguely felt Cindy's peck of a kiss on his cheek, her soft 'good night', and felt the cool draft from outside as the car door opened and she got out.

Someone else slid into the driver's seat and the car started up again, winding down into the underground parking under his condo. Good, they'd get him close to the elevator. He wasn't sure how well he could walk. Then it seemed like they'd turned around again and come back up the ramp, out of the garage, but he wasn't sure.

He was so tired now. Everything seemed to fade into grey… and then… nothing.

CHAPTER 42
WEDNESDAY
8:00 A.M.

The Judge was dreaming. Or maybe it was a nightmare. He wasn't sure. He was hot and he was dry. Like a dry sauna. How'd he get in a sauna? Who cranked up the heat so high? Why was he so dry? His mouth felt like it was full of sand.

And there was something else. A weight was on his back, pressing him down. Making it difficult to breath. The weight shifted. That was strange too. What a strange dream.

Suddenly there was a stabbing pain in the back of his hand; like a chunk of flesh had been ripped out. He screamed in pain. *Ah… fuck!* And then there was pain on the back of his neck, smaller, but like a nasty, deep nip. *God damn it!* He needed to wake up.

He was on his stomach. He spread one arm up and around toward his back. The weight moved slightly. He was horrified; his hand encountered feathers. A large bundle of coarse feathers. He slammed the back of his hand into the bundle with what little force he could muster, almost twisting his arm from the socket. It slashed into the soft feathers, ricocheted off a boney ribcage underneath, and bounced into a boney head with a sharp point.

CA Caw, CA Caw, screeched whatever was on his back. It hopped off to have a look at him. A lean pock-marked red neck extended down almost to the ground in front of the Judge's face, then the tip of a nasty looking beak, and finally a single mean flicking eye.

The Judge punched at the head with all he had, smashing into bone and cartilage, sending a jolt of pain through his knuckles and up his arm. Knocking the bird ass-over-teakettle in a flap of feathers and screeching. It unsteadily hopped off a few hops and then took to the air, its great black wings spreading like death, briefly blocking the sun.

The Judge looked down at the back of his hand. There was a quarter's worth of flesh gone. Shit, he'd just interrupted the buzzard's meal.

He sat up, discovering he was fully clothed and sprinkled with sand. Well of course he was. He saw he was in the middle of a desert. How he got here he wasn't sure. But swinging his head and then his body around, he saw a 360-degree perspective of desolation. No people, no structures, no cars, no highway, no nothing. Just sand and rocks and a bit of scrub here and there. And the buzzard some thirty feet away, back now for what it hoped to be a third bite. A bite of him.

The movement had started his head aching. It felt like a melon-sized anvil on which someone was pounding, waves of migraine spreading through his sinuses and up and over the top of his head. It was hard to think, to grasp where he was, what was going on.

He shaded his eyes with his hand from the bright morning sun and looked out to the horizon. It was there. The skyline of Las Vegas. Perhaps thirty miles away. *Damn, damn, damn.*

He tried his cell phone next, prying it with unsteady hands from his back pocket. There was no service.

He looked around for a water bottle, or maybe a canteen. There was none. *Jesus...! Shit.* He'd been dumped. Dumped just like Bob Hanson. Left here to wither and die. Here, on the desert floor. And then consumed by the buzzard and its compatriots.

He leaned over and, with supreme effort, got himself unsteadily to his feet. The buzzard bounded into the sky, disgusted by his recovery, giving up for now. Good. At least one good sign.

He looked again at the distant city shimmering in the desert's heat like a mirage of salvation. He'd not make it if he tried to walk. He'd end up like Bob. But no one knew he was out here, knew to look. What the fuck was he going to do?

But there was something. Something in the back of his mind somewhere. Something about Bob. What was it? He wished his brain would work.

Suicide. They'd labeled Bob's death a suicide. Why? Why? He could almost remember. And then he did. Bob's car was left behind a hill, out of sight, in the opposite direction from the Vegas skyline. And the keys had been in it.

He swung around to look away from the city. Yes. There was a large dune back there. Had they tried the same trick again? Should he go in the wrong direction, away from civilization, on the chance they might have left his car? He checked his pockets. No car keys there. He considered his odds in heading for the Vegas skyline. They were non-existent. What choice did he have? The opposite direction was his only chance.

He staggered around, turning his back on the skyline, and began to walk in slow steps toward the dune. He started up its casual incline. It quickly turned steeper and steeper as he climbed until he was slipping back in the sand, one step back for each two he took up. And the crest of the dune didn't seem to be getting any closer. He could feel his strength ebbing, each step harder than the last, his throat dry and caked with dust, his eyes swollen for lack of moisture. The top edge of the dune was a mirage, drifting away, seemingly more out of reach with each costly step.

And then he was there, feet straddling the top, sending rivulets of sand down both sides. There was a dirt track of sorts behind the dune, mostly covered by the sand. And his car stood there, way down there, glistening dully in a coat of dust. He scrambled, fell, and slid down the back side of the dune, getting himself upright again with great difficulty, to continue, slip and fall again. But gravity was his friend. He ended up in a sore ball at the bottom of the dune, closer to the car.

But if there were no keys in the car he was still screwed. He staggered up again, noting the shadow of the buzzard above, tracking him, optimistic.

He limped slowly toward the car. It seemed like an inch at a time. Its windows were open, it wasn't unlocked. Encouraging.

He reached the window and looked in. The keys were there, thrown on the seat. Thank God. But would it start?

He fumbled with the key to get it in the ignition, his hands shaking, his eyes almost shut, mere slits. Got it. Turned it on. Half a tank. He sat back, pressing against the back of the seat, exhausted. He found the switch for the trunk, popped it, and forced himself to get out of the car instead of drifting into the beckoning black.

Using the roof of the car to prop himself up, he slid along its side to the back, to the open trunk. With his last shred of energy, he felt inside for the water bottle he usually kept there. And by God it was still there.

He twisted off the cap with difficulty and brought it to his mouth, letting the hot stale water poor down his throat. Then thought better of it as he bent in a wrack of coughing, almost spilling some of the precious liquid on the sand.

He slid back around against the car to the driver's door and crawled back in. He took a big gulp of the ugly water, took a deep breath, mentally said a small prayer. Then he turned the key in the ignition and the engine roared to life.

It wasn't going to be his day to die.

He turned the car around, carefully, trying to keep the wheels on the faint track and out of the surrounding deeper sand, worried that it might strand the wheels for good. He steered the car back the way it had come, over its inbound tracks, praying that he and the car would hold together until his journey out of this Hell was complete.

CHAPTER 43
WEDNESDAY
12 P.M.

An hour and three quarters later, after steering the car with intense concentration as though his life depended on it, because it did, he carefully drove the car up and onto a highway. Deserted, grey and cracking, little used, but still asphalt by God. An hour later he was on a major highway and pulled into a small gas station. Relative civilization in this part of the world.

He filled the car up with gas, bought a case of water, a semi-frozen ham sandwich out of a vending machine, a banana, and called Katy. He still had his credit cards and his cash. After all, he was supposed to have been another suicide. Just like Bob. He also got directions to the Vegas skyline, still well off in the distance.

An hour later he eased the car into the Meridian Project and pulled into a guest parking lot. Katy was there, waving her arms and jumping up and down. She took it all in, scared, angry at what had been done to her man, joyful to see him, tears streaming down her face.

She helped him up to their condo, mothering him all the way, showered him, bandaged his hand and neck, put aloe vera on the parts of him burned to a crisp, and put him to bed. Sitting down in the chair beside the bed, not letting him out of her sight as he blissfully dozed off.

He slept until four, awoke from a bad dream thirsty as Hell, and consumed two more bottles of water. Water never tasted so good. He got up, ravenously wolfed the chicken soup Katy had made from scratch, her answer to all things 'sick', and went back to sleep.

By the next morning he was feeling his old self again, as long as he didn't think about the desert dreams he'd had or bump his damaged hand. They had Starbucks and ham and cheese croissants Katy picked up, settling into their small breakfast across their small antique table in their small condo. It was good.

"So many things we take for granted, Katy. Things which might never happen. Like seeing tomorrow's sunrise. The last twenty-four hours have been closer than I'd like. I'm so happy to just be here with you."

"Aww, Judge. You're going to make me blush. What would I do without you, you silly old goat?"

"Can you take the word, 'old' out, and just call me your goat?"

"Sure, Judge. Whatever floats your boat."

They laughed.

Later the Judge called Cindy to ask what had happened the night before.

"You got plastered, Judge." Cindy giggled. "You're lucky I didn't take advantage of you."

"You drove me, my car, back to the Meridian?"

"Of course. You couldn't drive. I think a little pink kitty got its claws into you."

"And then what?"

"I parked in a guest space like you said. Then a nice man pulled up next to us. Said he was your neighbor. Said he would take over, drive you and your car into your underground parking and hoist you up to your unit."

"How did you know he was a neighbor?"

"He said so, Judge. And he clearly knew you. Called you the 'Judge'. Said this happens a lot with you and he knew the drill."

"What did he look like, Cindy?"

"Oh, you know, regular. I didn't really look at him. I watched him drive you down into the garage and then I was off to catch my Uber."

"Can you remember anything about him?"

"Ah, about your age I think, not quite as tall but close, blond hair, a little pudgy… and oh, blue eyes. It was dark. So, it was hard to see."

"What was he wearing?"

"A white dress shirt, open at the collar, and, and … that's all I can remember. He looked familiar though, Judge. I think I'd seen him before with you, but I don't know where. Is there a problem, Judge? Did he ding your car?"

The Judge decided Cindy didn't need hear that she'd delivered him into the desert, maybe even spoken directly to one of the people who had killed Bob. At least not now. Maybe not ever. He said there was no problem, thanked her for her help, and hung up.

Later that afternoon, Katy and the Judge settled into their lawn furniture on their little balcony and watched the sun disappear over Caesars Palace two blocks away, leaving a soft blue desert sky behind. They chatted about not much at all for a while, each basking in the glow of the other, while the alcohol settled into their systems.

"So, Judge. Did the Spider arrange for you to be dumped in the desert?"

"I'm sure he did, Katy."

"How can the police contend Bob committed suicide, when the same thing almost happened to you?"

"I don't know, Katy. I guess they have their procedures."

"What does your detective friend say, Barry something?"

"Barry Marsh? He's certain Bob was a suicide."

"But you're certain it was murder, Judge.?"

"Yes."

So, who do you think killed Bob, Judge? You've been chasing around after this mythical Spider. Is he's the one that gave the order?"

"Yes."

"But you haven't been able to identify this Spider, Judge. And you haven't been able to identify the hired help that picked up Bob and drove the car. Maybe it's time to give up. If we're just tilting at windmills here and making you a target, maybe it's time to call it a day and head back to Malaga Cove."

The Judge smiled. Katy still wanted the Judge to go home. She was eager to go back to the cool air of Malaga Cove and the scent of the sea. And most of all she wanted him out of harm's way. But unfortunately, it wasn't that simple.

"I have made progress, Katy. This pimp guy is a good candidate to be one of the contract killers. This Arney Gunn. I think he was the bag man for the Spider, delivering part of the loan money in cash to Bob. He's the sort of roustabout the Spider would pick to drive someone into the desert. And I had him at my feet briefly. I didn't know his significance then. Now I can't find him. I think he took orders from someone else, a second guy who was in charge, the two men hustling Bob into a car in Vegas and tying him up for a several-hour drive into the desert. They took two cars, one drove Bob in their car, and the other one drove Bob's car out into that desert."

"Any idea who the other guy might be?"

"No. But as to identifying the Spider, I have a person of interest."

"Who?"

"Shorty Calkin. He owns the Buoys and Gulls Casino."

"Why is he a possible candidate?"

"He knows computers and the Dark Web, he's greedy and unscrupulous, he's been expanding his activities in the Dark Web. Forrest Langley thinks it's him. Angelo thinks it's him. He gets a lot of votes."

Katy sighed. She knew when to give up. "Okay, Judge. I can see you're staying. And if you're staying, I'm staying. Someone's got to protect you from the floosies in this town. So, let's think about this some more, Judge. You always say at some point the pieces are all there; it's just a matter or turning them around until they fit into a complete pattern."

"You're right, Katy. And there's something in the back of my mind troubling me. I just can't quite put my finger on it."

"Relax, Judge. Enjoy your drink and the sunset. Step back from the problem. Give it room to breathe. It will come."

The Judge slid down in his chair and watched the Vegas lights come on. The sky slowly shaded to light violet and then purple as the dark swallowed the light. He could feel the single malt loosening the tension behind his eyes, relaxing his neck, helping his body slip into a less stress-locked state.

"So. Judge, we're certain Bob was dumped out there?"

"Yes. Certain."

"Bob should have used his cell phone to call for help, Judge. That's what I would have done."

"He tried, Katy, just like I did. But there was no service out there, out in the middle of nowhere. Bob did try to text me."

"The poor man. What an awful way to die. And there was nothing on his body. No note or sign he intended to commit suicide."

"No. There was nothing on the body. Wait a minute. Shit. That's it, Katy!"

"What?"

"What wasn't on the body! Jesus, Katy, I'm such a dunce. I think I know who the other guy was who drove Bob out into the desert! He was the boss, picking up Arney Gunn as an assistant. The two of them arranged to meet Bob that night. Bob thought he was meeting the Spider. But it was a trap. They just snatched Bob and he disappeared. Jesus! But I just don't know how I can prove it."

The Judge jumped up, started to go back into their unit, turned and came back to put his hands on either side of her head from behind and give her a kiss on top of her head. He dashed off for his phone. He dialed Cindy back for a brief confirmation. He made one more call. Then he dialed his police contact, Barry Marsh.

"Hi, Barry. Some interesting new information has come to light. I think I know who drove Bob Hanson out to his death in the desert."

"We still think it was a suicide, Judge."

"I've always known it wasn't suicide, Barry. And now I think I can prove it. Let's meet and let me convince you. Can we meet tomorrow morning, early, maybe about eight a.m.? I'm going to need your help."

"Sure, Judge."

"Are you still working your case out in Sumnerlin?"

"Yes."

"Why don't we meet at the Red Rock Canyon Marker? Should be pretty quiet then. I'll bring Starbucks."

"Done, Judge. See you in the morning."

CHAPTER 44
THURSDAY
8 A.M.

The Judge pulled into the turnout at the Red Rock Canyon Marker. Red Rock Canyon jutted up from the desert floor like an island of toppled Stonehenge monoliths, a majestic pile of rocks that caught the sparkle of the early morning sun. The turnout was deserted except for Barry's dust-covered car, a dark green Ford that had the look of County issue.

The Judge slid into the passenger's seat in Barry's car and adjusted the seat for more room. The last occupant must have been a shrimp.

"How are you, Judge?" asked Barry. "You look a little weary around the edges. Perhaps this case is becoming an obsession. Perhaps you should just let it go."

"Can't do that, Barry. You know that."

Barry sighed. "Okay, what's up in the case?"

"I was thinking through all the facts I have in the case, puzzling how they all fit together. And…"

"And…?"

"Well, why didn't Bob just use his cell phone to call for help?"

"That's an easy one, Judge. There's no cell coverage out there."

"But he had the cell on him you said."

"Yes, wallet, cash, cell phone, no indication of foul play."

"That's what I recalled you said. And I'm sure you're right, Bob had his cell phone when he was dropped off in the desert."

"Yes, Judge. How's that relevant? There was no coverage to make a call."

"I'll tell you, Barry. It leads me to think you must have had a really good laugh when I originally called you to see if you could keep an eye out for my missing friend, Robert Hanson."

"How's that, Judge?" Barry sat a little straighter in his seat, turning to face the Judge now.

"Because you and Arney Gunn were the ones who hauled Bob off and dumped him in the desert."

"What the fuck? What are you saying, Judge?"

"You and Gunn were the contract killers hired by the Spider to give my friend his last ride."

"That's crazy, Judge. You've been in our desert too long. Why on earth would you think that?"

"Because of what wasn't on the body, Barry."

"I don't understand."

"At the morgue you said Hanson had been shoved out of a four-wheel vehicle intact, with *'his cash, driver's license, Social Security card, triple A card, cell phone, small change in his pocket, just as he must have been when he was picked up somewhere in Vegas.'*"

"So? So what? That was correct, what I said."

"Yes, Barry. It was a correct statement of what Hanson had on his person when he was grabbed in Vegas. And a correct statement of what he had on his person when he was dumped out of your SUV into the desert."

"Hold on…"

But it wasn't a correct statement of what he had on his body when it was brought in from the desert."

"What do you mean?"

"There was no cell phone on the body."

"Sure there was. There had to be. I examined it myself."

"No. I went out to the desert. To the place where Bob's body was found. And I backtracked some distance backward, toward where Bob had come from, from where his car had been."

"So…?"

"I found this lying under some shrubs." The Judge took Bob's cell phone out of his pocket and laid it on the seat beside him. "The only way you could have known Bob was dumped with his cell phone is if you were there, Barry, with Bob, the night he was dumped."

"He must have had two phones."

"No, Barry. No cell whatsoever was found with the body. I checked with the coroner."

"Sometimes you're just too damn clever, Judge. I like you. Enjoyed our association. But a liability is a liability. I'm a firm believer in eliminating liabilities."

Barry had put his hand inside his coat and now pulled out a snub-nosed revolver and pointed it at the

Judge's chest. It was surprising how big the hole in the barrel of a small handgun looked when you were staring down the barrel. The hole looked like a God damn cannon.

"Why, Barry? Why'd you do it?"

"For the money of course, Judge. My young wife sticks by me only for the money. Likes the big house high above Summerland. Likes the fancy trips and the expensive swanning around social events. I have to feed the dragon. It's the way the game's played. And the Spider pays well for running errands, very well."

"Errands like killing people. Dropping them off in the middle of the desert to die of hyperthermia."

"Yeah. Me and Arney did that. But your friend didn't cry at the end. Didn't whine, didn't whimper. Took it like a man. I respected that. No fight either. Just got out of the car and did what he was told. I didn't know he'd lost his cell phone along the way in his little hike. Tough to remember and check everything. Must be getting old. Nothing personal against your guy, Hanson. He just welshed on the wrong guy. The Spider doesn't mess around."

"And you gave me a similar ride, didn't you Barry?"

"Yeah," Barry laughed. "The Spider got tired of you sniffing up his ass. I would have just shot you, but the Spider thinks he's a god-damn artist or something. Thought it poetic justice for you to go out the same way as your friend. Load of crap if you ask me. I used more stuff for your drink. You were still out of it when Arney and I dumped you."

"Where is Arney?'

"Arney was going a little sideway, first falling all over himself for Hanson's stupid bitch daughter, then getting caught by you. And all the while yacking around about Hanson. Bragging about it. Stupid little fart. Spider and I agreed on that. Arney had to go away. I shot him in the face last night, Judge. Buried him in the desert. None of this *'Make a statement…. Make an example…. Make it look like suicide….'* crap the Spider spouts. One clean shot and one deep hole filled. Efficient. The way the game is supposed to be played."

"But you left a witness at the Meridian when you grabbed me, Barry. She recognized you. Saw you with me sitting in the hospital cafeteria the day Robbie overdosed."

"I've thought about that. Hanson's ex-old lady. Thinking I need to clean that up after I finish here. And surprised, surprised, Judge, you figured it all. You're a clever bastard. I'll give you that. This time it's going to be like Arney, Judge. I won't screw up again. Quick like. One clean shot into the back of your head. Play the game right with you, Judge." Barry smiled; it was the smile of a happy-go-lucky Sociopath.

"Who's the Spider, Barry?"

Barry laughed. "Who the fuck knows? I don't. Don't want to know. You know too much, suddenly you're dead. But he's one clever son of a bitch. Smarter than both of us."

"So, you're going to shoot me here?"

"If I have to, Judge. Prefer not to mess up my car, but it's your choice."

"Can I just show you one thing, Barry?"

"Careful, Judge. No tricky moves."

"Just thought I'd show you this, Barry."

The Judge slowly brought his two hands to his chest and unbuttoned a center button of his shirt. He stretched the fabric wide to show a white bulletproof vest under, and strung across it, a thin white wire.

Barry's eyes widened, his face turning beet red. He started to gasp for air, swinging his eyes around behind the Judge, out around the Red Rock Marker.

That's when Captain Edwards, Barry's boss, rapped on the driver's side window with his service pistol. Barry twisted around in a panic.

Two blue suits appeared at the passenger window with guns drawn, another at the front of the car and one at the back. A patrolman opened the passenger car door and grabbed the Judge, quickly sliding him out and around to the back of the car, and then away to a cluster of three patrol cars hidden behind adjoining rocks.

It was over. Barry slowly got out of his car, hands raised. He was handcuffed and marched past the Judge to one of the patrol cars. He gave the Judge a look of daggers as he passed.

"It's the way the game's played, Barry," the Judge said with a shrug.

CHAPTER 45
FRIDAY
8:00 A.M.

The Judge was up the next morning and on the road early, the Mercedes' top down, the desert air streaming across his face, drying his hair from a quick shower. It felt good to be alive. And good to be finally doing something to put things aright. Rather than chasing around after information like a bewildered squirrel searching for nuts. He looked in the rear mirror at the two cars behind him, a modern day mini-caravan streaming across the desert to the outskirts of civilization on Interstate 15. He was going to introduce Sam and his cold-calling partner, Jerry Brown, to some very special investors.

Sharry, the receptionist, gave him a big smile when he walked in. She apparently favored older men. It felt good to be noticed.

One of the gentlemen with the Judge looked expensive, older, mid-sixties, with a generous paunch well disguised in a finely tailored suit, grey stripe. The Rolex on his wrist spelt money, as did the large gold university ring on his other hand with its Cornell logo. He walked with assurance and authority, his keen eyes missing nothing. He was the money man the Judge was introducing to Sam Compton and Jerry Brown.

The other man was tall and scrawny, wore steel-rimmed glasses and a brown sport coat over a cream shirt and dark brown jeans. He had the feel of the prairie, maybe Texas, and looked like an accountant. The numbers guy.

Sam Compton and Jerry Brown came steaming into the lobby, ignoring the Judge, all eyes on the money guy. They could barely restrain themselves from fawning and scraping, wide shopkeeper smiles pasted on their faces.

"Hi, Sam, Jerry. This is Mr. Randoph, the possible investor I told you about, and his associate, Neil Carson."

Jerry's eyes jollied up to match his smile, his small hand coming out to give a solid handshake to each man, and then, almost an afterthought, to the Judge. Sam followed right behind him, all kissy friendly.

"Thank you so much for the introduction, Judge," said Jerry. "Gentlemen, right this way. Sharry, buzz us in, will you? Let me show you a well-oiled precision machine for generating cash flow."

Randoph and Carson followed Brown through the door into the cavernous room with the 100% air conditioning and the rows of desks and stations, the Judge and Sam bringing up the rear. The same crew was manning the stations, again looking haphazard and relaxed. The same air of expectation permeated the room.

But as Jerry strolled into the center of the room, all heads straightened up as though a burst of raw energy had suddenly detonated and spread to every corner of the vast space…. Jerry launched again into his motivational sales talk, haranguing the assembled cold callers, egging them into excitement, building to his finale when he jumped up on one of the tables and started to dance around as he yelled.

And they reacted the same as before, diving for their computers and cell phones at the end, hitting the desks, dialing for closure and dollars.

Jerry jumped off the table, dusted his hands together, and ambled over to Sam's little group, all smile and teeth. Randolph congratulated Jerry on his motivational talent, his eyes still carrying amazement at what he had just seen.

"What are they selling today?" asked the Judge.

"What are we selling?" asked Sam, turning to Jerry.

"Well, half the group is selling the art done by… you know, the 'No-Name' artists we buy from. We buy cheap and mark it up two thousand percent."

"Sold as an investment?" asked Randolph.

"Of course. Of course, all these modern pictures are useless to look at, you can't make heads or tails of them. Don't know why anyone would buy one just to hang on a wall."

"And the other half of the group, what are they selling?" asked Carson.

"Rare coins, kind of. Not really so rare, but they look old, and we have a dynamite script about how they're going to appreciate tenfold and more over the coming months. We buy them in bulk, dirty them up a little, and encase them in plastic for display."

"Also sold as an investment?"

"Of course. We canvas a lot of people, and then we harvest the addresses of the people who show interest."

"How does that work?" asked Randolph.

"Our third partner, the silent one, buys these contact lists off the Dark Web. That's what we use to email and to call. When we get any sort of nibble, whether a live one or just a looky-loo, that person's contact goes into a special folder, labeled susceptible contacts. That's our full pressure sell list.

And to reduce costs, we turn around and sell out contact list back over the Dark Web. That almost covers our overhead right there. This is a very lucrative business."

"Who handles the Dark Web part of the business?"

"Our third partner."

"He's good with the Dark Web?"

"He's a genius. He gets the good contact lists for us. Our entire computer and email system here is on the Dark Web and essentially untraceable. Funds get forward to the account our partner controls, and he arranges to wash the money and return untraceable clean funds here. He is literally Mr. Dark Web. He's automated our entire system and eliminated the risks."

"You have an interesting business, gentlemen," said Randolph, turning slightly to include Sam in his comment.

"So, what do you think, Mr. Randolph? Can we count on you for a significant investment so we can expand?" asked Jerry. "We were thinking in the neighborhood of five million, perhaps part loan and part equity."

"Why isn't your third partner stepping up with the cash?" asked Randolph.

"He would in a heartbeat if he could," said Sam. "But he had a five million loan go south this month, and he's scrambling to recover, close his shorts, get everyone paid off, you know, stuff. He doesn't have it right now and we can't wait."

"Who is your third partner?" asked Carson

"He prefers to remain anonymous," said Jerry.

"I'm afraid I can't do business with you unless I know who I'm doing business with," said Randolph. "I make that a cardinal rule I never break."

"We've sworn to never reveal his name," said Sam, desperation spreading across his face.

"That's too bad. I guess that concludes our conversation."

"Wait, wait," said Jerry. "Perhaps we could quietly disclose it to you since you want to move forward with an investment. You just can't tell our partner, or anyone, that we said anything."

"Alright."

Jerry stepped close to Randolph and said something in a whisper the Judge couldn't make out.

"So, who is he, exactly?"

"He owns an off-the-strip casino in town, 'The Buoys and Gulls'. Has a sports book there and has various real estate interests around Vegas. He's solid. And technically brilliant. An expert at manipulating the Dark Web to keep our affairs secret."

Randolph and Jerry began to haggle about the terms for a five million capital infusion. How much equity, how much by loan, what interest rate, what share of profits. Sam was almost panting, slavering at the thought of the additional capital and his share of the cash flow it would produce.

It was then that Sharry from reception showed up and tugged at Sam's arm. "Mr. Randolph's two additional gentlemen have arrived," she said.

"Oh, yes," said Randolph. "I'm sorry they missed the show. I guess they got a little lost."

"Show them back, Sharry," said Sam.

The two new guys ambled through the door and into the warehouse, sharp eyes taking everything in from corner to corner. They muttered "Blake" and "Stevens." Hands were shaken all around.

Randolph said, "Well, Sam and Jerry, as I said, you have an interesting operation. But I don't think I fully introduced myself."

Sam looked up sharply, something in Randolph's voice triggering a chill.

"I'm Jacob Randolph. I'm an attorney with the SEC. Mr. Carson here is with the IRS. And Blake and Stevens… well, you see, Blake is from the Justice

Department; and Stevens, and his crew waiting in your parking lot are with the Clarkson County Sheriff's Department. They specialize in white collar crime."

The Judge nodded at Randoph and faded from the room, through the lobby, out to his car, and on to Interstate 15, satisfied he'd played some part in reducing a little the investment losses suffered over the Dark Web.

CHAPTER 46
FRIDAY
10:00 A.M.

As the Judge fought late-morning commuters back along the freeway, his cell phone made a screeching sound like a pouncing hyena. The damn phone was getting more and more independent, picking up sounds from everywhere to offer up as its call announcement. He'd have to trade the thing in soon, before it started nibbling on his ear. He allowed his car to pick up the call over the car's Bluetooth and said, Hello."

"It's Angelo. I've got him, Judge. I've found the Spider!" Angelo's voice crackled with excitement.

"Who is he, Angelo?"

"You were right, Judge. It's Shorty. The bastard has gone way off the reservation."

"How do you know?"

"When Shorty came to Vegas ten years ago and opened his little casino, it was with a specific understanding with the powers that be. He'd pay the usual tariff monthly, a small percentage of the gross quarterly, and he'd limit his territory interests to gambling and girls at his casino, a little hard money lending on the side, and assist in certain monetary chores."

"Like money laundering."

"We don't use that term. Anyway, the deal was he was not to poach into other people's business, like drugs, online gaming, offsite woman, and so on. Come to find out he's doing all these prohibited enterprises secretly over this Black Web thing you've been talking about. The boys here in Vegas are incensed. He's been carving into their revenues right under their noses. And cheating on his quarterly gross percentage payments."

"That confirms what I just learned, Angelo. Sam Compton, and his partner, Jerry, let it slip this morning. Shorty and his money are behind their cold call operation over the Dark Web. And I think Shorty funded the second trust deed on The Spire, a five-million-dollar loan which is now worthless with The Spire in bankruptcy. You said you wouldn't put it past Shorty to eliminate a defaulted debtor."

"Shorty has a real temper, Judge. Doesn't always think things through. Acts on the spur of the moment. He would think nothing of giving your friend a one-way ride into the desert. Come join me for brunch at Caesars at noon. I'm buying. I'll detail what I've found, what Shorty's into, and how it's all going to be settled. Give some closure for you and for your friend's family. Not a big fan of these conversations over my cell phone."

"If you're buying, Angelo, it's a date."

CHAPTER 47
FRIDAY
11:45 A.M.

The Judge settled into a low overstuffed chair in the lobby of Caesars facing the lobby entrance. He was a little early. Between rushing around on this case, the early meeting this morning, and his desert ordeal earlier in the week, he was very weary. He found himself starting to doze, until the hairs on the back of his neck suddenly stood up. He eased his head around to look at the large glass wall a foot behind his chair. And froze.

The huge wall was clear glass, one side of a very large aquarium. And pressed against the glass on the opposite side was a grey nose and two dark flat eyes staring at him with malice. Eyes that didn't catch the light. Eyes that looked dead.

As he watched, the snout opened to show two rows of needle-sharp teeth. They made a grotesque smile as the creature's head pressed harder against the glass, seeking to reach flesh. The shark was big, perhaps eight feet long, with white tips on its fins. Another one was coming up behind, also interested in the potential menu. He worked at quelling his panic and made his head rachet back to the lobby. But he knew the whitetip was still there, seeking some way to get at him. He shuddered and took hold of himself as Angelo came through the casino entrance.

Angelo plopped down in the chair next to the Judge, a small, battle-scarred coffee table separating them, and gave a slight smile to the predator looking over the Judge's shoulders. Professional courtesy mused the Judge.

"What's Chicago say?" the Judge asked.

"They're livid. Everybody was wondering why the gross has been sliding downhill for some years. Everybody was complaining. Here, Chicago, L.A. I had to do some deep digging. We squeezed one of Shorty's lieutenants until the guy sang the whole tawdry story. There's no honor among thieves anymore, Judge. In the old days there was mutual respect. One could shake hands and trust a firm deal had been made. But these kids coming up, this Shorty.... No class. No understanding of our history or of our calling. They think they can just rip fruit from everybody's trees without consequences. Justice is being arranged. It will be swift and complete."

As Angelo spoke, the Judge's eyes ranged the room out of habit, briefly settling on a man in a long overcoat who'd just walked in through the hotel's revolving door. The man stood there, blinking, adjusting his eyes to the glittering lights. He looked somehow out of place. Was it the dark overcoat he wore after walking in from a 96-degree afternoon? Or the funny way he held his hand and arm, mostly covered under the folds of his coat?

His eyes swept the lobby, finally resting on the Judge and Angelo, focusing there.

He took four steps farther into the lobby toward them, then brought his hand out from his coat, awkwardly producing a small handgun with a long silencer on its end. He pointed the pistol at the Judge.

Everything seemed to move in slow motion as the Judge watched Angelo dive flat onto the floor, marine style. Surprisingly agile for an old guy. And the Judge instinctively followed, crashing heavily on to his paunch, losing his breath.

Four shots rang out, *pop, pop, pop, pop*. People in the lobby screamed and started to scatter.

The Judge felt something sting. His hand flew to his head in shock, coming away with sticky fingers, warmth starting to trickle down the side of this neck... a lot... his blood!

The shooter turned and darted for the front door, careening into an older gentleman who tumbled to the floor in a scramble of old bones and cane. The shooter disappeared back through the revolving doors into the daylight and was gone.

The Judge felt moisture soaking down his back and along his arm, his white dress shirt suddenly dark with moisture. Was he covered in blood? He looked at Angelo, who was shifting up to his knees. Angleo looked at the Judge, apparently unharmed, but still with fear in his eyes, almost panic. Why? The shooter was gone. Angelo was looking at the Judge... and behind him.

The Judge, still flat on the floor and a little dazed, swung his head around, following Angelo's gaze. There were four little holes in the shark tank's wall of glass. Spray running out from the holes had wetted the back of his shirt and pants, mixing with his blood. He'd been shot somewhere.

Now there was a cracking noise and two long jagged fractures appeared in the glass, connecting the four holes and working their way out to the tank's corners.

A second later there was a larger crash as the entire panel of glass turned into a spiderweb of lines and then shattered, releasing a huge wave of water, shreds of glass, and the snapping jaws of two angry sharks down on top of the Judge.

The Judge shrieked, throwing his hands up over his head to protect his face and neck, pulling his legs and elbows into a ball and desperately trying to roll away as two sets of double teeth in matching rows angled and thrashed closer and closer on the wet floor to get a taste.

CHAPTER 48
FRIDAY
12:15 P.M.

The Judge rolled away and then scurried onto all fours, putting distance between him and the snapping jaws. The two sharks looked disappointed, even as they twisted toward the Judge's direction, slowly dying from lack of water over their gills. He started to get his dripping frame up, still in shock. Angelo, standing now, looking dapper and dry... reached down to give him a hand.

"You okay, Judge?"

"I don't know, Angelo. I'm wet and bleeding somewhere. You?"

"I'm okay, just wet like you. It looks like one of the bullets nicked your left ear."

The Judge reached around and touched his ear lobe, his fingers coming away sticky with blood.

"Was that meant for me?" asked the Judge.

"I thought it was met for me, Judge, or maybe both of us. The guy sure had bad aim."

"Why now?"

"The word's out, Judge. Shorty's done in this town. Done everywhere, done permanently on the

Davis MacDonald

planet. He knows it's you and me that's set the dogs on him. I think that was his effort at payback. We've found this Spider of yours. And the Spider found us!"

"But that wasn't Shorty shooting at us."

"Oh no. He'd never come himself. Did I tell you one of his unsanctioned businesses is Murder for Hire?"

"The bastard."

"Sorry for your bath, Judge. But it was a last hurrah of a floundering scum. Shorty will shortly be no more. I guarantee it. The people in charge here are already jockeying to see who takes over his casino and its assorted onsite business. You don't need to worry about the police or the courts now, Judge. Our... er... fraternity has its own way of administering justice. This will all be handled discreetly and with finality. Shorty's killing of your friend has generated a shitstorm that's going to bury him quickly and quietly. Literally."

The police arrived then, and the Judge spent the next hour squashed, soaked clothes and all, in a small, padded armchair while he recited over and over what had happened. The nip out of his earlobe was surprisingly superficial for all the blood it produced. A medic stopped the bleeding with a spray-on bandage. Between questions, he considered what he would tell Katy when he was finally allowed to leave. To tell her he was shot at would lead to an endless discussion in which she would lecture him that she had been right, they should have gone home yesterday. He just needed a good explanation.

He decided that he'd accidentally tripped and fell into Caesars' swimming pool. It sounded weak. But he figured if he stuck with his story long enough, she'd stop circling around and peppering him with questions to pry out the truth.

CHAPTER 49
FRIDAY
7:45 P.M.

After Katy was through interrogating the Judge about his wet clothes, noting his evasiveness with suspicion, the Judge quickly changed out of the evidence into dry clothes. The Judge and Katy then settled again on their condo deck to enjoy some freshly squeezed orange juice Katy had made. They watched the cars and pedestrians file along Flamingo Road, buzzing among the several off-strip casinos there. It was like a toy world for adults. The Judge was feeling smug. He'd brought the Spider and his henchmen down. Not to justice in the court system as he'd intended. But to a far swifter and more brutal end.

Bob was gone. Poor Robbie was in the hospital on life support while Jackie still struggled with the decision to shut everything down. The Judge had no sympathy for Shorty and what would befall him.

"Judge."

"Yes, Katy."

"I still don't understand. Why did the Spider have to kill Bob?"

"Bob borrowed this chunk of money over the Dark Web from the Spider, Katy. The Project consumed it and Bob couldn't pay it back."

"And you said this chunk of money was secured by a pledge of Bob's life ?"

"That's right. When Bob couldn't pay, his life was forfeit."

"But why wasn't it like Angelo said? Better to keep Bob working and some day he might pay off his debt?"

"I don't know, Katy. Perhaps there was bad blood between the Spider and Bob."

"Well, that's obvious, Judge. The Spider sent his goons to kill Bob. The question is, what was the bad blood over? Maybe we should turn the board around. Look at it from the other side."

"What do you mean, Katy? How?"

"Well, we've been looking at your puzzle from Bob's perspective."

"Yes."

"This loan secured by a pledge in Blood is all very suspenseful, and draconian, Judge. Almost like pirates and secret handshakes sealed by a drop of blood. Something out of Captain Kidd. All very romantic."

"Well, I wouldn't call it romantic," huffed the Judge.

"No, I know dear. It's quite serious. But your Mob friend, Angelo, said no one kills debtors anymore. The Mob are like bankers now, take a longer view, figure they own you forever and can collect at least a little periodically if they keep in close touch."

"Yes. That's what he said."

"So why would the Spider want to kill Bob just because he can't repay the loan right now?"

"Well, the Blood pledge, and all the stuff you just mentioned." The Judge unconsciously crossed his arms, signaling things were all settled, and more discussion wouldn't be helpful.

"I know, Judge, but that wouldn't be very good business, would it? You're forever out your money, no one around to work off the debt, plus you have the expense of hiring two killers. And the legal risk that something goes wrong, and the hit gets traced back to you."

"Well… well…"

The Judge was sputtering and he knew it.

"That's what I mean by turning the table and looking at it from the Spider's point of view."

"Okay, Katy. How do you see it?"

"Looking at the table from the Spider's point of view, what would stir him up so much he felt compelled to do away with Bob?"

The Judge frowned. "I don't know. I don't know how the Spider thinks."

"I can think of only one thing, Judge. One thing that would jump start your Spider into action to take Bob off the board. And hang the costs, loss of his loan money forever, and the risks."

"What, Katy? What are you thinking?"

"Bob somehow found out who the Spider was!"

The silence was deafening then. The Judge was so startled he was at a loss for words. He opened his mouth, but no words came. He was supposed to be the clever detective.

But as usual, in her non-assuming way, Katy had followed her unerring instinct to the core of an issue he hadn't thought about.

The issue she raised was relevant, even key. Why did the Spider decide he had to kill Bob? And her answer, once uttered, was obvious. It was the only thing that made sense.

"You're absolutely right, Katy," he finally admitted. "Your insight is one of the reasons I love you so much. That must be what happened."

"So, that opens a whole new avenue to explore, Judge. What did Bob find out? And how did Bob find out? And did Bob leave tracks behind to follow to the Spider's identity?"

"But does it really matter, Katy? Now we know Shorty's the Spider?"

"Do we?"

"Do we what?"

"Do we know Shorty's the Spider?"

"Well… Angelo's convinced Shorty's the Spider."

"But perhaps Shorty's not the Spider, Judge. How can you really be sure?"

"Well, Angelo said…"

"Angelo's got the Chicago Mob on his back. He had to act fast and solve their problem or it was his neck.

He needed a candidate in a hurry. But maybe he reacted too fast. Maybe he's wrong. Maybe Shorty isn't the Spider."

"Oh, I don't know, Katy. Shorty meets all the criteria. And he's a mean, angry little animal. Just the sort to be the Spider."

"We don't have any actual proof, do we Judge? Just Angelo's opinion on it."

"And Jerry Brown and Sam Compton's statements."

"Yeah. Real straight-up and objective witnesses they are."

"Well…"

"And Judge, you never found why Bob's office was ransacked. What were they were looking for?"

"I… I don't know."

"Maybe the Spider's men were desperately looking for the evidence Bob was holding over the Spider's head. Evidence of his identity."

"I guess anything's possible."

"You said Jackie had her own unit at The Spire, after she moved out from Cindy's."

"Yes."

"Was her unit searched too?"

"I don't know. But if Bob had given her something to hide, she would have told me."

"Maybe she didn't know. Maybe Bob just slipped in and hid something in her unit."

"You think I should check?"

"I think we should check."

As they grabbed their coats and walked by the TV through the living room, the Judge saw his own face flashed on the screen on the two o'clock news, his boyish smile and aw-shucks countenance belied by the bloody patch on one ear, his soaked shirt and pants, and his dripping hair.

Katy screeched to a halt in front of the TV, her hands going to her hips, her eyes alternately watching the screen with amazement and flashing up at the Judge as the whole tawdry story came out. Then she wrapped her body into a powerful swing and landed a punch on the Judge's shoulder.

"Ouch," the Judge yelped, more for effect than anything else, since a punch thrown by a lightweight little thing like Katy was still a lightweight punch, regardless of how she tried to add power and heft to her blow. But the Judge backed up, explaining in rush of words his version of what had happened at Caesars, downplaying the danger wherever he could. Katy was incensed. Angry at Shorty for trying to kill her Judge; angry at Angelo for dragging the Judge there to be shot; angry at the Judge for making himself a target again; and particularly angry at the Judge for not telling her what happened.

They took the elevator down and left the Meridian, Katy raging at the Judge like the mother lion she was. Finally winding down after they'd settled into the car.

CHAPTER 50
FRIDAY
8:45 P.M.

The Judge brought out his cell phone and dialed Jackie. She came on at once.

"How is Robbie, Jackie?"

"Oh, Judge. I don't know what to do. Robbie's the same. They're pressing me to unplug him. Damn doctors! We have such a fucked up medical system in this country. It's not about the patient anymore, Judge. It's only about the money."

"I'm sorry, Jackie. I'm so sorry."

"Guess it's time I grew up, Judge."

"Yes. You have some tough decisions to make."

"What do you need, Judge? Have you caught this ugly Spider that killed Dad? Put my son in this awful condition?"

"Some of us think so, Jackie. And some of us aren't so sure. You moved into The Spire with your dad when you left home, didn't you?"

"I did. Dad gave me the unit next to his. It was a furnished model, so it worked out great for a while."

"What was the unit number?"

"2024."

"Have you been back since that night when they dragged you out of your dad's unit?"

"No. I couldn't. There's only a handful of clothes there. It was all so terrifying. I'm just not quite ready to go back."

"I understand. Did Arney and his muscle search your unit that night?"

"No. I mean… not that I know of. I don't think they knew about it."

"Did your dad ever give you anything to hold for him? Maybe keep in your unit for him?"

"No."

"Okay. Jackie, do you mind if I look in your unit?"

"Have at it Judge. The code on the keypad lock is the same as Dad's. His birthday."

"Thanks, Jackie. If you want to talk… about Robbie… about stuff, call me anytime. Day or night."

"Okay, Judge. Thanks."

The Judge turned back to Katy. "We have permission to go search Jackie's unit."

"Let's go, Judge. Let's go right now."

The Spire was as dark as ever. A slim silhouette against the purple sky from their angle of approach. It looked spooky. They crept through the dark lobby feeling like burglars and rode up the elevator to the penthouse suites. The Judge punched Bob's birthday code into the 2024 keypad and the door to the unit swung open. The Judge stepped in and turned on the lights.

It was the same size as Bob's suite, laid out in reverse order, non-descript furniture from the staging company in whites and beiges. There was nothing personal that said 'Jackie'. They did a systematic search, coming up with underwear and socks in the bedroom chest of drawers, a couple of outfits in the closet, some mostly dried out cosmetics in the bathroom, and little else.

They returned to sprawl on the beige sofas across from each other, disappointed.

"Okay, Judge. You knew Bob better than I did. If he wanted to hide something here, something critical, something he'd certainly not want his daughter to find…. For her to see it might mean her death. Where would he put it?"

The Judge leaned back in the sofa, closed his eyes, and thought about his lost chum. He slowly sat up straight and looked at Katy.

"Jackie's five-foot four. Bob was six foot two. He'd hide it high."

They stood up and walked through the unit again, looking along the upper walls. There were a selection of paintings depicting various famous Vegas casinos. And one family picture of Bob and Jackie on a ski slope.

Katy stopped at the ski slope picture, saying it seemed, "Out of place. Doesn't match the other pictures."

The picture looked great to the Judge. He would have put the same picture there had he been Jackie. But he'd learned over the years to go with Katy's instincts.

He lifted the frame from the wall and looked at the back side of the frame. A small envelope was tucked in there. The Judge opened it. There was nothing in it. He opened it wide and rattled it at Katy.

"There's something written on the flap," she said, unperturbed.

Scrawled in light pencil in Bob's hand, hardly noticeable, were three lines. The first looked like an account number. The second looked like a password, consisting of a series of twelve words: *'witch collapse practice feed shame open despair creek road again ice least.'* And the third line bore a name: Sammy the Geek.

"It's a block chain account," said Katy. "The first code is the public key, and the twelve-word string is the private key. But I don't know what Sammy the Geek means."

"I do," said the Judge. "And that may explain how this whole mess got started." The Judge folded the envelope in three and tucked it into his pocket. Then replaced the picture. "I'm going to visit a talented young man who is actually an old friend. He owes me a favor."

"Who's that, Judge?"

"Sammy the Geek of course."

CHAPTER 51
SATURDAY
8:00 A.M.

The Judge pushed the door into the Computer Fixit Shop, hidden in a dilapidated strip mall on the East Side of old Las Vegas. He hadn't been here for awhile, but some things never change. The aged proprietor behind the counter, Sammy's uncle George, looked up from his racing form with mild interest. Visitors were few and far between. This was the age of the use it and dump it consumer.

The shop was cluttered; refurbished laptops lined the exterior window, their lids opened beckoningly, pleading to be taken home as though they were puppies in a pet store. White wire bins lined the center of the store in three tall rows, filled with dusty parts and gadgets, some used, some new, all pertaining to computers.

George sat behind the counter on a tall stool. He slowly took off his reading glasses for a better look, his face lighting up as he recognized the Judge.

"By God it is you, Judge. What the Hell you doing slumming down here in our hood? I thought you'd be on the Supreme Court by now."

The Judge smiled. Some old friends were so comfortable you could walk out their door two years earlier, and when you walked back in you just picked up the conversation from where it'd been dropped. As though you'd never left. He reached across the counter to give the old man a pat on the shoulder.

"You haven't changed a bit, George. Just as crusty as ever."

George smiled. "You probably want Sammy? Just go through that curtain at the back, you'll find him at his bench."

Sammy the Geek, as he was known in the trade, was one of the foremost computer experts the Judge knew. He'd been a hacker in his teens, got caught a couple of times, but the authorities couldn't make anything stick. Now in his late twenties, he'd matured into a computer consultant, accepting delicate jobs from big boys all over the country. He mostly worked online, made a ton of money for his time and expertise, and preferred to hang here, in his uncle's fix-it shop, as he'd always done. He must be even more busy now since hackers were picking on important businesses.

The Judge pushed through the curtain, and Sammy immediately got up from his bench to throw his arms around the Judge, practically squeezing the breath out of him. The Judge had helped make some small hacking charges go away once, and as a result they'd become fast friends.

This space in the back of the shop was the storeroom and Sammy's workspace. Sammy made tea at a small kitchenet in the corner, and they caught up on family, friends, current work roles, and other issues of life, as friends do. They sat across from each other at a small table, and Sammy produced soda crackers, butter, and strawberry preserves. Sufficient for a mini feast.

After they'd caught up, recalled some funny stories they'd shared, and had a couple of good laughs, the conversation died down a little and Sammy said, "How can I help, Judge? What do you need?"

"You know me too well, Sammy. You're right. I came for help."

"Your wish is my command."

The Judge started to explain about Bob Hanson, The Spire, Bob's untimely death.

"Say no more, Judge," Sammy put up his hands to stop the Judge. "I know all about it. I met Bob on one of your fabled yacht parties in Marina Del Rey. He was pure salesman, could charm a toad off a log. A real nice guy. And then he came to see me about eight weeks ago. Had a small assignment for me."

The Judge's head went up, his eyes narrowing. "What did he ask you to do?"

"It involved his Spire Project and some financing for construction. He received a large sum in from a lender, but in bitcoin. He wanted to know the best way to liquidate into U.S. currency."

"That was all?"

"Slow down, Judge. There's more. The bitcoin came in from the Cayman Island Crypto Exchange. He wanted me to try and find the initiating account where the bitcoin came from, and its ID and password."

"He wanted a hack?"

Sammie looked around. "Let's not call it that. He was a friend of yours, a nice guy, he just needed a little help."

The Judge pulled the empty envelope out of his pocket and opened its fold to display its writing. "Was this the information you got for him?"

Sammy looked at the writing, frowned a little, and said, "I don't really remember. Could have been."

"How can you track a bitcoin account, Sammy?"

"Easier than you think, Judge. Look at the FBI in the Colonial Pipeline case."

"Were you involved helping the Bureau on that one?"

"Not allowed to say, Judge. But it was a Dark Side case. A Russia-based cybercrime group hacked Colonial Pipeline and caused turmoil on the East Coast. A four-point-three-million-dollar ransom was paid by Colonial in bitcoin. But two-point-three million of it was recovered by the FBI."

"How was the FBI able to recover more than half of the ransom?"

"There's quite a bit of speculation about that. There are two issues, tracking the bitcoin, and recovering the wallet to open the account."

"And?"

"Tracking the movement of the bitcoin was relatively easy. That's what I did for Robert Hanson. You simply review the bitcoin public ledger and track where the bitcoin went. In Robert's case, the bitcoin moved through at least six different addresses before it reached his Spire account, but on the public ledger you can follow it. That's the whole point of validation. The big mystery in the Colonial Case is how the FBI was able to get the key for the wallet holding the two-point-three million."

"How do you think?"

"There's been a lot of speculation about that too. Some people think it's all a U.S. plot to discredit bitcoin, and there never was a hack. Others speculate the FBI had an inside man in Dark Side who got the wallet key and sent it back."

"And what do you think, Sammy?"

"I believe it was more direct. I think the FBI knew where this two-point-three million was sitting and used a combination of certain outside computer security consultants and their own supercomputer to access the site and extract the key. Course I can't say I was involved helping or anything. But that's the way it would have been done."

"What about the identity of the wallet holder in the Colonial case? Did the FBI get that?"

"I believe not, Judge. It would be under a false identity somewhere. They wouldn't be able to identify him. They might have got a location where he was when he transferred money in or out, just saying. But the blackmailer was on the move all the time. It didn't help."

"Is that what you did for Bob Hanson, Sammy? You located the end account in the Caymans where the funds came from, and hacked the wallet to get its key?"

"Judge. We don't use the word 'hack'. Please."

"Okay…. Okay…. But this is the address and the key in the Caymans for the Spider's account where the bulk of the seven million in bitcoin came from?"

"Might be. If that's the info I gave to Bob. But I'd have to check my records to see if these are the same numbers. I've been through too many projects since to remember."

"Did you get a real name for the lender/owner who transferred the bit coin to Bob's account?"

"Let me think. Nope, no name. Just some phony ID and a storefront downtown where he was when he made the transfer… Nothing useful. But I gave it all to Bob."

"Can you check your records and call me with the exact information you gave Bob?"

"Sure, Judge. I see no harm. Bob's gone now and I know you guys were close. Sorry about your loss."

"Thank you, Sammy. How long will it take?"

"Just got to go into my log and look it up. But I've got another rush project for the same Bureau I don't work for that I have to get out first. Give me maybe an hour or so."

"Thanks, Sammy. You're doing me a great favor."

The Judge gave Sammy a big smile. And there was a gleam in the Judge's eye that spelt serious trouble for a certain arthropod.

The Judge waved to George as he traversed back through the dusty shop and out into the desert air, feeling quite giddy he was finally taking an initiative that might validate Shorty's identity as the Spider and perhaps even locate the bastard for Angelo.

CHAPTER 52
SATURDAY
10 A.M.

The Judge balanced his two plates and maneuvered toward the table where Katy awaited. They were having breakfast at the Wynn. It was a massive buffet, probably the best in Las Vegas. The Judge's plates were loaded with eggs Benedict, thick bacon, sausage, a slice of ham, hash browns, and of course the mandatory two waffles, golden brown and dusted with powdered sugar. And that was only the first plate.

Katy looked askance at his second plate as the Judge approached their table, loaded as it was with three kinds of coffee cake and a slice of Key lime pie topped with extra whipped cream.

"If you don't die from overeating, you're surely going to be in misery for days from the indigestion," Katy said tartly.

He looked at Katy's plate, one egg scrambled and a piece of dry toast. "We have different philosophies," said the Judge smugly. "Nothing is better for a man than to eat and drink and enjoy his work. Ecclesiastes, Chapter Two."

"Are you enjoying your work?" shot back Katie.

The Judge sat his fork down, suddenly losing his appetite.

"You know I'm not. I'm frustrated. I know Shorty's the Spider. I know he had Bob killed. I know he's responsible for a twelve-year-old boy who's now a God damn vegetable. But I can't prove any of it. The Dark Web is like a cesspool at the bottom of the internet; it hides everything. And I can't even locate Shorty. Neither can Angelo. Shorty's gone to ground, buried himself deep. I want to wrap my hands around his neck and squeeze, but I don't know where he is. I am so frustrated I could scream!"

Katy immediately reached over to put her hand on his arm, calming him as she always did "Keep at it, honey. You'll find Shorty. And if he's the Spider, you'll prove it."

The Judge's cell phone went off with a buzz. The Judge recognized the number. It was Sammy the Geek. "Excuse me Katy, I'd better take this."

As the Judge listened to Sammy, his jaw tightened, and he pushed his plate away.

When he hung up, Katy put her arm back on his. "What's up, Judge?"

"Sammy confirmed what Bob had written down on the envelope we found was the public password and private key for the Spider's offshore account. Sammy was never able to give Bob the true identity of the account's owner, only a location, a public storefront where the Spider used his laptop to transfer bitcoin."

"Does that help, Judge?"

"Oh yes. Oh yes…. So very much.

"So, you know where Shorty is right now?"

"Not exactly, Katy. I was wrong. You were right."

"What, Judge. What are you saying?"

"It's not Shorty. Now I know for sure who the Spider is!"

"Holy shit, Judge. That's great news. Who is it?"

"I don't want to tell you right now, Katy. Knowledge of the Spider's real name can be a death sentence."

"Well, let's go to the police."

"We can't."

"What? Why not?"

"Because I know for certain who the Spider is. But the evidence wouldn't hold up in court. It's all circumstantial."

"What are you going to do, Judge?"

The Judge's mouth turned into a hard grim line. His eyes blazed.

"I think there's another way to bring things to a 'just' conclusion. It will have to be choreographed carefully, but I'm going to bring the Spider's existence to an abrupt end. I'm no longer hungry. Let's go back to our condo. I want to set this up. I need to talk to Angelo and I'm going to need my computer and printer."

CHAPTER 53
SATURDAY
12 P.M. Noon

The Judge and Angelo huddled together over the small corner table in Mothership Coffee Roasters. Angelo had gone on for five minutes about how he'd almost caught Shorty.

"We almost had the bastard, Judge. But somehow at the last minute he managed to slip away. Now he's gone to ground. We're turning Vegas upside down looking for him. And putting out feelers across the country and internationally. We'll find him, I'm certain. And when we do, punishment will be quick, severe and complete."

"It's not Shorty, Angelo."

"What?" Angelo's eyes puzzled.

"I know who the Spider is, and where he is."

"And it's not Shorty?"

"No. Shorty tried to do away with us both because we were pressing him. But he's not the Spider."

"For God sakes, Judge. Are you sure?"

"Yes."

"How do you know, Judge? How can you be sure it's not Shorty?"

"Because I found a hidden note left by Bob. It led me to the address and private key of the Spider's offshore bitcoin account, and to his identity. That's why Bob had to be killed; because he knew the name of the Spider."

"Santa Maria, Madre di Dio! Who is it? Let's go get him."

"He's right here, Angelo. I'm looking at him."

Angelo's face changed then, his smile disappearing into a grim line of a mouth, his jaw stiffening as he leaned over the table closer to the Judge, the laughter and good cheer in his eyes turning to a smokey glint. Harsh lines etched under the pockets of his eyes. The smile lines, almost the trademark of the Silver Fox, were gone.

"How'd you find out?"

"The tech who ferreted out your bitcoin account couldn't give Bob an owner's name, but he could give Bob the location of the account owner at the time he moved the bitcoin loan into The Spire's account. It was done here, Angelo, on your laptop, at this table, in Mothership Coffee Roasters."

"Shit! I should have been more careful."

Angelo's face filled with anger now as he slowly slid his hand inside his coat.

"You just wouldn't leave it alone, would you Judge? You had to keep pulling at the fabric of the thing. Couldn't let it be. And you're a son of a bitch who seems to have nine lives. But I think your ninth life has just run out."

Davis MacDonald

Angelo pulled out a .38 caliber Beretta automatic from his coat.

CHAPTER 54
SATURDAY
10:30 P.M.

Angelo watched them approach across the parking lot toward the diner: four shapes lit in the garish overhead lights, dark suits under dull green overcoats that flapped in the desert breeze.

He thought about the end of his conversation with the Judge. He'd had his gun out; flourished it under the Judge's nose. He could have taken care of the business himself, right there, no more Judge.

But then the Judge had said, "I wrote up my findings in an extensive report, Angelo. All the facts, all the evidence, all circumstantial of course."

"To the police?" he'd asked

"No."

"To the press?"

"No."

"Then where?"

"Chicago."

The Judge had pushed his report across the table, slid out of the booth, and just walked away. Leaving Angelo stunned, frozen.

He could have run then, tried to disappear. Perhaps he should have. But he knew it would be futile. The Mob had a worldwide network; there was really no place to run. Particularly if you were a high-profile capo caught with your hand in the cookie jar. He'd screwed up. He'd been caught with an extensive illicit business empire outside the Mob's direction and control, funded with embezzled mob money. A vast business enterprise on the Dark Web he'd thought was totally private and totally secure.

He'd been wrong. It hadn't been secure. God damn the Judge. God damn him to Hell. If the Judge had only kept his nose out of it, things would have been okay. And if Angelo had only made a deal with Hanson after Hanson had found out his identity, paid him off, left him alive. Then the Judge wouldn't have come. Damn, damn…! Damn…! Damn…!

If…. If….

He though back to what his mother use to say in that dingy little apartment in Little Sicily where he grew up:

"If… but…if… but…. If all the ifs and all the buts are packaged up as candied nuts, it'd be a wonderful Christmas."

Well, it wasn't going to be a wonderful Christmas for him. In fact, there wasn't going to be any Christmas. He felt… surreal, like some twisted morality play was happening in front of him and he was merely an observer. He looked around the diner. It was empty. His guard-dog guys had melted away. They weren't paid to fight lost causes.

The delegation of four quietly escorted him out of the diner, out across the half-lit parking lot, out to a black SUV. He was deposited in the middle of the second set of seats, a large-shouldered guy on either side and one behind.

They offered him a sack to put over his head. He tried to decline but they insisted. The SUV rattled on for four hours on good pavement, and then another two and a half over rough terrain at a high speed, bucking and bouncing like a bronco, desert dust seeping in from myriad small fissures, making it hard to breath in his sack.

Then they stopped, the door opened, and they slid him out to stand on the sand. He stood there, disoriented, heard the doors slam again and the SUV roar off, its noise quickly fading into desert silence.

He took the sack off and blinked into the beginning light of sunup, his eyes adjusting to focus on the way-distant horizon. In the clear morning air he could faintly make out the blinking lights of the Vegas skyline. Perhaps forty miles out. There'd be no car waiting for him behind a hill here.

He sank down on the sand. It wasn't going to come easy. Of course, that was the point. A sort of cosmic justice he supposed....

CHAPTER 55
6 MONTHS LATER

The Judge and Katy sat on silver stools at the La Fontaine de Belleville, an Italian Coffee Bar affiliated with the one in Paris. They were in a corner of the interior patio of The Spire Guest Hotel. It was a beautiful spring day in Las Vegas. Not too hot, not too cold, and the snowbirds were still flocked here, nesting in what had become one of the hottest boutique guest hotels in the Southwest. Bob Hanson would be proud.

His estate was all settled and Jackie Hanson and Bob's girlfriend Elka had inherited The Spire and were now operating it together. They had become fast friends and partners. And they'd done a beautiful job. All the units were complete, and 90 percent were sold. The swank Italian restaurant on the second floor of the lobby was operating full tilt, already having made a name for itself with its two Michelin stars. The third floor had been licensed as a small casino, with slots, craps, blackjack, and a sports book. Money was pouring in from all directions and the two partners were happily awash in it.

The Judge had gone to the authorities about the dirty tricks of Building Department Head Regie Jones, attorney Darrel Hurtz, and Supervisor Harry Jessup. And Darrel had copped a plea, identifying the banker behind the conspiracy. They were now sweating the unsealing of an indictment for racketeering and fraud. Jessup had already lost his seat on the Board of Supervisors.

Once they'd been exposed, the construction loan bank quickly reversed course, extending the construction loan for an additional two years, and groveling at the feet of Jackie and Elka in the hope of avoiding litigation.

The Judge had introduced the stalled project to a smart family office which immediately saw the opportunity and were only too pleased to pick up the slack, providing the additional cash to complete the hotel and provide working capital until The Spire broke even. And The Spire quickly flashed past breakeven, once freed from the bankruptcy court by a new attorney the Judge brought in.

Sam Compton and his partner, Jerry, were in jail for selling fraudulent securities, and violating various other provisions of state and federal securities and fraud laws. They'd each have a minimum five-year vacation at the expense of the Federal Government once they were convicted. What assets they had were gathered into a fund and would be distributed to victims. Sadly, there was only about a 10 percent recovery, testimony to the age-old caution not to make investments over the phone, or the internet, with people you don't know.

Cindy Hanson had collected the full value of the insurance policy on the life of Robert Hanson and disappeared. There were rumors she'd bought a hilltop house overlooking Trunk Bay on St. Johns in the Virgins. The Judge couldn't blame her.

Bob Hanson, although a great guy and the Judge's dear friend, had not been one to settle down in domestic bliss. He was, what was the expression...? 'A good timing man.' Their marriage so many years ago had been a mistake from the beginning. But Cindy had steadfastly put up with his frequent default in alimony, had even advanced Bob money from time to time to keep him going as he pursued his rollercoaster real estate developer business, and never taken him to court. She was entitled to taste some of the fruit of their love affair that had been so hot but so wrong for so long.

Angelo Rosolino, the Silver Fox, had simply disappeared from the Vegas scene, simultaneously with the disappearance of the Spider. There were rumors of course. A concrete kimono at the bottom of Hoover Dam, a long one-way ride out into the desert, an unmarked grave somewhere on the outskirts of town, or perhaps a place in the sun in some colorful hammock on the beach in Taormina, Sicily. No one really knew. The Judge was of the view that the Mob was very efficient in disposing of one of its own.

Shorty had disappeared too. His casino was sold by his family for a modest price to a consortium of East Coast and L.A. investors.

Jackie had been off drugs since Robbie's overdose. And with the help of regular consulting and hard work creating The Spire in all its splendor, she'd managed to reorder her life. She even had a regular boyfriend who thought she walked on water. Well, of course she did.

Elka had a new baby boy, with the same vivid blue eyes that had belonged to his dad. It looked like he'd be a towhead too.

And little Robbie? Despite pressure from the doctors, Jackie had refused to give the order terminating life support. Robbie had lingered in an unconscious state on the edge of death for four weeks. Then suddenly regained consciousness and managed to make a slow but determined recovery.

The Judge and Katy watched him bounce around The Spire's lobby now. At thirteen, taller and still growing, he made a cutting figure in his new suit as the junior bellhop for the hotel. His part-time job after school. He'd settled in with Jackie in her Spire unit, and his happy smile as he greeted guests told everyone he was right with the world.

"In that white suit and sailor's hat, he looks like a monkey in search of his organ-grinder," whispered the Judge... followed by an "Ouch!" as Katy's sharp elbow lashed into his rib.

They all missed Bob, of course. But six months had given some time for some healing, some adjustment, and some new growth.

The only continuing discouragement was the Dark Web, which continued to operate and churn, dealing in drugs, loan sharking, murder for hire, blackmail, and the newest techniques for hacking legitimate businesses for ransom. Its dark fingers continued to invade the computers and bedrooms of the youngest to the oldest, like a spreading fungus, searching for anyone it could snare.

THE END

XXX

Further Notes for the Reader

Robert Frost's poem, *Design*, published in 1932, is one his most controversial, dealing with themes of religion, life, and death, and depicting God not as a benevolent being, but rather as a malevolent spirit. Consider the last two lines, a rhyming couplet, suggesting a dark design and a creator creating to 'appall' and instill fear. Here is *Design* again:

DESIGN

I found a dimpled spider, fat and white,
On a white heal-all, holding up a moth
Like a white piece of rigid satin cloth--
Assorted characters of death and blight
Mixed ready to begin the morning right,
Like the ingredients of a witches' broth--
A snow-drop spider, a flower like a froth,
And dead wings carried like a paper kite.

What had that flower to do with being white,
The wayside blue and innocent heal-all?
What brought the kindred spider to that height,
Then steered the white moth thither in the night?
What but design of darkness to appall?--
If design govern in a thing so small.

Robert Frost 1932

Davis MacDonald

SOME ADDITIONAL NOTES
For those who'd like to read more about some of the topics raised in this Novel:

-Mother says her son died of overdose on drugs bought over social media: Link
https://abc7chicago.com/dr-laura-berman-son-fentanyl-overdose-buy-drugs-social-media/10324555

-7 Tips for Using the Tor Browser Safely: link
https://www.makeuseof.com/tag/tor-browser-safety-tips/

-How to Access the Dark Web Safely and Anonymously: link
https://www.makeuseof.com/tag/how-to-access-the-dark-web/

-Nevada: Morgue Employee arrested for pimping out corpses for sex
Link: https://worldnewsdailyreport.com/nevada-morgue-employee-arrested-for-pimping-out-corpses-for-sex/

-About bitcoin keys: link
https://www.oreilly.com/library/view/mastering-bitcoin-2nd/9781491954379/ch04.html

ACKNOWLEDGEMENTS

Thanks to those good friends who helped me to write and edit THE DARK WEB - VEGAS. Dr. Alexandra Davis, who was the first to see every word; my amazing editor, Jason Myers, who did yeoman work on the edits and kept me on the straight and narrow; my daughter, Katherine Davis, who had the final say on all grammar and editing, the multiple good friends who agreed to read and comment on the early draft, and Dane Low, (www.ebooklaunch.com), who helped me design the distinctive cover.

Thank You All.

Davis MacDonald

Davis MacDonald

This is a Work of Fiction

THE DARK WEB – VEGAS is a work of fiction. Names, characters, businesses, organizations, clubs, places, events, and incidents depicted in this book are either products of the Author's imagination or are used fictitiously. Any resemblance or similarity to actual persons, living or dead, or events, locales, business organizations, clubs, or incidents, is unintended and entirely incidental. Names have been chosen at random and are not intended to suggest any person. The facts, plot, circumstances and characters in this book were created for dramatic effect, and bear no relationship to actual businesses, organizations, communities or their denizens.

About Davis MacDonald

Davis MacDonald grew up in Southern California and writes of places about which he has intimate knowledge. Davis uses the mystery novel genre to write stories of suspense, love, and commitment, entwined with relevant social issues and moral dilemmas facing 21st Century America. A member of the National Association of Independent Writers and Editors (NATWE), his career has spanned Law Professor, Bar Association Chair, Investment Banker, and Lawyer. Many of the colorful characters in his novels are drawn in part from his personal experiences and relationships (although they are all entirely fictional characters).

Davis began this series in 2013, with the publishing of THE HILL, in which he introduces his new character, the Judge. Here is a bit about each book in the Series in the order they were published:

THE HILL, set in Palos Verdes, a suburb of Los Angeles, is a murder mystery and a love story which also explores the sexual awakening of a young girl, how sexual manipulation can change lives forever, and the moral dilemmas love sometimes creates.

315

THE ISLAND, set in Avalon, Catalina, continues the saga of the Judge and his love Katy, as the Judge finds himself in another murder mystery, and forced to make some key decisions about his relationship with Katy. The story explores the dysfunctional attitudes of a small town forced to drop old ways of thinking or face extinction.

SILICON BEACH, set in Venice, Santa Monica, Playa Vista and Marina del Rey, opens with a sundown attack on the Judge on the Santa Monica Beach, and carries the reader through the swank and not so swank joints on the Los Angeles West Side, as the Judge tries to bring down killers before they bring him down. The book takes a close look at the homeless, who they are, where they came from, what their lives are like, and offers a novel political solution.

THE BAY, set in Newport Beach, Balboa, and the Orange County Coastal communities, finds the Judge pressed into service by the FBI to solve a murder of one of their own, and stumbling into a terrorist plot that could devastate Orange County. The story takes a close look at Islam in its many strains, as it exists in the United States.

CABO, set in Mexico, finds the Judge and Katy on a holiday in Cabo San Lucas which turns deadly as they unravel a stealthy double murder, and go head-to-head with human traffickers in Baha California.

THE STRAND, set in Manhattan Beach, Hermosa Beach, and Redondo Beach, involves a murder, as well as a controversial case centered on a pre-school and alleged child-abuse; a case that triggers prosecutorial misconduct and a rush to judgment by the D.A.'s Office and the Press, ruining reputations and destroying the lives and assets of the accused in reliance on 'creditable' sources that are not creditable, long before the defendants are ever brought to trial.

THE LAKE is set in the mountain community of Lake Arrowhead. A best friend dying in your arms. His last desperate words a cryptic message of death to thousands. What would you do? The Judge sleuths out the facts, exposing the shocking private lives of people he thought he knew, uncovering the greedy that would risk the world for financial gain. Blind-sided along the way by Katy's sudden unhappiness, the love he expected to last forever seemingly unraveling, the relationship wobbling. What are the right words, the right steps, to touch her heart again? To put something fragile back together and fuse it so strong it lasts a lifetime ? Can the Judge hold off the dark in his personal life, while exposing killers so cold, so calculating, they give the word Evil a new meaning?

THE CRUISE. The Judge and Katy are on a relaxing cruise to Hawaii when one of their fellow passengers has a deadly accident. And then a second deadly accident... and a third. As the number of 'accidents' becomes statistically improbable, the Judge weaves his way through the conflicts, animosities and rivalries of a fractured business family and the Ship's guests and crew, seeking the truth. But the more the Judge learns, the more he puts himself in harm's way. When the ship is blown off course into the Great Pacific Garbage Patch, business partners become adversaries, family members become enemies, old lovers become bitter, and polite facades are dropped to reveal ugly motives, jealousy and hate.

Theft, embezzlement, avarice, greed, infidelity, sex, and of course... 'accidents. Lots and lots of suspicious accidents. The primal violence seething underneath humanity's surface comes to a boil in the pressure cooker of a six-day cruise across the Blue Pacific. Follow the Judge as he risks all to ferret out the truth, on... THE CRUISE!

THE DARK WEB – VEGAS. The Judge's best friend is dropped off alone in the desert, thirty miles from any road. So begins a hazardous investigation into what the

Vegas Police call 'suicide' and the Ex-wife calls murder. The Judge finds himself entangled in the Dark Web, dodging deadly assaults by a malevolent "Spider". When his friend's twelve-year old grandson becomes an overdose victim of the Spider's Dark Web drug trade, the Judge must somehow breach the secrecy of the Dark Web to identify the Spider and put an end to his reign of destruction before the Spider puts a permanent end to the Judge.

THE CITY BY THE BAY. The Judge and Katy, on a combined business and pleasure trip to San Francisco, stumble into a series of murders beginning with a wild cable car ride in which the Judge almost loses his life. The Judge and Katy become targets in an orchestrated effort to cover up an evolving scandal involving US Corporations and China. The Mystery Novel will be published in the Fall of 2022. The first two chapters are included at the end of this book.

All books are available digitally on Amazon for Kindle, and in paperback in fine bookstores and online shopping platforms. Audio books are available for the first six books in the series. Watch for forthcoming audio books for the remainder of the series.

HOW TO CONNECT WITH

Davis MacDonald

Visit my website: http://davismacdonald-author.com/ or Google **Davis MacDonald-Author** to see information on each book, Video Trailers for each, and posts about new books coming out.

Email: Don@securities-attys.com

Twitter: https://twitter.com/Davis_MacDonald

Facebook: Davis MacDonald, Author

Blog: http://davis-macdonald.tumblr.com/

LinkedIn: Davis MacDonald

Amazon Author's Page: Davis MacDonald-Author

Davis MacDonald

What follows are the first two Chapters of THE CITY
BY THE BAY – A MYSTERY NOVEL

THE CITY BY THE BAY
A Mystery Novel

BY

DAVIS MacDONALD

CHAPTER 1

Fog rolled up the hill toward Chestnut Street in thick cotton waves from the bay, filtering the early morning light into a spidery web of shadows and rays. The Judge snuggled deeper into his overcoat as he walked, wishing he could have spent another hour in bed pressed up to the side of Katy, his young bride, warm, soft and feminine smelling. But the case was a big one with international ramifications, and today's deposition was key.

As usual it was 7:30 a.m. when the Judge climbed from wet slippery pavement on to the Hyde cable car at the top of Chestnut. He took his favorite seat at the front in the lower end of the car, where he could look down the steep street to the foggy city below. This was his fourth and final day of depos at the law offices of Madison, Weinstock & Chan. And the big fish was going to be interrogated today.

He was going to nail the defendant scientist's ears to the barnyard door this morning, making a record of his collusion.

He looked around the car. It was almost empty. There were two young men in spiffy suits and college ties who looked to be novice brokers or venture capitalists, likely working together somewhere. They were sharing their ride to the office, as they had each of the prior mornings, by comparing notes in not so discreet tones as to their success in female chasing the night before.

There was the old Chinese gentleman sprawled across two seats behind the Judge, arms spread out, his expensive grey silk suit open to display a large chest and tummy covered by a starched white shirt with a personal monogram on the pocket, open at the collar, showing his thick neck. He had puffy eyelids, mostly covering slivers of eyes that peered out from under his heavy brow. But he had looked quite cheerfully back at the Judge as the Judge boarded. He was a regular too. They'd exchanged pleasantries the morning before about the weather; it had been sunny then.

There was a young blonde, mid-twenties, medium height and slender, wearing a faded blue London Fog, open at the front to show the top of a black cocktail dress with an attractive décolleté of her small breasts. Her tousled hair, which she ran a hand through now to take control, suggested she'd spent an exciting night somewhere, but now, sadly, had not been asked to stay. The slash of grim lipstick marking her mouth, recently added, implied she might be pissed.

And finally, there was a middle-aged man in whites wearing a white apron, perhaps a baker coming home after a long night shift making the city's bread. He was a regular too.

As the car lurched away from its Chestnut stop, there was a sharp popping noise, like a tiny firecracker. It came from beneath where the gripman stood.

"My God, I've lost the rope!" yelled the gripman. "Oh no… Oh my God!"

The cable car suddenly started careening down the steeply sloped Hyde Street Hill with increasing velocity, faster and faster, shaking and wobbling from side to side, throwing the passengers to the floor. The young woman screamed as she was slammed to the floor. One of the stockbrokers whined , "Oh shit… oh shit" in a high-pitched squeal.

The car smashed into and through a station wagon in front of it just before Bay Street, triggering a fiery explosion as the cable car knifed through the wagon's gas tank, spewing a wave of gas over the street and inside the cable car.

The Judge exchanged a grim look with the Chinese gentleman whose knuckles showed white, both on the floor and holding fast to poles which ran from the floor to the roof.

A river of flames jumped down Hyde Street from the gas and leaped onto the upper end of the cable car. Everybody aboard started to yell, including the Judge.

By the intersection of Bay and Hyde Streets, flames had completely enveloped the upper half of the plummeting cable car. The two stockbrokers, both in flames, jumped in desperation from the car, landing hard on the pavement and then twisting their bodies in a futile effort to extinguish their flames.

The gripman followed and managed to roll his flames out on the slick wet street. The baker was not so lucky, bailing off the side of the car but getting his foot caught in its steps; slamming under the rear wheel as the car gyrated on its tracks, his single long piercing scream cut off as the wheel ground over him.

The car sped another two blocks before jumping its rails and slamming into the corner of a building at Hyde and Jefferson.

The Judge was thrown hard against the front of the seat where he'd been sitting, smashing his head. But he managed to crab-crawl his way out the open door and on to the wet payment, rolling away as the flames swept through the lower half of the car.

The Chinese gentlemen, less agile, got caught under the seat in front of him and screamed once, twice, three times, before the blazing inferno engulfed him. The woman disappeared in the ball of flame that exploded into the lower half of the car, her cries gone silent.

CHAPTER 2

Hands out of nowhere reached the Judge from either side, gently rolling him into a blanket, half carrying half dragging him further along Jefferson, away from the scorching flames. Sirens were wailing up the hill from all directions. Residents were pouring out of their stacked flats to see what had happened and how they could help. It was a nightmarish scene as greasy black smoke etched up through the rolling fog.

The Judge carefully stretched out one leg and then the other. They both seemed to work. So did his arms. But his hands encountered warm wet across the front of his overcoat, apparently from the bash at the top of his head that was spurting blood, repetitively flooding one eye as it ran down his face and he wiped it away.

"Just hold still buddy, don't move," said a male voice above him. "You're losing blood from your head wound, and movement is aggravating it. The medics are coming."

The Judge stopped all movement and tried to lie perfectly still, willing the bleeding to stop.

Time went by. Someone in a fireman's suit leaned over him and gently took his vital signs before slapping a square patch of band-aid aid on his head. Then, suddenly, Katy was there.

His young wife had her overcoat wrapped around her blue pajamas with yellow canaries, hair tousled, no makeup, tears running down her cheeks. She must have run all the way down the hill from Chestnut.

She held his hand in one hand and gently stroked his cheek with the other, whispering, "It's okay, Judge. You're in shock. But you're all in one piece. You're going to be okay."

He had the feeling she was saying it to calm herself, as much as she was to reassure him. Over her protest and the clucking disapproval of a young rescue truck worker, he got his arms down to his sides and pushed himself up into a seated position. Wiping the blood from one eye, he surveyed a scene that looked right out of Hell. The twisted and smoldering carcass of the cable car was twenty feet away. They'd pried one body out, likely the old Chinaman by the size and shape of the green tarp they had covering the body. And they were now searching in the wreckage for the woman.

Up the street, the twisted hulk of the station wagon was still on fire as a Company engine maneuvered near to deploy foam. There had to be bodies trapped inside, but it would take a while to untangle them. Below to the left were two mounds covered by green tarps, the stockbrokers. And to the right, a shorter bundle, but piled higher under its green tarp... the scraps of the baker.

The gripman sat on the tail gate of rescue truck; his uniform pulled down while a fireman dabbed his burns with something antiseptic. He looked to be in shock. The Judge turned his body sideways, got one knee under himself, and with Katy's help rose unsteadily to his feet.

XXXXXX

A Personal Note from the Author

I hope you enjoyed your read. Here are the other books in the Judge Series, (in order). If you've enjoyed one or more of these mystery novels, please leave a review on Amazon and help us spread the word.

Davis MacDonald

THE JUDGE SERIES

Book 1: THE HILL

Book 2: THE ISLAND

Book 3: SILICON BEACH

Book 4: THE BAY

Book 5: CABO

Book 6: THE STRAND

Book 7: THE LAKE

Book 8: THE CRUISE

Book 9: THE DARK WEB – VEGAS

Book 10: THE CITY BY THE BAY (out in late 2022)

(On Amazon search under 'books' for **Davis Macdonald** to find a complete list of the books.

All are available in paperback and on Kindle. Books 1 through 6 are also available on audiobook, and book 7, **THE LAKE**, will be out on audiobook shortly.)

www.ingramcontent.com/pod-product-compliance
Lightning Source LLC
Chambersburg PA
CBHW062019170626
46813CB00001B/220